STAIRWAY OF THE GODS

STAIRWAY OF THE GODS

A NOVEL BY

VIC WARREN

TURNING HEADS
KAILUA-KONA, HAWAII

Turning Heads
73-1104 Nuuanu Place
Kailua-Kona, Hawaii 96740

Second Paperback Edition: April 2012

ISBN 978-0-615-62388-7

Printed in the United States of America

1. SAUSALITO

The band was playing "Satisfaction." It was a local band. Not one of the local San Francisco bands that would make it big, like Jefferson Airplane or Big Brother and the Holding Company. More of a Sausalito-style local band, which was what they were. Four guys who could play pretty well, keep a steady beat and who knew at least the top half of the Top 40. And, since they were friends of Anne Bellamy, they were set up in one corner of the houseboat's giant living room, close enough to the open bar, playing for free. You never knew who might discover you at Anne's.

Anne Bellamy's houseboat--actually, houseboat doesn't really conjure up the proper image of the place--was more like a ferryboat, or a warehouse on a barge. Brand new and covered inside and out with two stories of unfinished split shakes and stained glass windows that looked like the glass was still molten. During the day, pools of green and yellow and orange melted down the walls and slid across the floor. If you weren't careful, it seemed, you would track multicolored footprints across the broad living room floor and up the shag carpeted stairway to the rooms above.

Tonight, the splashes of color had receded to their proper places in the glass, barely visible against the darkness outside. Now the color was supplied by a couple hundred closely packed bodies, filling the room and spilling out onto the spacious deck. Anne Bellamy knew just enough of the kind of people everyone loved to say they knew. Artists, critics, a few writers and dancers, some of the theatre people who were hot right now--like a couple of guys from the cast of "The Fantasticks." And that was sure to attract the friends of friends and the groupies and the occasional crasher who really made her parties work.

The deck on the bay side of the house was big enough to play badminton on, and it was full, too, but a little less ferociously. Clusters of guests sat at the half dozen umbrellaed tables. More of them stood nearby, jealously watching and waiting to grab chairs if one of the sitting groups foolishly decided to go inside to dance.

At least it's cool out here. And the smoke isn't so stifling, Paul thought, as he lit a cigarette to add his bit to Bay Area pollution. The Malibu lights around the edge of the deck and the oil candles on the tables created the feel of one of those posh outdoor restaurants in Tiburon. He was sure if he waited long enough a white-coated maitre d' would come by and ask him if he had a reservation.

Paul Webster was not one of the writers who knew Anne Bellamy. But like they say, everyone is only six acquaintances away from the President of the United States. And Paul was only twice removed from Anne. He supposed that put her only four from the president. He'd come with Alberto Mendoza, the Berkeley literature professor and playwright. Paul had taken a couple of classes from Mendoza during his last year at the university. It was Mendoza who'd steered him away from a life in a garret and into advertising.

"Prostitute thyself," Mendoza had said. "At least until you learn to write."

And the advice hadn't been half bad. Paul liked trying to come up with fresh, new slants for the charter airline account that was now his alone. He had learned to put up with the give and take with the art directors. He'd work up a rough draft and give it to the account's senior art director, who'd give it back and say, "Cut about a third of this. And can't you make this headline shorter?" Actually, he spent more time editing and cutting than he did writing. But the money was good, and it was just a start, anyway.

Mendoza had called him that day at work and invited him to dinner. They'd eaten at Solomon's, where Mendoza had cajoled him into doing a couple of free lectures on the ups and downs of a beginner writing for a living, while Paul nodded with a mouth full of pastrami. Yes, Mendoza agreed, ordinarily they paid their lecturers, but there would be a couple of important contacts attending, and this was a tight budget year. As they waited for the check, Mendoza mentioned Anne Bellamy's party. He'd been invited, and there was always plenty to drink and plenty of people for Paul to add to his notebook for the real writing, later on.

They had split up once they got inside--Mendoza had to find somebody--and Paul hadn't seen him since. He looked around the deck. No sign of him. No sign of any familiar face. And Paul really wasn't very good at walking up to strangers with easy-going chitchat. He'd have one more drink and drive back to town. It was still early enough to catch the second show at the El Matador. There was a new Brazilian band there called Brazil 65. They were supposed to be pretty good. He wondered which was correct, El Matador or the El Matador? Translated, the latter read, "the the Matador." He'd have to look that one up.

Paul ran his hand through his dark brown hair. Time for a haircut, he thought. Or maybe he'd let it grow even longer. It seemed to be the thing to do nowadays.

Just in front of him, a couple was actually getting up from their table to go inside. As they pushed their chairs in, he looked on either side of the soon-to-be-available space. On the left, the beautifully tailored suit and wavy silver hair of a captain of industry, sitting with his wife. On the right, long, straight blonde hair and a sleeveless minidress. He reached for the right chair. But the girl was too fast for him. She pulled it in and wrapped a slender arm protectively around its back.

"I'm sorry, but this seat's taken," she said.

"How can it be taken? It's not even cool yet," argued Paul. He waited for a response, but the girl stayed glued to the chair. "Well, I guess I'll just have to take this other one to help you protect your prize. Between the two of us, we should be able to ward off any invaders."

"Help yourself, I only need one. I've been sitting here for an hour waiting for it."

"An hour? You must have wanted it pretty badly," Paul said as he sat down. He wanted to put his arm around the chair *and* the girl, but he didn't. I will in my notebook, he thought.

"I told my roommate I'd come out here and get us a place to sit. But I don't know where she's gone." She relaxed her grip on the chair, but it was still obviously her territory.

"Well, I hope she's not over on the other side of the deck holding onto a chair for you."

She frowned. "I hadn't thought of that. But I can't go look for her, or I'll lose both my chairs."

Paul smiled. What an amazingly silly dilemma, he thought. "I'd save them for you, but I don't think I could protect all three," he said.

"No, probably not," she sighed. "And my glass is empty, and I can't even go get a new drink."

She picked up her glass and tipped it to her mouth. It was still empty. She frowned and set it back down carefully in the water ring it had left on the glass tabletop. She was slim and tan, her sun bleached hair pulled back from her face, hanging perfectly straight halfway down her back. He had heard that some girls ironed their hair to get it straight like that. He wondered how she looked leaning down, her hair stretched out on the ironing board. It sounded difficult. There must be an easier way, he thought. He'd have to look that up. "I'll tell you what, Miss...?"

"Davis. Joanie Davis."

"...Miss Davis, Joanie. I have an idea. Let's give up all three chairs and go someplace where we can sit down, where they will actually serve us drinks."

"Maybe we should," she said. "I've been here almost two hours and you're practically the only person I've met."

"Well, I've proven to be a reliable chair guard. That's a good sign, isn't it?"

"Oh, I didn't mean, well, you know...," she smiled. "Yes, it is a good sign."

They got up and started to thread their way through the crowd. She was tall. Maybe too tall for him. He was six feet, and in her flats she was nearly his height. Wearing high heels, she'd probably be an inch taller than him. Oh well, swallow your pride, Paul thought as he followed her, wondering why someone with legs like that hadn't met a lot more people. Behind them, two couples fought over the chairs, neither wanting to settle for the leftover single.

As they entered the darkness of the houseboat, the smoke and the smell of the dancers hit them. It was even more crowded than before. She turned and said, "Don't lose me."

"Don't worry," Paul answered and took her arm, the slender arm that a few minutes ago was only notebook material.

They worked their way through the dancers and past the band that was shouting its way through "Woolly Bully." Outside on the dock a line of guests and other hopefuls was still waiting to get in. As they reached the street, she said, "I'd better leave a note on my roommate's car, so she'll know not to look for me."

* * *

"How'd you happen to come to an Anne Bellamy party?" Paul asked as they approached the Golden Gate Bridge on their way into the city.

"My roommate works at an art gallery on Union. Her boss was invited, but he couldn't make it. He asked her to give the hostess his regrets."

Funny, Paul thought. I never met the hostess. As they crossed the bridge, Paul could see a funnel of fog stretching under the bridge, sucked into the bay by the pull of heat reaching from Oakland and the mainland. At the city end of the bridge, it was ten degrees cooler, but still remarkably warm for a spring night in San Francisco. He loved the feel of San Francisco at night: the red-sauce smell of Italian family restaurants shoved up against the gaudy strip joints of Broadway and the cool, beat coffee houses and bookstores, the three separate personalities of North Beach jammed back to back to back with exotic Chinatown, that was piled high on Monday nights with stacks of empty wooden grocery boxes, filled earlier in the day with everything from bok choy to jasmine tea, all fresh off the ships and into the stores. He had learned long ago that the best of these boxes made terrific, not to mention free, furniture: bedstands, bookcases, coffee tables, planter boxes. Levitz would have given a lot for the shoppers who worked Grant Avenue on Monday nights.

"What's your name?"

He was back in the car. He glanced down and saw Joanie's long legs stretching from her short skirt down under the dash of the MG. The street lights created bands of artificial moonlight sliding down her long legs--one, two, three, slide, slide, slide. He grimaced with guilt. Here he was, with this beautiful girl, and what does he do? He daydreams about Chinese boxes! "What?" he asked.

"I just realized I don't know your name."

"Oh, I'm sorry. It's Paul. Paul Webster."

"Glad to meet you, Paul Webster. And don't be sorry," she smiled, blowing smoke up into the night air. "What do you do?"

"I graduated from Berkeley last year. I'm working at an ad agency as a copywriter for the time being."

"I take it you'd rather be doing something else?"

"Kind of. I think I'd like to do some real writing--you know, serious writing, books and such--some day."

"So, a writer named Webster. Maybe you should write dictionaries," she laughed and threw what was left of the cigarette out into the street.

"He's no relation, but we do use a lot of the same words."

* * *

The Matador--he had decided to Anglicize it until he checked it out--was even more crowded than Anne Bellamy's. A double line stretched outside and halfway up the block. Damn those newspapers, he thought. One good review, and jazz fans come out of the woodwork. It was only Monday night, but tourist season had started, and Broadway was crawling with them. He crept along with the traffic, wearing out his clutch and braking for jaywalkers, past Carol Doda's show at the Condor, past Finocchio's, and finally out of the crowd and into the Broadway Tunnel.

"Why don't you take me home, Paul. It's getting late, and I have classes in the morning," Joanie suggested.

"Okay," he replied. The 11 pm rush hour traffic had tired him out. "Where to?"

"Just off Geary. Right near Mel's Diner."

"What are you studying?" he asked.

"Art history, anthro, archaeology. All the A courses except astronomy. USF has connections with some good museums. I'm especially interested in primitive art and culture. I'll get my BA next June, but I'll probably have to go on to graduate school. At least for my Masters. You can't really get anywhere without it."

The house was a wonderful Queen Anne Victorian, painted yellow with white trim and, unexpectedly, a black front door. Joanie shared the second floor. She let them into a long hall that ran the length of the flat to the kitchen at the back. Off of it to the right were arched doorways to sitting room, then living room, then dining room. Farther back on the left were the bedrooms.

"This is quite a place. How'd you get all this great furniture on a student's budget?"

"We lucked out. The place came furnished. Mrs. Mencken, our landlady, lives alone downstairs. Her husband died a few years ago. He was the curator at the de Young Museum. This is all their stuff. You should see the things she has downstairs. She has trouble getting around, so we help her with shopping and the lawn work. She's a dear, but it's getting more difficult for her. I don't know how long we'll be able to stay here." She ran her hand down the wooden molding of the living room doorway. "How about a glass of wine? I think there's some in the fridge."

Paul took off his jacket and laid it on a chair, then sat down on the couch. He noticed that his new gray summer weight slacks were already wrinkled. He tried to smooth them, then crossed his legs. Maybe she wouldn't notice.

The coffee table was topped with two panes of glass, sandwiching a large, hand drawn manuscript, some kind of music. She brought in two glasses of wine, handed him his, then walked across to the stereo. "Isn't that a great table?" she asked. "It's a page from a book of Gregorian chants, twelfth century, part of a manuscript from Strasbourg that was unfortunately broken into individual sheets. Beautiful, isn't it?"

The record started. Bossa nova. The girl singer had a light and airy voice, and the Portuguese words sounded thick and soft. "What's the record?" asked Paul.

"Sergio Mendes and Brazil 65, In Person at El Matador," she smiled, holding up the album cover.

"You're kidding."

"No. It was recorded during their first visit here. They just released it. I got it the other day."

I guess Atlantic Records must know how to handle the name, Paul thought to himself. That was one item he wouldn't have to look up.

They sat and talked about school and work and home and San Francisco. Half a dozen times Paul nearly worked up the courage to put his arm around her and pull her to him, but he sat and sipped his wine and listened instead. Joanie was from back East. She had moved out here to go to school. She liked it here and would probably stay. Or maybe she would go to Europe. Her Spanish was okay, and there were plenty of wonderful museums in Spain, if she could get a work permit. She turned the record over for the second time, brought in the bottle from the kitchen and refilled their glasses. Paul stretched his arm out on the back of the empty couch. He wondered why such a simple act seemed so terrifying. If she rebuffed him, it wouldn't be the end of the world. He had only known her a couple of hours. But she was so beautiful, and how did she iron that hair, anyway?

Joanie sat back down on the couch, a little closer, it seemed to Paul. She leaned back, and his fingertips brushed her bare shoulder. Maybe she wants me to..., maybe she's as nervous as I am, he thought. He moved his hand half an inch. She leaned forward and put her glass on the table, neatly placing it to fit between two lines of music. He moved his hand down, thinking, if she bumps into it, it could just be an accident. She turned toward him, and, taking his face in her hands, she kissed him, his arm still stretched out in surprise.

* * *

He lay on his back in her bed, a sheet covering him. The flowered wallpaper and the dark furniture made it a warm, comfortable place, like a room he had been in before. Joanie came in from the bathroom. The light from the little porcelain lamp on the bedstand and the tan lines from her bikini turned her an even darker golden bronze. She slipped under the sheet and rolled over against him. He held her close, his mind racing through waves of thought, yet thinking of nothing but the feel of her. Her mouth was still tangy from the wine, and her skin was so soft and smooth he could only think of clichés to describe it.

She was surprisingly strong. She rolled back, and he followed willingly, until he was on her and in her. Falling and rising, he felt her hands sliding down him, pulling him to her. He raised himself up and looked down at her, unable to believe she was there. Her white breasts glistened, their small nipples hard. Her long hair was a tangle on the pillow. He bent down and kissed her warm, wet mouth. She moaned with excitement and pulled him down again, harder, wrapping her long legs around him. The pleasure stretched out nearly full circle, approaching a place he'd never been before, so unbearable and so delicious.

Later they lay side by side, kissing and touching each other softly. Not wanting to ask her if it had been good for her--he'd read that too many times--Paul tried to relax instead. He decided he could trust Joanie. She knew her own mind, and she wasn't afraid to share her convictions. And right now, the way she moved her body against his told him she had enjoyed it as much as he had. This could be habit forming, he thought.

"What about your morning classes," he asked, already knowing what she would say, but dreading the thought that he was wrong, that he would have to end the evening by getting up and driving home through the night and the lonely city.

"I'll borrow somebody's notes. Just go to sleep," she said, stroking his dark hair as she reached behind her to turn out the light.

* * *

When Paul woke, the sun was streaming through the shutters. He looked up at the strange ceiling, then remembered where he was. He felt like he'd been in some kind of time machine. Go to sleep in 1965 in San Francisco, wake up in 1990 in The Philippines. The clock next to the bed said eight o'clock. He rolled over. She wasn't there. Just then he heard her walking down the hall. She came into the room wearing a bright turquoise robe that matched her eyes. She was carrying a steaming cup of coffee.

"Here's your coffee, sir," she smiled. "Breakfast will be arriving in just a few minutes." She put down the coffee and leaned over and kissed him.

He reached up for her. "Ummm, I want you for breakfast."

"Food first, then sex," she laughed, as she left the room.

He leaned up on one elbow and sipped the hot coffee. Dark and strong, European style. He could hear kitchen noises in the distance. He heard plates being taken out of the cabinet, the clink of silverware.

Outside, birdsong, faraway traffic, a horn honking. Life starts again, he thought.

She came back in with a tray overflowing with rolls and butter, fruit, a pitcher of milk and a pot of coffee. Even fresh flowers in a small vase. She put the tray in the middle of the bed and slipped off her robe. The little nightgown underneath barely covered her hips. Her bare shoulders and long legs gleamed bronze in the morning sun as she climbed up cross-legged on the other side of the bed.

She was radiant this morning, he thought. The food was good, but he barely tasted it as he ate, anxious to set the tray aside and take her in his arms again.

"How are you feeling?" she asked.

"Wonderful."

"You seem very far away."

"No, not really," he said as he picked up the tray and put it on the floor. He leaned across to her and pulled her down onto the pillows, kissing her. "I was just thinking about our first night together, and then our first breakfast in bed. It's hard to believe that was twenty-five years ago."

He lifted up her nightgown. She raised her arms as he took it off, then reached out for him. He put his arms around her and held her, dizzied by her presence again. He never tired of the fragrance of her, or the feel of her. Whatever else was right or wrong with his life, she was his foundation, his raison d'être. He wasn't sure what kind of danger they might find tomorrow on their journey into the northern mountains, but today was for just the two of them. They spent the rest of the morning in bed.

2. PAUL

Twenty-five years. It couldn't have been that long. True, there had been the big party last week. Their twenty-third wedding anniversary/going away party. Hosted by their own children. And this fall their baby was starting college.

Why, they were just getting started. He was still a young man. Maybe there was a little gray at his temples. Maybe he didn't have quite the stamina he'd had when he was younger. At least they'd both slowed down the aging process.

Several years ago, Joan had started running; she averaged fifteen miles a week, jogging San Francisco's hilly midsection. She would pull back the halo of honey-colored hair, permed into waves since the tight curls of seventies' afros had become defunct, and fasten it into a loose ponytail with a wide rubber band. She ran by herself, since Paul hated running. Up Larkin, watch out for the broken sidewalk where the pin oak roots were breaking through, left on Washington, race the cable car clanging its way through the intersections, right on Jones and up to Grace Cathedral, around the Fairmont and down Powell. Or any one of twenty other routes.

Paul was glad that Joan ran. It kept her slim and fit, not the straight-haired slender girl she had been at twenty, but a mature and lovely facsimile.

And, besides, he loved the smell of her sweat. Often, when she came in from her run, her gray Cal t-shirt soaked through, he'd give her a massage before she showered. Just another little way of keeping love alive in their marriage.

Paul wouldn't run, though. He had tried it for a few months, but it bored him and did bad things to his knees. But he did keep in shape with racquetball and a nautilus routine. The racquetball was more than exercise: it was a great game, a good competitive sport, and the chance to work out his aggressions on a ball instead of a person. He had started the nautilus when he turned forty, in an attempt to keep his chest from sliding down into his stomach, and in seven years he hadn't lost too much ground.

Well, he was certainly getting better. And look at the crowd growing old, or older, with him. Every day the papers had major articles on the growing number of mature adults. That didn't sound so bad-- mature adults. He hoped the writer who had coined that expression had gotten paid for it. Yet, in the evening, television was full of youth. Full of thong bikinis and seventeen-year-old tennis stars and well-dressed young men racing around in cars that could do twice the speed limit without even trying. He wondered if there would ever be a war between the generations. They'd had civil wars. World wars. Holy wars. The war between the sexes. Why not the war of the ages?

They had done a lot. Seen a lot. Been through a lot. He wondered how many breakfasts in bed they'd had, and which one of them had carried in the tray more often. Probably a tossup. Definitely, she'd carried the first one, and the last one. He'd have to think of something special for the next one.

He had moved in with Joanie in her wonderful Victorian flat, putting up with her roommate until she moved on to her next boyfriend. He went to work at the agency, write, edit, write, edit.. He learned that Joanie never ironed her hair, she simply had very straight hair. In fact, she was jealous of his wavy, almost curly hair. She finished her BA and started graduate school. In the evenings, when she was done with her homework, they talked and read and listened to music and made love, sometimes not in that order. He loved reading out loud to her, especially erotic passages from whatever he was reading—particularly when she was in the tub or the shower. Later on, they would sleep in what was by then the guest room, because the bed in their room was soaking wet.

They were married about two years after the night at Anne Bellamy's. Their friends all said they knew it would happen eventually. After all, they were made for each other. Paul was happiest about the fact that the wedding hadn't changed anything. The vows they made to each other had been spoken in so many words so many times that nothing was really different except their tax status. They still celebrated their first night anniversary with more feeling than they did their wedding anniversary, which was hard for some of their friends to understand. Paul's mother was completely confused by the whole thing. Last week at their anniversary party, she had drawn him aside.

"Paul, darling, someone just said this is your twenty-third anniversary."

"It is, Mom," he replied.

"But last month I called, and Joan was telling me about the wonderful pearls you gave her for your twenty-fifth anniversary."

"That's right. See, it's simple. We celebrate two anniversaries."

"Then which one did I miss?"

* * *

A year after they were married, Mrs. Mencken died, and her children sold the house. Some of the more special pieces in the house went to the museum. Most were auctioned off. They found a little place in Pacific Heights. It was a great neighborhood, but only an average place. She got her doctorate. Dr. Joan Webster. She had decided that Dr. Joanie Webster didn't sound right. During the Seventies, when it was all the rage, she toyed with the idea of a hyphen--Dr. Joan Davis-Webster. But she came to the conclusion that it was too much work to change over. And besides, it took longer to write.

Two babies came, a girl and a boy. They needed more room when the second arrived, so they joined the exodus to the suburbs. Contra Costa, then Marin. Joan's work demanded more time traveling. Paul's didn't change much. The agencies changed, and so did the clients. He had to look at his resume to count them. But the work didn't change. He enjoyed the challenge of a new client's problems, learning the ins and outs of a new industry. But when you got right down to it, writing about concrete technology wasn't that different from selling blue jeans. At least every time he moved to a new agency, the money got better.

At times, he still longed to really write. Over the years, he had taken a stab at writing at home. He'd started three novels, in fact, but set each one aside because he was too busy at work, or because they'd decided to move to a new house, or because the ideas just dried up. He had all the words he needed, he just hadn't been able to put them in the right order. He knew he had all the words he needed. Once, about a week after he'd moved in with Joanie, she came home with a large, gift-wrapped package. She put it on the coffee table in front of him and sat down next to him. She was happy and excited.

"What is it?" he asked.

"Go ahead, open it."

He tentatively lifted it. It weighed a ton! He untied the ribbon and ripped the wrapping paper away. It was the recently released Webster's Third New International Dictionary.

"Thirteen-and-a-half pounds of words," said Joanie, smiling. "All the words you'll ever need."

Since then, whenever a new, addenda edition came out, she got it for him. He had the original dictionary and four Addenda Sections now. They were getting to be a burden to move. He remembered Jack Burden in *All The King's Men*, saddled with the burden of history. He felt like Jack, carrying with him the weight of all the words in the world, still trying to figure out what to do with them.

* * *

Politically, they had survived. Paul's introduction to politics came just after his twenty-first birthday, when he managed to get a press pass when the Republican convention came to the Cow Palace in 1964. This would be exciting--history in the making, and his first chance to vote in a presidential election. His parents had always voted Republican, but here was an opportunity to see the machine in action and to decide for himself.

It was Tuesday the 14th, the night before the nominations. The moderates, led by the Scranton delegation, had challenged Goldwater to a floor fight over some of the more hotly debated planks in the party platform.

The press pass worked fine. He passed the civil rights pickets demonstrating against Goldwater's opposition to integration and walked right in and was handed an information packet, all the background he would ever need, down to the electrical capacity of the Cow Palace, with various suggested layouts, depending on whether he wanted to rent space for a trade show exhibition or a corporate banquet. Things were well under way. As Fats Waller said, the joint was jumpin'! The floor was a sea of state delegates, all more or less identified by show cards with each state's name. Paul looked around and wondered what the plastic boater concession had been worth. A lot of the delegates waved posters for their states' favorite sons. The podium was empty as he threaded his way forward along the side wall, past Delaware and Arizona, Kentucky and Washington State.

Chairman Thruston Morton of Kentucky turned the podium over to Senator Hugh Scott of Pennsylvania. Scott was a moderate promoting an anti-extremism amendment aimed at defusing the John Birch Society and its power with the Goldwater camp. The galleries booed and chanted, "We want Barry!" The moderates followed Scott with their trump card, Governor Nelson Rockefeller. He approached the podium to a round of boos and catcalls. Chairman Morton pounded his gavel for order. Rockefeller started to speak in favor of the same amendment, but each time he began, the noise from the floor drowned him out. Each time he waited, calm and poised, for the noise to subside. But with his next words, the galleries stepped up their booing. Twice Morton, urged by someone from backstage, tried to get Rockefeller to cut his speech short, but Rockefeller kept doggedly on, delivering a phrase at a time. As he finished, he set aside his speech and said, "It's still a free country, ladies and gentlemen."

As he left the podium, the mob roared, and Paul was ashamed for every one them. He started to leave, but encountered a wall of bodies at the rear of the Cow Palace, all trying to move forward. He twisted his way through the crowd to the exits. Past the exits, he could see several thousand more outside the gates. He stopped a security cop to see what was going on. He had to shout to be heard.

"All hell's broken loose," the cop yelled back over the din. "Somebody with a real cute sense of humor printed a few thousand fake tickets and sold them. Now we've got people standing outside with real tickets, people who've driven halfway across the country to be here, and they can't get in. And we don't know how many inside have fakes. We've gotta go through and check every one." He pulled out a handkerchief and wiped the sweat from his neck. "Problem is, most of the people with the fakes thought they were OK and paid good money for them. It's a real pisser!"

The angry crowd outside let him through, since he was actually leaving and creating some space. The civil rights pickets were calm and polite and totally outnumbered and unheeded. The ticket scam was much more important to all these folks than a few liberals.

The next day Paul watched the convention on TV. He wept with frustration when he heard Goldwater pound the podium and say, "I would remind you, extremism in the defense of liberty is no vice! And let me remind you that moderation in the pursuit of justice is no virtue!" He wondered if the American writer who'd written those words actually believed them, or was just doing his job, selling another product.

They had survived sex. Twenty-five years of sex with the same person had to be something of an accomplishment. They'd watched over the years as friends married, divorced, tried again. Keeping the romance alive wasn't teasy. Especially if, as with some of their friends, the romance was all tangled up in a desire for mystery and danger. And greener grass.

Or rather, he had survived sex. Joan thrived on it. She was the one who always seemed to be able to keep the whole thing together. If she had operated like Paul, they would have been another one of those statistics in the newspaper like so many of their friends. Joan's ability to make sex work for them wasn't really because of anything she did. It was simply because of who she was. She was open and honest to a fault. She always told Paul what she felt and asked for what she wanted. But Joan never used her honesty to hurt him, only to reach him.

And when it came to sex with Paul, Joan wanted it. She liked it. Maybe she had studied enough primitive cultures to assimilate the idea that sex wasn't something to be ashamed of, or afraid of. It was a natural act, a statement of love, and it was fun! Paul kicked himself for always getting so serious and solemn when they made love. Of course, he liked it, but there was always that gnawing worry underneath that made him feel like he was searching for the Holy Grail. How could you laugh and joke at a time like that?

Once, sometime during the late Sixties, when San Francisco was at the height of its love-in period, and Haight-Ashbury had been transformed from a rundown, neglected neighborhood into the Love

25

Capital of the World, they went to another party at Anne Bellamy's. LSD was still legal medicine, and Anne's parties had become not only a place to see and be seen, but a place where anything was allowed, so long as it felt good.

They were sitting at a table on the deck talking to a classmate of Joanie's from graduate school and his girlfriend and sharing a joint and some wine. Joanie's friend, Norman Diakhata, was from Senegal, very tall and very black. He was wearing a white Nehru jacket, and his melodious voice was a wonder to Paul, his English almost sweet with resonance in the way that each syllable was so lovingly uttered. His girlfriend was a tiny Japanese-American from Seattle named Joyce Tanaka. Stepping out of a soaking tub, she couldn't have weighed more than a hundred pounds. She was a few years older than Norman, already out of school and a successful stock broker.

Norman was leaning, with his arm around Joyce, talking shop with Joanie. Joyce and Paul sat in the middle, and Paul, in the midst of the conversation, was totally removed from it. He sat, soaking up the sound of Norman's voice and trying to cope with the buzz in his head from the pot and the wine. Joyce bent over and whispered in his ear. He straightened up, blushing, although it was so dark no one could tell, as the buzz seemed to become a roar.

Joanie put her hand on his shoulder, "Paul, are you all right?"

Joyce giggled, "Oh, he's just embarrassed. He's so cute. I only asked him if he'd like to make love."

Joanie smiled, "Well, if he isn't too crazy or too high, I'm sure he would. Wouldn't you, Paul?"

Paul choked, giving himself time to think of something to say. But before he could open his mouth, Norman joined in on the fun and suggested he and Joanie go find themselves a quiet corner.

As if she had just been invited to dance, Joanie got up and said, "I'd love to." Then, turning to Paul, "If it's all right with you, Paul. You go enjoy yourself with Joyce."

Paul, not knowing why, except that it seemed to be the heroic thing to do, nodded.

The four of them got up from the table, starting a major stampede for the vacated chairs, and worked their way inside the houseboat. Norman pulled Joanie on ahead, and she turned back to say, "See you later, darling."

The acid rock assailed his ears as Joyce took him by the hand and led him safely through the crowd to the stairway to the second floor. She seemed to know her way around the houseboat. She passed the bedroom at the top of the stairs, saying, "That room's always too crowded," and led him into the darkness of a second bedroom. One candle flickering in the corner of the room barely illuminated the movements of two other couples already there. They cautiously stepped over one couple near the door and crossed to the back of the room. She quickly took her clothes off, while he stood there numbly. He kept thinking to himself that this should be wonderfully exciting, but all he could feel was terror. Was Joan feeling terror? Was she doing this for him? Or was she really enjoying herself?

Joyce unbuttoned his shirt, and helped him pull it off. He came to when her hands reached for his belt buckle. "No. I'd rather do it myself," he mumbled.

He took off his clothes, listening to the urgent sounds of a climax from the couple near the door. Joyce was sitting on the floor, and she reached up and took his hand and pulled him down with her onto the deep shag carpet. Her hands and mouth explored his body. Her hands were cooler than Joanie's, but her mouth was wet and warm. She kissed his chest and then his mouth, and he began to relax. Or rather, as he remembered it later on, he began to feel the stirrings of passion. She moved her mouth to his ear, and her hot breath and tongue made him shiver with excitement.

She was lying on top of him, light and soft. He felt he could lift her with one hand and hold her at arm's length. He began to run his hands over her satiny back. He felt himself growing hard, so hard that it hurt. He rolled her onto her back and caressed her small breasts and bent down and kissed her hard nipples. She moaned softly and said, "Eat me up, baby." He moved his lips down her body to the soft mound between her legs. She spread her legs for him, and he stroked her soft thighs and searched her with his tongue until she cried for him to stop. She took his hands and pulled him up onto her, and, as he entered her, and their bodies met in a frenzy, a tiny corner of his mind kept telling him to be careful, she's so small. Don't hurt her.

They were back out in the hall, heading for the stairs when Joyce stopped, and reached up and kissed him. "Joanie's a lucky girl. And you're a sweetheart for trying something so new and scary."

He returned the kiss, feeling a strange, intimate yet platonic nearness to her. He felt like a schoolboy who'd just lost his virginity. He kissed her again, saying, "Norman's a lucky guy." He almost said, "Thank you," but decided not to. For a long time after, he wondered if he should have said thank you after all.

She smiled and said, "Let's go find those lucky guys."

And then, as they headed out to the deck to find Joanie and Norman, his mind began to race. Maybe he'd enjoyed it too much. Did Joanie enjoy it more than he had? They weren't out here on the deck. How much was she liking it? Maybe she would fall in love with Norman and leave him. Hadn't their whole relationship started with a night of sex?

When Joanie and Norman did arrive a few minutes later, he was sure he could sense a distance that hadn't been there before. She and Norman were acting like great friends, and when he asked her how it was, she simply answered, "Wonderful!"

That was it! She had fallen in love with Norman. Their marriage was over, he was sure of it. Yet when he asked her about it at home that night, in their own bed, she laughed and said, "Oh Paul, don't be so ridiculous! Norman and I just had sex, just like you and Joyce. Are you going to run away with her?"

Well, it made sense, he had to agree.

But for weeks afterward, he refused to let it go. He worried it like a terrier, shaking it this way, then that. And the more he chewed on it, the bigger it got. He waited in trepidation for something to happen. Any day now, he was sure, Joanie would come home from school and announce that she wanted a divorce. Would his life be totally shattered? Would he have the nerve to call up Joyce and ask her out? Why would he want to call Joyce? They'd only had sex together--he didn't even remember her last name. But then, Joanie'd only had sex with Norman, although she did see him every day at Berkeley. Maybe she was having lunch with him right now. Maybe she was at home with him, in his bed! The thoughts crowded his mind, especially when he and Joanie were making love--one night he called her Joyce!

Joanie sat up and looked at him with concern. "Paul, is there a problem? Are you still worried about Joyce and Norman?"

He started to cry. "Oh, I'm sorry, Joanie. I wasn't thinking about her, I mean not thinking about making love with her. I can't get it out of my head that something's wrong, that you've found someone else, and you're going to leave me," he blubbered, wiping his nose with the back of his hand.

She put her arms around him. "Don't say you're sorry. I'm not going to leave you for anybody. Nothing's the matter, except that you've got this whole thing all blown up out of proportion." She rocked him in her arms while he wept, all the suspicion and guilt he'd been nurturing pouring out in a torrent.

"Go to sleep," she whispered. "You'll feel better in the morning."

"But we were making love. You don't want to stop, half-finished like that, do you?"

"Lie back and close your eyes," she said, running her hand across his stomach. "I'll finish for both of us."

When Paul woke up the next morning, he felt great. He brought her breakfast in bed and made love to her with more passion than he could remember. They became great friends with Norman and Joyce and saw them regularly until Norman took Joyce back to Senegal with him. They still exchanged two or three letters a year and had spent a couple of vacations together. And eventually Joanie taught him to smile when they

30

made love (he was still working on laughing). He had a lot of names for his wife, his lover, his soul mate, his miracle, his woman, his life. He called her Joanie, Joan, Baby, Babe, Sweetheart, Honey, Darling, Juanita (when they were in Mexico), Sexy, and Wonderful, but never again did he call her Joyce.

* * *

They had survived children.

After Joan received her doctorate and became assistant curator at the Museum of Asian Art, she quit taking the pill. Megan McDonald Webster was born eleven months later. They'd just started getting the hang of day care, dealing with a swift succession of nannies, when Eric Livingston Webster came along, only a year and a half after his sister. Paul had accumulated a stack of books on names, and with each pregnancy he had typed columns of promising combinations.

"A person's name can determine their whole outlook on life," he said. This was serious business. "We can't overlook anything. I don't want to be responsible for saddling our kids with names they'll hate us for."

So the favorites were selected and dissected. Lauren, Laurie, Laurel, Emily, Emmy, Rose, Rosie, Rosalind, Ros, Scott, Scotty, Sean, Shaun, Shawn, Tracy, Trace, Mark, Martha, Marty, Kirk, Curtis, Curt, Jennifer, Jenny, Jen, Jesse, Jessie, Pamela, Pam, Pammy, Samantha, Sam.

"Beware of those diminutives," Paul warned. "Make sure nothing's hidden in the initials, like MAW, PAW, LOW, COW or RAW." Joan's initials were JEW, now that she had become Joan Elizabeth Webster. Of course, that hadn't occurred to them until Paul had gotten them each monogrammed towels, and it became a bathroom joke whenever they had company.

As a tribute to the women in their families, they chose their mothers' birth names for the kids' middle names (Their mothers still referred to them as their maiden names, but Joan and Paul were beyond that.)--McDonald was Paul's mother's, Livingston Joan's. Besides double last names sounded educated and successful.

Joan thought that Paul was taking the whole thing a little too seriously, but they ended up with names that sounded good, and neither of the kids had been ruined by them. They'd grown up being called Meg and Meggie, Erico and Airhead, and anything else their friends could think of, and, in spite of it all, they'd become well-balanced, intelligent young adults.

* * *

They had even survived parents.

Joanie's folks lived in New York, or rather just across the river in New Jersey. Paul thought they were great on the rare occasions they got together. Joanie could only cope with them for three or four days at a time, but since that seemed to be the chosen length of stay on either side of the continent, everything worked just fine.

Paul's parents had a cattle ranch in Kansas. Paul's dad was also the only attorney within a hundred mile radius, so he handled his friends' legal problems, which primarily amounted to wills and minor disputes. Like when John McDowell's dairy herd knocked down the Heidenreich's fence and ate up the clover planted for the Heidenreich bees. Obviously, a case for Ted Webster. Of course, in most of these disputes, both parties were friends of Ted's, so he spent more time mediating over a kitchen table than he did battling in court. So, the McDowells built a new fence, the clover grew back, and the Heidenreichs got a year's supply of the sweetest milk around.

In 1978, Ted Webster fell off a combine and never regained consciousness. Paul's mother, Tess, sold the ranch and spent a few years traveling, or rather visiting her other three children, all of whom still lived in Kansas, punctuated by cruises in the Mediterranean and the Caribbean. She loved to cruise and was a card-carrying Skjäld member. In 1986, she came west for the first time to discover Alaska on the Royal Viking Star, and she stopped for a visit with Paul and Joan. On her way back from Alaska, she decided to buy a condo in a seniors' community in Rollingwood. They saw her about once a month when she came to the city, usually fleetingly, since she mainly came to scoop up her grandchildren, "her joys," as she called them, to take them exploring San Francisco. Paul was sure that it was the kids who took her exploring.

* * *

The Philippine sun had moved halfway across the sky, leaving the slotted shutters in shadow and making the bedroom cool and dark. Joan was asleep under the sheet next to him. He looked up at the ceiling and realized that now he had no excuse not to write.

And now he was finally going to tackle real writing. He was sure a change of scenery would help him break out of the mold the agencies

33

had fashioned for him. He had quit his job and come with Joan to the Philippines, where she was collecting pieces for a show of primitive Asian art. They had spent a few days in Manila, and, while Joan met with bankers and patrons and the directors of several local museums, he roamed the teeming city, soaking up the strange smells and sounds, the light and the color. It was the middle of the rainy season, and every day the clouds rolled over the bulge of the island from the southeast and dumped sheets of rain on the city, washing a year's worth of dust and litter through the streets, down the storm drains and on into Manila Bay.

Manila was a sweet-scented flower, bright and seductive, pungent and throbbing, and her exotic sensations intoxicated Paul. Instead of the air-conditioned car and driver at his disposal, he swam headlong into the humidity and the heat that he'd never felt before, outside of the tropical conservatory in Golden Gate Park. He spent hours walking through streets crowded with traffic—Manila traffic: jeepneys bright with chrome and black with exhaust, taxis, chauffeur-driven limousines, buses and trucks choking out diesel stench, pedicabs, horse-drawn calesas and private cars, all honking and clattering and maneuvering their way across the city in near gridlock. The steady vehicular stream was cross woven with dense threads of pedestrians, courageous and foolhardy in their dance with death or disfigurement, sidestepping puddles and streams as well as traffic. He discovered the bar district of Ermita and strolled the narrow streets, watching the couples walking arm in arm, the men of every age, size and nationality, the women all young, slim brown girls. He learned to ride the jeepneys, sharing the jeep/bus hybrid with another dozen or so riders, climbing up the back and making a space for himself on one of the bench seats, traveling through whole sections of the city for a couple of pesos. He took notes on the way each driver decorated and named his jeepney: Rambo, Mango, Good Luck, Hermanio, Linda, Monna Lisa, Quezon Lady, Sweet Pea. He started a list of the collections of items proudly displayed on dashboards and hoods: chrome-plated horses rearing on their hind legs, plastic models of Ninja Turtles, figures of the Virgin Mary. He grabbed cabs and rode, his head straining out the open window like a golden retriever, inhaling the essence of miles and miles of corrugated metal and clapboard crazy-quilt shacks, of Coca-Cola and San Miguel Beer signs nailed to banana trees, of sari-sari stores and corner cafes offering pansit and fresh lumpia and green mango juice, of a dozen kids racing scrap wood boats across a flooded street, and gigantic painted Arnold Schwarzeneggers and Michael Jacksons and Chuck Norrises at every major intersection, larger than in their latest movies and larger, certainly, than life.

Most evenings, Paul and Joan were guests at cocktail parties and dinners thrown by members of Manila's 400. On these occasions, they were picked up at their hotel by the hosts' chauffeur and assisted into the back seat of what usually turned out to be a large, shiny Mercedes sedan, its leather seats deep and fragrant, its air conditioning humming softly. As they drove through Manila to one walled community or another, the thronging, steaming metropolis moved by outside, muted and distant as television screens in a store window. Sometimes rain streaked the windows of the car, and, as the wipers carefully and silently swept the water from the windshield, Paul found himself leaning forward, looking over the driver's shoulder out through the metronome of the wipers over the long hood, as if he were six years old and standing on the floorboards in the car behind his father.

The limo was an extension of the hosts' home, street, family, country club, polo grounds, stomping grounds. The Mercedes was West Berlin, an island of tranquility in a sea of economic depression. The car would slow as it turned into the community's guarded entrance. A wave of recognition from the security guard to the driver, and the gates would lift. Paul would breathe a sigh of relief--they'd made it through Checkpoint Charlie, and they were safe now, along with the vital information they'd brought with them. Up the long, curved streets, past rows of sprawling estates, walls, fences, hedges and gates, they'd glide into their hosts' driveway. Doors would open, smiling servants with umbrellas ready to usher them safely inside, through a few feet of open air, hot and moist as a greenhouse, into the cool of the air-conditioned and marble-floored entryway, welcoming handshakes and the usual apologies, "The August weather, it is so bad. You really should come back and visit us in December, or January."

One night they relived this ritual at the home of Bonifacio and Victoria Vital. He was a powerful man, in stature and politics. The Vital family were wealthy landowners in southern Luzon, with vast holdings of sugar cane and coconuts, and now Bonifacio Vital was a member of the Philippine Senate, one of only twenty-four elected nationwide. Victoria Reyes Vital was the third daughter of the influential Manila banking family, had received degrees at Mt. Holyoke and Cornell, and was on virtually every arts advisory board in Manila. She was a slim, attractive woman who selected her wardrobe during her annual trips to the designer shows in New York, Paris and Milan. In spite of their power and wealth, they were young and bright, and completely unprepossessing.

"Call me Boy," smiled the senator as he and Paul shook hands. He was dressed in a crisp, white *barong Tagalog* and black silk slacks. The barong Tagalog was the well-dressed Filipino's very comfortable answer to a suit or a tuxedo. It was a crisply starched, slightly transparent shirt, worn with dress slacks and never tucked in. "All my friends call me Boy. What will you drink?"

"Gin, on the rocks with a twist," answered Paul. He remembered how he had worried over his kids' names years ago. But here in the Philippines, it seemed to Paul, the more powerful the person, the friendlier the nickname. All the way at the top, it was Cory, not Corazon, or President Aquino. And major members of her government were called Boy, Sonny, Bobbit and Joker.

"Boodles, or Bombay?" asked the senator, and when Paul said Bombay, the waiter standing behind him disappeared before he could turn and repeat the order.

"So, this is your first trip to the Philippines. What a shame to have to visit in the middle of the rainy season. And, I'm afraid the rain is especially bad this year. This is the time of year when most of us either leave Manila or settle for inside activities. Do you play squash? Perhaps you'll have time for a game at the club before you leave for Baguio?"

Paul could guess that Boy was a good squash player, in spite of his size. The waiter materialized next to them with Paul's gin and something and tonic for the senator. Paul glanced around the spacious living room. Joan was at the other end of the room with Vicky, who was introducing her to two matrons in very expensive dresses and even more expensive jewelry.

"I'm not sure," said Paul. "We leave the day after tomorrow. But we might have more time on the way back. By the way, I read in the paper today there was a military skirmish near Sagada. Is it safe to travel farther north than Baguio?"

"The mountains to the north are never completely safe. The Gran Cordillera Central are extremely rugged, and they've been home to some of our most primitive cultures for thousands of years. For over three hundred years, while virtually all the rest of the Philippines were governed and baptized by the Spanish, the mountain people, or the Igorots, as the Spanish called them, maintained total autonomy except for a few scattered successes by Dominican and Franciscan missionaries. When the Americans arrived in 1900 after the Spanish-American War, they managed to establish some basic government and, in building a network of trails and roads, even put an end to the highlanders' traditions of headhunting." He paused to sip at his drink, then patted his mouth with his napkin.

"But the Cordilleras' terrain is so difficult," he continued, "the region has never been totally civilized. During World War II, Japanese troops occupied the mountains, as well as the rest of the Philippines, but the area also served as the primary hiding place for American and Filipino guerrillas. At the end of the occupation, General Tomoyuki Yamashita, the 'Tiger of Malaya,' retreated into the Cordilleras. The Americans bombed every major village in the mountains until Yamashita and his last 16,000 men made their final stand on Mt. Napalauan. Napalauan was a forbidden area to the highlanders, a sacred place in their mythology, and the Japanese took advantage of this, digging into the deep ravines and sheer cliffs. They honeycombed the mountain with gun emplacements, tunnels, barricades and fortifications. It took three months of continuous bombardment by the American planes and artillery before Yamashita finally surrendered."

The waiter appeared, taking orders for fresh drinks. The senator nodded to him and included Paul with a wave of his hand. "Today the mountains are refuge to Communist insurgents--the NPA, the New People's Army. They're little more than thugs and bandits, and they often prey on travelers on the lonely roads in the mountains, then force the local people to hide them and feed them. But my driver, Rudy, will take you and Joan to Banaue. He knows the roads and the people. Once you're in Banaue, you'll be guests of the wonderful Ifugao people there. I have friends in Banaue. You'll be fine."

"Darling, enough history for tonight," said Vicky, as she and Joan joined them. "Paul, you must be hungry. She took his arm and asked, "Would you escort me in for dinner, sir?" Squeezing his arm she said, "You know, they say that the Japanese hid a great treasure in the mountains. If you find it for me, I'll love you forever."

They left Manila for the five-hour trip north to Baguio through a downpour that blurred their views of the sugar cane and rice fields and towns crowded with explosive growth that stretched to the foothills of the Cordilleras. An hour from Baguio, the base of the mountains interrupted the broad plain of central Luzon, and they climbed through steep jungles of narra and palm and banana trees, the nearly vertical hillsides choked with vines and foliage as exotic as a dream. Water from the monsoons rushed down every ravine, and waterfalls tumbled through rocky gorges, adding their spray to the beating rain on the windshield, which somehow the wipers of the big, brown Mercedes sedan were able to keep clear. Far below, the streams and cataracts dumped their accumulated mud and silt into the Bued River as it twisted through rocky canyons, choking it with the rich lode that fed the paddies and fields below every year during July and August.

The road left the dense jungle behind and climbed into the pine forests that covered the hills around Baguio. The first shops, or last, if you were leaving Baguio, clung to the slopes like goats. Between them, the metal- and plywood-roofed houses of squatters littered the hillsides. They passed the clubhouses and golf course of John Hay Air Base--once the R&R center for American military in The Philippines, now jointly managed by the Armed Forces of the Philippines and a popular spot for vacationers' picnics. They turned east, away from the city, and circled up to an open, grassy hilltop.

Stretched across the western slope was a modern wood and glass home. Its wide eaves and timbered construction felt vaguely Japanese, and the meandering pine grove below, between the house and the misty view of the city, looked like a painting on a Japanese screen. The driver pulled up next to the house, and they ran through the driving rain and under the eave to the open door. The maid who greeted them at the door was a small, pretty Filipina who curtseyed and said, "Welcome, mum, sir," as they entered.

The house was primarily two rooms, large enough for entertaining quite a group. The outer room was walled on all four sides with rows of glass doors, closed now against the rain. With good weather, this became a large covered porch that could seat 40 guests for dinner. A massive stone fireplace connected the two rooms, opening into each. The inner room was smaller and more intimate, with rattan couches and conversation groupings for about twenty people. Off this inner room at the south end of the house was the master suite. At the north was the kitchen, and beyond it, a smaller building with rooms for the servants. These people live damned well, thought Paul. Nothing but luxury. He wondered what the road tomorrow into the real mountains would bring, then smiled as he remembered Vicky's description of this rest house, "Please do not expect too much. I'm afraid it is very quaint and small."

3. MT. POLIS

The lizard lay at the edge of the road, its white belly shining against the rain-darkened rock face that stretched up to the switchback above. From the dark gray wedge of its head to the tip of its tail it was over two feet long. It was a small casualty of progress; it had been hit by a car or the Dangwa bus that serviced this part of the Ifugao Province--between Talubin and the Mt. Polis summit. Here, the road cut into the side of the mountain was so narrow that gates were placed at each end of the section to control the one-way flow of traffic. If your timing was bad, you'd wait up to half an hour until the oncoming car traveled the distance and the guard opened the gate and turned the road over to you, phoning ahead to the guard at the other end that a car was on its way.

Looking out the side window of the Mercedes, Joan watched the still figure of the lizard, until it disappeared around a bend in the road. The Ifugaos honored this lizard and attributed special powers to it. They carved its likeness on many of their storage boxes and ceremonial items, and, even today, many of the women wore a necklace of its vertebrae in their hair to ensure their children's good health.

Paul hadn't seen it, and Joan hadn't felt it necessary to point out a dead lizard to him. This section of the drive put him on the view side, and he was leaning out the window with his camera, shooting the beautiful mist-shrouded slopes of Mt. Polis. Joan moved across the wide leather seat and looked out over his shoulder. Even though the major peaks only reached from seven to nine thousand feet high, in all of her travels she had never seen a mountain range as varied and impressive as the Cordilleras. And this mountain, of them all, conjured up feelings of magic and mystery. She could understand why the Bontocs, as well as the Ifugaos, revered this mountain as sacred.

"Beautiful, isn't it?" she asked, leaning against Paul's back to get a better look out the window. The rain had stopped, and the sky had brightened, warming the colors of the alpine slopes across the valley from them.

" Breathtaking," Paul turned his head and kissed her on the cheek.

* * *

He was having such a great time on this trip, thought Joan. She was really glad he'd come. She hadn't seen him so enthusiastic about what he was doing in years. She was amazed at the way he had thrown himself into experiencing Manila. Every evening, getting ready for that night's dinner party, he'd come in from a day in the streets, wet with rain and sweat, full of the day's discoveries. While he showered and shaved, he'd rattle off the highlights of his adventures like a kid just back from summer camp. And the next morning, he'd leave the hotel coffee shop to head back out before she could finish her breakfast.

She thought back to Paul's musings during yesterday's breakfast at the Baguio rest house. Twenty-five years did seem like a long time. An especially long time to set aside your true creative urges and sacrifice yourself and your talent for someone or something else. Which was exactly what Paul had done--first for her, then for the two of them, then for the kids. She knew a lot of women who had put their husbands through college, and graduate school if necessary, to help build a future for them both. Then, once the career was started, and the money began

43

to roll in, the marriage fell apart, and suddenly the future they had built was for him alone. Or more often, for him and some new and invariably younger trophy wife. In their case, it was Paul who ground away at the office, then usually ended up cooking dinner for them both when he got home, while she studied. And after the kids arrived, it was probably Paul who got up in the middle of the night to calm a fever. If she was out of town on business, it was Paul with the hot fudge sundae in the Dixie cup at the ice cream social, and it was Paul filling a seat at the junior high school spring concert.

A vision of Paul's dad flashed through her mind. She rarely thought of Ted Webster; she had only visited with him a half dozen times. She smiled, thinking of him. If he had been Irish, they would have said he had the gift of the Blarney about him. He had been a smooth talker, with a keen, incisive mind. He had also been an incredibly demanding parent, and he had pushed Paul toward those mutually unattainable goals of perfection and tolerance. Paul had inherited his father's ability at negotiation, and he had stretched himself between what his clients and co-workers asked for and his vision of what they really needed. Over the years his ability to negotiate had developed into pragmatism and acquiescence. Long ago, he had reached the point where he stopped really caring about what he wrote at work, and Joan had watched him try to escape into the real writing he had always wanted. But the deadness from the continuing work and the demands of the home and the children held him from finding relief with his own writing. Three times he had given in, and each time some of his drive had been imperceptibly drained away. The changes had been so subtle that, for a long time, Joan hadn't noticed them. Until last June, when she came home from the International Design Conference in Aspen.

Joan had been asked to lead a discussion on museum exhibition. She had intended to fly back to San Francisco on Saturday afternoon, following the closing ceremonies in Aspen, but she met the head of a Bay Area design firm who was flying home Friday night in his own corporate jet. He offered her a lift; it was an offer she couldn't pass up. She called Paul before she left the hotel in Aspen, but only reached the answering machine, so she left a message that she'd be getting in late that night, that she'd take a cab from the airport, that she loved and adored him.

They made it through the light fog into San Francisco International around eleven. She rolled her suitcase into the terminal--the best thing about flying in a private plane, she thought, was no waiting for baggage. She promised to call her newfound friend when the museum was ready to discuss exhibit design for the upcoming primitive Asian art show and got a cab for the ride up the Bayshore Freeway to the city. After the dry climate of Aspen--hot during the day, cold at night (they even had snow one night)--San Francisco's evening air felt moist and refreshing. She remembered the feeling of her bare arm trailing out the window of Paul's MG as they crossed the Golden Gate Bridge for the first time so many years ago. The cab turned off the freeway onto an exit dominated by a huge Frito-Lay billboard and entered the slow street world of the city.

It was after midnight when the cab pulled up in front of their house, but Joan could see light coming through the beveled glass windows of the living room. Paul must be waiting up for her. Her heart beat with excitement as she paid the driver and carried her bags up the steep steps to the porch. She knocked, not feeling like fumbling for her keys. No answer. She found her keys and let herself in. She put her bag and briefcase by the brass umbrella stand in the entry way and kicked off her shoes. The soft, dove gray carpet felt familiar and welcoming under her feet as she walked to the living room doors. She turned the corner and screamed at what she saw.

The room was a shambles. Books were scattered everywhere, dominated by the massive bulk of Paul's dictionary collection. A favorite piece of Chinese porcelain lay shattered on the marble hearth, its bright blue pieces mixed with the clear glass shards of a broken gin bottle. Paul was stretched out in the middle of the room, his face lying in his own vomit.

"Paul!" cried Joan. "Oh my God, what's happened?" She held onto the doorjamb to steady herself, started toward him, then thought, don't panic...get help. She turned back into the hall, picked up the phone and punched 9-1-1.

"Police and fire, two-four," answered the operator.

"There's been an accident!" Joan said, hurrying back into the living room with the remote. "My husband's unconscious. I don't know what's wrong."

"Yes, ma'am," said the operator. "What's your name, please?"

"Webster, Joan Webster." She threw herself down next to Paul, cutting her knee on a stray fragment of vase. "My husband is..."

"What's your address, please?"

"We're at 2510 Evergreen Place. Please hurry!"

"Stay right there. We'll have someone there right away."

She turned off the phone and dropped it on the carpet, putting her arms around Paul and pulling him up. She cradled his head in her lap,

46

rocking him like a baby, wiping the vomit off his cheek as the tears streamed down hers. "Ohh, baby, baby, baby," she whispered.

In what could have only been three or four minutes, there was a knock at the door. Joan lowered Paul gently to the floor and ran to the door.

Two paramedics, one a tall and gangly redhead, the other a burly young Asian, stood on the porch. The flashing red lights from the aid car backlit them and gave them both a surreal, menacing aura.

"Mrs. Webster?" asked the Asian.

"Yes," said Joan, throwing the door open and motioning them in. "Paul's in here," she said, leading them into the living room.

The redhead knelt down, avoiding the broken glass, checked to make sure Paul was breathing all right, and asked, "Does your husband drink a lot?"

"No," answered Joan. "This isn't like him at all."

The two men returned to the aid car and brought a stretcher back in. "We'll take him to Metropolitan Emergency to have him checked over," said the Asian. "It looks like he's drunk himself unconscious, but we don't want to overlook anything. Would you like to ride with your husband or follow us in your car?"

"I'll ride with him," said Joan. She got her coat and followed them out to the aid car, climbing in after the stretcher and sitting next to Paul.

The Asian got in behind her, and the redhead slammed the rear door shut. He jumped into the driver's seat, shifted into gear and turned the siren on as they approached California Street. Traffic slowed for them, and they ran the red light and swung left onto California, heading up Nob Hill. As they climbed the steep hill, the Asian checked Paul's

47

blood pressure and temperature. He picked up his radio. "Webster, Paul, two-five-one-oh Evergreen Place, bp one-two-four over seven-eight, temp nine-eight-five." He turned to Joan, smiling reassuringly. "Both normal. He seems OK. They'll probably just keep him a few hours for observation."

Four hours later, Joan paid the cab driver, then led her husband, half-awake and wholly chagrined, into the house. She helped him upstairs to their bedroom, where he stripped and rolled groggily into bed. She covered him, then went into their bathroom. She looked in the mirror and couldn't believe what she saw. Her face was swollen from crying and streaked with mascara and eye shadow. She took off her clothes, breaking open the cut on her knee as she pulled off her shredded pantyhose. She stepped into the shower and let the water massage the back of her neck. She toweled off, bandaged her knee, put on her robe and went downstairs.

The living room was still littered with broken glass and scattered books. She started to pick up the books lying about the room and noticed for the first time that all of them were lying open, with a word or a phrase marked with yellow highlighter. She started to read them and at once realized that Paul had been frantically crying for help. The yellow accents lighted up words in the dictionaries: *dried, wither, shrivel, wasteland, juiceless, lifeless, numb, dead end, catatonic, comatose.* Two books stood on the mantel in place of the porcelain. They were *The Dead Father* and *A Burnt-out Case.*

The next day Joan convinced Paul to quit his job.

* * *

The Mercedes came to a stop, and the driver turned to look at Joan. "Trouble ahead, mum."

From her comfortable back seat, she couldn't see anything wrong. She leaned forward and asked, "What is it, Rudy?"

Paul opened his door and started to get out.

"Careful, sir. Don't get too close."

Joan searched the road ahead, and suddenly realized there wasn't a road ahead! Or at least, not a whole road. The rain had washed out part of it; it must have happened since the last cars had passed, less than an hour ago. Landslides and mud slides were common during the monsoon season, and Rudy had warned them before they left that they might not be able to get through, but Joan was anxious to reach Banaue, and this was the shortest way when, and if, it was open.

She got out of the car and followed Paul and Rudy to the edge of the slide. Below them, the collapsing road had tumbled down the steep slope, leaving a narrow smear of mud and gravel until it disappeared into the vegetation below. She leaned to look closer.

"Careful, mum," warned Rudy. "The edge could give way also." Rudy is a born mother, Joan thought. He had been driving for Boy and Vicky for many years now, and he did his job well. He was amiable and agreeable, with a smile that lit up his square face. But he took his job very seriously; he was an excellent driver, with little time for chitchat. He answered, when spoken to, then went on with his work. And, judging from his broad, muscular physique, when conditions warranted it, he was probably a devoted bodyguard as well.

Joan stepped back as a handful of pebbles slipped away from beneath the road and clattered down the mountain. She turned to Paul. "We don't have room to turn around and go back."

Paul shrugged. "No, and we can't expect any help. Rudy, how far are we from the gate ahead?"

"About ten kilometers, sir. We're just halfway through this one-way section."

"Well, Rudy, we're in your hands. Any suggestions?"

"Yes sir. If you would both walk up ahead to that next turn, I will join you shortly." He turned and started back to the car.

"What about our luggage?" Joan called after him.

"I will see that it is taken care of also."

The two of them skirted the cave-in and walked up to the next curve. When they reached the turn, they stopped and looked back. Rudy had gotten in the car and was carefully backing it down, away from dangerous ground. The car stopped, then suddenly lunged forward, picking up speed as it approached the slide.

"Paul, he's going to try to jump it!" shouted Joan.

Rudy pulled the big Mercedes far to the right, nearly grazing the mountain's rocky face. He kept the pedal to the floor as the front wheels reached the washout. The car shot forward, its left front wheel spinning in thin air. It hit the other side while the rear wheels were still on solid ground and pulled ahead until the left rear sailed across, dug briefly at the collapsing edge of tarmac, and then lunged up onto solid ground. Joan's heart pounded as the car approached them, slowing to a comfortable pace and then stopping. She and Paul opened their doors and got in.

"Rudy," said Paul, "you could have been killed!"

"No," answered Rudy. "Many times I've seen much worse. And what is more, it is important for you to reach Banaue. Besides, the Senator would not wish for me to leave his car here for the thieves or the NPA."

Behind them, an even larger section of pavement crumbled away and roared down the mountain. They would have to give notice at the gate: no more cars on this road until the crews came after the monsoons.

* * *

It had taken a long time for Paul's desperation to surface. Joan could see their careers translated into graphs, tracked and plotted by some graduate student writing a thesis on the relative aspects of fulfillment in work and psychological well-being. The graph measuring Joan's job involvement over time would be a series of steadily rising plateaus, each jump coinciding with each promotion or move she made during her career. Paul's curve, on the other hand, started up immediately, then leveled off and gradually began to decline, broken here and there by upward blips representing new clients that had piqued his interest for a while. Figure 2.2, measuring Paul's level of frustration, was a mirror image of his career curve, increasing with each passing year. The end of this line was marked with a date and the notation, "Breaking Point." Joan wondered about the accuracy of the dotted line into the future labeled, "Marked Improvement--Projected." She looked again at her own career curve and the significant dates where the line jumped up.

December, 1965. It was Christmas break, a few months after Paul moved in. She had taken the bus downtown with Mrs. Mencken to do some Christmas shopping. Mrs. Mencken wanted to get something for her granddaughter, and she was sure Joanie could help her choose just the right gift.

"Richard always loved City of Paris at Christmas," said Mrs. Mencken. "It was his favorite store in San Francisco. Why, even the year that he passed on, he insisted that I bring him here so he could see the Christmas tree. I pushed his wheelchair on and off of the elevator, so he could see the tree from each floor. On and off, on and off, all the way to the top."

They were standing at the foot of the great tree that City of Paris had installed this year. It towered above them, reaching up four stories into the rotunda of the store. Thousands of white lights twinkled on it, and the huge glass ornaments at its base reflected the crowd of shoppers that milled around it on all four levels. Joanie had fond memories of Christmas in New York, with the decorated windows and the lovely chill in the air, but there was something really special about the City of Paris tree, glittering up through that beautiful building, scented by the cosmetics department with all those extravagant fragrances.

They picked out some perfume for the granddaughter. Mrs. Mencken had wanted to buy a bottle of Joy, but Joanie convinced her that a young woman would prefer Ambush. As they left the store, Joanie let Mrs. Mencken enter the revolving door first, then slowly pushed the door around for both of them. The December afternoon was crisp and bright, and the tangy smell of the bay was sharp after the sweet pungency of the store. They waited at the light, shading their eyes from the glare. Across the street, a cloud of pigeons rose from Union Square and banked across the facade of the St. Francis Hotel.

"Joanie, dear, I'm so grateful to you for coming with me today," said Mrs. Mencken.

"It's really nothing. I'm enjoying it."

"Yes, but it makes me feel younger somehow, just having you with me."

"You're still young."

"Don't be silly. But...Joanie, will you do an old woman a favor?" The light changed, and Joanie took her arm as she stepped carefully off the curb. "Will you take me to City of Paris next Christmas, even if you have to push me in a wheelchair?"

Joanie's eyes welled up with tears. "Of course I'll come downtown with you. But I'm sure we won't need a wheelchair."

"Thank you, dear. Oh, and by the way, can you and Paul come down for a glass of sherry tonight? There is someone I'd like you to meet."

At six o'clock sharp, Joanie and Paul knocked on Mrs. Mencken's door. Whenever she had people over for cocktails, it was always at six o'clock. Cocktails were invariably over by seven, and Mrs. Mencken was in bed by eight-thirty or nine. Then she was up for her morning routine at five the next morning. Joanie wondered why so many elderly people had clocks that put them to bed so early and got them up so early. There was no compelling reason to get up, and there were so many things to do in the evening.

53

A silver-haired man answered the door. He was tall and lean, and natty in English tweeds. His pale blue eyes sparkled in his tan, weathered face. He stepped aside and motioned them into the foyer. "Come in. Come in! Natalie's in the sitting room."

As they stepped into the vestibule, he extended his hand to Paul, then to Joanie. "Paul, Joanie, it's a great honor to meet you both. I've heard so much about you. I'm Emory Barclay. Please call me Emory."

They crossed the hall past a pair of Goya sketches and entered the sitting room, Emory Barclay following them. Mrs. Mencken sat on a green cut-velvet sofa that flanked the opposite wall. "Good evening, children," she said. "I'm so glad that you could come."

"Thanks for inviting us," said Paul, as he took her hand and bent to give her a peck on the cheek.

The room was festive with holiday trimmings. Swags of cedar boughs were draped on the mantel. A large cut crystal bowl filled with holly dominated the mahogany coffee table, which gleamed richly in the firelight.

"Sit down, sit down," said Emory Barclay. "Some sherry, Joanie? Paul? Or would you prefer scotch?"

It was a simple question but the tone in his voice made it sound as if he were asking Paul to join him in some kind of a radical political party. Joanie knew this man, she thought. Or at least she was sure she had heard his name. She found it impossible to take her eyes off him. He had such a strong personality, she could almost see the energy radiating from him. Surely from his eyes, at least, which glittered in the firelight. And as they talked, it seemed to her that he was observing her, anticipating her thoughts, reading her mind. Yet somehow she wasn't offended by his scrutiny. In spite of his intensity, there was something kindly, no, strong and reassuring about him.

"Natalie tells me your future is to be in museums," Emory Barclay said.

"Yes," replied Joan. "But that will be a long way off. I'm only completing my undergraduate studies this year."

"Oh, if you only knew how fast time goes by! But at any rate, you're young and bright and--forgive me, Paul--very lovely. Not that beauty should in any way be a requisite for success. If such were the case, I certainly shouldn't have achieved what I have done in my life. Perhaps I only mention that to prove to you that I still possess a keen power of observation." He picked up a small cup from the table. "But enough about that. Natalie has shared with me some very high words of praise concerning you. And there is no one whose opinion I value more than Natalie's." He handed the cup to Joanie. "Do you know what that is?" he asked.

She turned it over in her hands. It was a small, yellow ceramic cup, with two flowers and a branch etched into one side. The flowers were crudely dyed a deep blue-green. "It's a Japanese tea bowl," she answered. "Yellow Seto style. A reproduction of a design from the Momoyama period."

"You're close," he said. "It's not a reproduction. It *is* from the Momoyama period. About four hundred years old. That particular granular finish in the glaze was known as 'fried bean curd.'

"I've been collecting Asian art like that for quite a number of years now. I've decided that it's time to turn the whole kit and caboodle over to the city. I have several capable people working to get it all organized and catalogued. But we're running out of time, and I find I need still more help. How would you like to work on this project with me?"

Joan looked at him in amazement.

"Before you answer, let me just say that I realize you need to continue your studies. You'll need to go on and get your doctorate if you want to work with me. And I'm sure that we can work out a flexible schedule to deal with that."

The cup in Joanie's hand nearly dropped onto the celadon and ivory Chinese rug. With great effort, she quieted her trembling hands, carefully placed it on the coffee table and looked into Emory Barclay's eyes. The whole room seemed to glow. A pair of crystal candlesticks on the bookcase behind him cast shafts of brilliant light that cut the air around him, creating an aura she felt she could touch.

"Mr. Barclay...Emory. I'm very flattered. If you're serious about this, I'd love to work for you."

* * *

Emory Barclay was serious. He had been collecting Asian art for more than forty years. He had amassed a treasure of over 10,000 pieces. Chinese jade, Indian polychromes, Japanese ceramics, Korean bronzes, Nepalese rugs, Persian miniatures. He had offered the entire collection to the City of San Francisco, providing the city build a proper museum to house it. A bond issue had been passed, and the new Museum of Asian Art was under construction in Golden Gate Park. The museum, with its collections partially displayed, officially opened in June. Joanie graduated from USF the same month.

Emory Barclay, however, was not quite ready to quit collecting. While the cataloguing went on at the museum, he was back on the road. Kyoto, Hong Kong, Kuala Lumpur, Tehran, Surabaya, New Delhi, Bangkok. He had contacts everywhere, and he knew the territory. It was like a game of Monopoly, spread across the globe instead of around the town, and dealing with art instead of real estate. Wherever he stopped, he bought. And he invariably bought the best, and at the best price. He had been doing this for so long that it was second nature. He found a fifteen-hundred-year old stone Buddha in Afghanistan, sandstone bas-relief sculpture in Cambodia, T'ang dynasty hand scrolls and Chou period lacquer ware in China, undiscovered woodcuts by Hokusai in Japan, a copper statue of Siva from the eleventh century in India, a bronze Walking Buddha in Thailand and illuminated palm-leaf manuscripts in Nepal.

While he was in Nepal, he fell from a stone wall and broke his arm. He got dysentery while staying with Kurdish rebels in Iraq. He lay all night in a jungle stream outside a ruined temple to escape sniper fire in Cambodia. If you asked him why he collected Asian art with such obsessiveness, he would probably answer that he loved art, but in all reality, he very likely loved the excitement, the exotic adventure and the people he met as much as the art.

* * *

May, 1969. Joanie lifted her hand and curled her knuckles to rap on the varnished mahogany door. She paused, her arm raised as if tentatively volunteering in class. She looked at the brass card holder on the door and the faded card in the holder: R. Singleton Waring, PhD. The sight of the name sent a shiver up her spine.

During her three years at Berkeley, R. Singleton Waring had been, if not exactly a roadblock to her career in museums, at least a very large obstacle. He was the one member of her advisory board with whom she had never been able to develop at least a professional student-teacher relationship. He was aloof, critical, and condescending. It was obvious that he thought little of her as a scholar, much less as a writer or a researcher. When she had announced to her advisors the proposed subject of her dissertation, he had derided the idea until the others very nearly agreed with him. Joanie's arguments finally saved her another four months work developing a new subject, but Dr. Waring seemed to have taken her victory as a personal affront, and he had been even more unequivocating and arrogant since that meeting.

Next Monday, the final revisions on her dissertation were due, and, if accepted, she would receive her PhD in June. And now, at the last minute, she had received a call from one of the art secretaries: Would it be convenient for her to meet Dr. Waring at his office on Tuesday at three? She had never been to his office before, never, in fact, even met with him alone.

Joanie took a deep breath and knocked three times on the door. She waited a few seconds and was about to knock again when she heard Dr. Waring say, "Well, come in."

She opened the door and stepped into the office. It was a warm spring day, and the two large sash windows across the room were opened wide. The breeze created by the cross-ventilation from the open windows to the open door ruffled stacks of paper on the desk and blew several pieces into the air toward Joanie.

"Close the door!" exclaimed Dr. Waring. "Hurry!"

Feeling like Alice being attacked by playing cards, she closed the door and it slammed shut from the breeze.

Rattled, she turned and hastily scooped up the papers from the worn Kilim that covered most of the floor. The last had blown under a ladder-backed chair that stood against the wall. As she pulled it out, it caught under a foot of the chair and ripped. She tried to shuffle them into a neat pile as she stood up and stepped across to the desk, where he stood waiting impatiently. He took the papers from her and said, "Sit down, Miss Webster." He called all his female students Miss, regardless of their marital status.

"I'm sorry, Dr. Waring," said Joanie, as she pulled up the oak armchair.

"It's all right," he answered.

R. Singleton Waring was a large, portly man with thin, white hair that he brushed straight back. He shopped at Brooks Brothers for his suits and had his shirts custom tailored in Chinatown. His shirts were starched, and his slacks pressed, but Dr. Waring was one of those men who always looked rumpled, regardless of what he was wearing. Even his face had a rumpled, slightly dog-eared, look about it. His cheeks were beginning to show their age, sliding down his face into jowls, losing inexorably their battle against gravity.

Dr. Waring's office was a mirror of the man, littered with piles of papers and strewn with books. Every horizontal surface, including the wide window sills, was a platform for books and notebooks stuffed with papers. Even the floor was rimmed with stacks of art magazines, folios and reports. The air was filled, too, with the sweet aroma of pipe tobacco. A rack of well-worn pipes and a can of Dunhill's Toasted Cavendish were squeezed onto the crowded desktop. But Joan knew that looks could be deceiving, and specifically, she knew that Dr. Waring was renowned for his knowledge of Asian, and particularly Japanese, art and literature.

He put the papers back on one of the piles on the desk and weighted them down with a small bronze figure of a dog, then sat down in his green leather armchair and leaned back.

Joan sat silently, watching him attentively.

"Miss Webster," he began, "this meeting is not an easy task for me, but I feel it's important that I tell you a few things about yourself.

"Three years ago, when I was asked to become one of the advisors of a certain Joanie Webster, a recent graduate of USF and a newly-hired assistant of Emory Barclay's, I was not happy about my commission.

"Emory Barclay and I are, in a word, enemies. I think he's a thief and a scoundrel, that his approach to collecting art amounts to nothing more than piracy, and his ideas of exhibiting art are sensationalist at best, and snake oil salesmanship at worst.

"He, on the other hand, will tell you that I am a dusty old monkey gathering data and cobwebs, that my method of research is antiquated and my style far too erudite to do anybody any good."

He leaned forward and picked up the can of tobacco and pulled a pipe from the rack. He opened the can, filled his pipe, closed the can, lit the pipe with a kitchen match and leaned back again.

"When I heard that you were Emory Barclay's protégée, I wanted to have nothing to do with you, certain that Barclay was merely wielding his power to create another clone, yet another successor to carry on his brazen style.

"Dr. Waring, I...,"

"Please, let me say what I must. Then argue with me if you choose," he demanded, then stopped to relight his pipe.

"You had nearly won me over, until you announced to us your choice of subject matter for your dissertation--Seto-style ceramic glazing techniques. Barclay's large collection of Seto-style teaware stands to benefit mightily from this study. Barclay has duped us, I thought to myself, into helping this young woman do his research for him .

"But I couldn't bring myself to announce my suspicions to the other members of the board, and they were finally convinced by your well-reasoned arguments. I assigned myself the role of watchdog, to wait for any sign of impropriety so that I could expose you and Barclay to the department, and eventually the world.

"I must tell you, I've lost sleep over this situation. A museum can't be a mere showplace for P.T. Barnum grandiosity. Collectors must adhere to high standards of ethics, especially when dealing with objects of a religious nature. Europe and America have, for centuries, taken the cream of other cultures and held it captive for the limited understanding and enjoyment of their own upper classes.

"A moth, mounted in a display of lepidoptera, fades to a dusty brown, papery shadow of itself. But when viewed clinging to a mulberry leaf in the moonlight, it's a wonderful and fantastical sight. The Japanese tea ceremony, while exotic and fascinating to Westerners, can never be appreciated as it is by people raised and nurtured with the teachings of Buddhism and Shintoism.

"I've finally come to the conclusion that you understand that. I'd like to offer you my apology. You are indeed a sincere and intelligent young woman who will bring a sensitive and knowledgeable commitment to some museum, somewhere. I look forward to our meeting next week, and I'll happily add my name to those recommending that the school award you your doctorate."

4. JOAN

Joan looked up and saw that the afternoon light was fading, bringing a sodden early dusk to the mountains. Rudy had turned on the headlights, and they shone through the stripes of rain still pelting the pavement. It would be another hour of so up the dangerous road before they would reach Banaue. Joan had time to reflect on those early years.

* * *

September, 1975. Joe Cocker was singing "You Are So Beautiful" on the radio, and Joan was making waffles. Paul sat in the glassy kitchen nook reading the paper. Outside, the golden Contra Costa hills looked like pale winter wheat under the dark gray sky. The windows wept with the first rain of autumn. Soon, the golden hills would change to their coat of winter green. Megan and Eric were on the floor with the Sunday funnies. Megan was reading, in the unique style of a four-year-old, to Eric, who was just about two and a half. Eric was bored and was trying to turn the page.

"So here's Charlie Brown, and here's Lucy with a football. Lucy says, 'Hey, Charlie, something something the something.' Charlie says, 'No...' Eric, leave the paper alone! Daddy, Eric won't leave the paper alone!"

Joan turned out two waffles onto two plates. "Kids, breakfast is ready. You'll have to finish the comics later." She put the plates on the table and returned to the island to pour more batter into the waffle iron.

The phone rang. "Paul, would you get that? I'm up to my elbows in these waffles."

"Sure, honey," said Paul, and he went into the family room to answer the phone.

Joan finished pouring the batter and started to help the kids butter their waffles.

"Joan," said Paul, returning from the other room, "that was St. Francis Hospital. It's Emory. He's had another stroke. They said it doesn't look good."

"Oh, my God," cried Joan.

Paul put his arms around her. "They want you there right away."

"Of course."

"What's the matter with Oji Emory?" wailed Megan. "Can I go, too?"

Eric threw down his spoon and started to shout, "Go! Go! Go!"

As she drove west on Highway 24 toward the city, the rain increased, and Joan turned the wipers on high, before she realized it was the tears in her eyes she couldn't see through. She had known Emory Barclay ten years this coming Christmas. He was her boss, her patron, her champion. Since she had gone to work for him, she had worked hard, and she had done a good job. She had rewarded his trust in her. And she had become his protégé and had moved up through the ranks faster than she ever could have alone. She had accompanied him on several trips, and he had introduced her to people everywhere they went, people with the power to accomplish things, people in all the right places. But Emory was more than just a convenient lift up the museum ladder. He had become like a father to her. He appreciated the passion she had for art, something his own son and grandchildren lacked. He was devoted to Megan and Eric as well, always bringing some special present for them when he was in town. When each one was born, he had sent strings of origami cranes to the house for good luck. He taught Megan words in half a dozen languages, and he would roar with laughter when she called him her Oji Emory, her Uncle Emory.

Joan drove into the hospital garage and found a parking spot on the third floor. The rain had subsided, but water still fell in huge drops off the eucalyptus trees outside. She found the information desk in the lobby and was directed to Room 610A, in the north tower.

The jalousies at the windows of the room shielded most of the light from outside, and a small lamp on the wall near the bed was lighted. Emory seemed to be sleeping. Emory's son, Frank, and his wife were there. Frank drew Joan outside into the hall. "This time it was really a bad one," said Frank. His left side is paralyzed. He can't talk. He comes in and out of consciousness without warning."

Joan put her hand on Frank's arm. Frank was trying hard not to cry. "Go in and sit with him," said Frank. "Barb and I will get a cup of coffee."

She pulled a chair up next to the bed and sat down. Emory's eyes were closed. The left side of his face sagged from the aftermath of the stroke. Half his mouth seemed curled into a frown. His deeply bronzed face and arms seemed yellowish in the light. Joan reached out and touched his cheek. "I love you, Emory," she whispered.

Emory's eyes opened and turned toward her. Joan smiled as she saw that incredible spark still glowing in them. She leaned across and kissed his cheek. He lay still beneath her. As she pulled back and sat down

65

again, he looked down at his right hand, and Joan saw he was pantomiming writing. She picked up the pad and pencil on the hospital tray, put the pencil in his hand and held the pad for him. In his clean and crisp style he wrote, "Good girl. It's yours."

* * *

Joan looked up from her thoughts and noticed that the road had crossed a ridge. She was on the view side now, although it was too dark to see much, and Paul leaned against the other softly upholstered sidewall, asleep. Rudy's hands were on the steering wheel, at ten and two. His eyes were on the road ahead. He was doing his job. The depressing weather outside made her shudder, and she pulled her coat closer around her.

* * *

Emory Barclay died three days later. The newspapers ran front page articles. The mayor made a statement to the press and offered condolences to the family. A mass was said at Grace Cathedral.

By Saturday, the weather system had passed through. It was hot and sunny. While most of the summer in San Francisco is cool and foggy, September often brings the city its warmest, most summery weather, and this day was no exception.

The large turnout for the funeral was a vivid demonstration of how many people thought highly of Emory Barclay. The services had to be delayed for nearly half an hour to allow friends and well-wishers time to find parking and walk to the graveside. As they left the funeral, Paul put his hand on the nape of Joan's neck. Her long hair was done up in a bun. Her eyes were red from crying.

A husky man with a gray crewcut stopped them. He was wearing a navy blue suit that seemed too tight for him. His face was ruddy, and his neck seemed to bulge from the starched white collar that showed signs of sweat. It was obvious that heat didn't agree with him.

"Mr. and Mrs. Webster? I'm sorry to interrupt you at a time like this. Mr. Barclay was a fine man. Many of us will miss him."

"Is there something we can do for you?" asked Paul.

"My name is Robert Woislawski. I'm an attorney with McDougal, McDougal and Finch." He handed Paul his card. "We're handling Mr. Barclay's estate, and we will be reading his will on Monday at two o'clock. I'd appreciate it if you could be there." He offered his sympathy again and left.

* * *

At ten to two on Monday, a secretary showed them into the McDougal, McDougal and Finch conference room. Frank and Barbara were already there. Frank's son from a previous marriage was there as well, but his daughter lived in Denver and had to return after the funeral. Emory had a younger sister living in a rest home in Arkansas, but her health hadn't allowed her to come west.

The secretary returned with a silver tray filled with coffee pot, china cups and saucers, sugar bowl, creamer, linen napkins and sterling spoons.

"I can get decaf if anyone would prefer that," she said. They were all fine with regular coffee, and she left.

A few minutes later, Robert Woislawski arrived and greeted everyone. He seemed more comfortable today, here in his own element. The heat wave continued, but the air-conditioning here on the thirty-second floor made it almost chilly.

Woislawski invited everyone to sit, then sat down himself at the head of the long, rosewood table. He looked around the room at the five people present, smiled and said, "I'd like to thank you all for coming today. Although you and I have never met before, I want to assure you that I knew Mr. Barclay quite well. He was a fine man. An extraordinary man, as you all know." He took a sip of his coffee.

"I met Mr. Barclay in Bangkok in '67 when I was finishing up my tour of duty with SEACOM command. When I told him I planned on returning to the Bay Area after my discharge, he made me promise to call him. I've handled an assortment of legal matters for him ever since I returned in '68. I'd like to extend to you the firm's, and my own, deepest sympathy.

"I have here Mr. Barclay's last will and testament, signed by him in January, 1970, and amended just last March. Mr. Barclay liked to keep things simple. This won't take long."

He read through the standard preamble, then continued, "First: I give and bequeath to my sister, Lucinda Maureen Mackay, of Fayetteville, Arkansas, the sum of Five Hundred Thousand Dollars, to be put in trust and to create a continuing income for her as long as she lives. Secondly: I give and bequeath all other assets and worldly possessions to my son, Franklin James Barclay, and his heirs..."

Woislawski stopped and referred to an attached sheet of paper. "This amounts to about twenty-two million dollars in round numbers," he said, looking at Frank. "I have the breakdown here for you."

Then he continued to read, "except, Thirdly: I give and bequeath to my friend, Dr. Joan Elizabeth Webster, the remains of my private collection of Asian art, which amounts to thirty-eight pieces (see attachment B). I also appoint Dr. Webster executrix of my entire collection of Asian art currently in the possession of the Museum of Asian Art in San Francisco. It will be her responsibility to ensure that the collection is kept and exhibited in a manner of which I would approve. If, in the future, it becomes her professional judgment that the collection would be better served in another location, the decision to move the collection rests solely with her. A trust fund will be established to ensure that she receives adequate compensation for the performance of these duties (see attachment C)."

Joan stared at Woislawski in amazement. He gave her a neat, professional smile and closed the file. "Mr. Woislawski," she demanded. "You can't be serious!" She turned to Frank and Barbara. "This is too much! I can't accept this responsibility!"

"It's what Dad wanted," replied Frank. "No one knows the collection like you do, and I doubt that anyone could come closer to handling it the way Dad would have." He started to get up from his chair.

"Then listen to me," said Joan. "No one outside of this room should ever know that I have the power to move the collection. If that news leaks out, I'll be hounded by museums all over the world."

"The museum commission will have to know. It's all linked to your becoming curator. I have to tell them," said Woislawski.

"Well," said Paul, "I'm sure they won't breathe a word of it. It's certainly not in their interest to do so."

"Mr. Woislawski," said Joan. "Can you keep this quiet for a couple of days? Just to let me get used to the idea before you break it to the commission?"

"I'd be happy to do that. I'll call you on Thursday before I call the commission to set up an appointment."

* * *

Woislawski and Joan met with the commission the following Monday. Most of the twenty-three members were delighted with the news until Woislawski reached the last clause. Joan strenuously pointed out to them that she had grown up with the museum and the collection, and that she certainly had no intention of moving it. She assumed, she said, that Emory Barclay had included that line in his will merely for insurance against totally unforeseen circumstances, and that she was sure she would never have to exercise that power. As long as the commission continued to respect the collection as it had for the first nine years, they had nothing to fear. Several members argued that the city had been foolish to build a structure for a collection it didn't have complete control over, and they were attacked by others arguing that the collection was too important, that they had had to accept Barclay's terms. Voices grew louder, the room was out of control.

Joan leaned over to Daniel Swanson, the president of the commission. "Dan, can I have a word with you in private?"

They left the fracas in the conference room and entered the office next door. Joan closed the door. "Dan, what do you think?" she asked.

"It's a bitter pill for some of them to swallow. It's natural that they'd be upset, losing control like this," he answered.

"They haven't lost control. They never had it. Don't forget," she said, "the museum has been at Emory's mercy all these years. He could have moved the collection at any time. So nothing's really changed, except that I am the new curator of the Emory Barclay collection. Everyone on the commission is a member for one reason: to do their level best to see that this collection is cared for and maintained for future generations.

"It was obvious when the mayor first approached Emory that San Francisco was the ideal location for his collection. Its large Asian population and their ties to their native countries, its location on the Pacific Rim, and the interest of its citizens in history and culture were important points no other city could match. Well, *nothing has changed!* The perfect place for this treasure is still here. You know that; so do I.

"I've been given a huge responsibility. It's one thing to travel around and buy pieces of great art. It's glamorous and thrilling to see your name attached to a prized piece in a museum. It's quite another thing to care for and maintain a collection of over 10,000 pieces, many of them thousands of years old. To see that temperature and humidity are kept at optimum levels for each type of material. Storage alone--we only have room to display about a tenth of the pieces--is a major job. Proper lighting, protection from pollution and earthquakes, cleaning, documentation and photography, packing and shipping of items shared with other museums, educational programs, cultural exchanges, continuing research on conservation methods.

"It's a big, expensive job. Very few philanthropists get excited about paying for heat or janitorial services or even printing costs. But when San Francisco's voters said they would invest in this idea, they created a legacy that's been entrusted to us. I plan on doing my best to deserve their trust, as well as Emory Barclay's."

In the end, there was nothing they could do but accept the situation and put their trust in Joan. They gave notice to John Terry, the current curator. Joan had liked working with John, and she offered him another position, but he was furious. He left immediately, but not before starting the rumor that Joan had wriggled her way into the old man's will by sleeping with him. In spite of the fact that Joan was well liked, he managed to create doubt in some minds, and Joan was forced to replace nearly a third of the staff during the next few months.

* * *

The dark was broken only by headlights and the glow from the dashboard. Rudy's head and shoulders were softly silhouetted by them. Paul was still asleep, unconcerned by the movement as they rounded yet another curve. Up ahead, a small deer, startled by the glare of the headlights, sprang sideways and crashed noisily into the bushes at the side of the road.

* * *

April, 1984. By now, Joan was Director of the Museum and a recognized expert on Asian art. She had been invited by the American Museum Council to join a ten-member group to work, in conjunction with the State Department, at developing closer cultural ties with China. Tomorrow, she was leaving for a three-week tour of northern China. The goodwill trip was wholeheartedly supported by President Reagan, who planned to visit China himself later that month.

Megan and Eric were staying overnight with friends. Eric was thrilled at the chance to spend the night playing with his friend Michael's new Atari. He had been badgering them to buy him one, but Joan wasn't sure that these new video games were of much use. Probably just another fad that would go the way of the hula hoop. By next year, he'd forget all about it.

Paul had fixed veal piccata for the two of them. Joan loved Paul's cooking, not just because she didn't have to cook, but when you haven't cooked something yourself, you're not already wrapped up in the food's odors and flavors, you don't know what substitutions have been made, you're not aware that the garlic browned a little too much. It was almost like going out to a restaurant. As usual, his cooking had encouraged her to eat too much. She was finishing with coffee, and just a spoonful of his zabaglione, while Paul put on another record--Tania Maria, his latest discovery.

Joan wondered about Paul's love affair with Brazilian music. If something ever happened to her, she could almost see him dropping out of the advertising business, holing up with a typewriter under some palapa on a beach near Rio, and immersing himself in native rhythms, a perpetual samba with dark-skinned girls.

She felt Paul's hands on her shoulders and purred as he began to massage her, "Ummm, that's good."

She turned to look up at him, and he took her face in his hands and kissed her. "I'm going to miss you," he whispered.

"I wish I could tuck you in my carry-on and take you with me," she answered. He had put on some cologne this evening. Joan wished he would use it more often, it turned her on so.

His hand slid down to her breast. She got up and led him to the sofa. They sank into each other's arms and held each other for a long time, kissing softly, content for now to be close, closer than close, as close as only two people who have loved each other for many years can be. The husky Portuguese lyrics in the background were an aphrodisiac. Later, as they made love, Joan's eyes filled with tears.

"What's wrong, Wonderful?" asked Paul.

"Sometimes I get so frightened. I think of losing you, and my imagination carries me away. I feel like I couldn't even breathe without you," she cried.

"Joan, sweetie," he soothed. "Don't worry. I'll still be here when you get back."

* * *

The next afternoon she had finished packing for the trip. Paul and Eric were carrying her suitcases to the car. She knocked on Megan's door. "Honey, we're going to the airport now."

"Bye."

She opened the door. Megan was lying on the bed, reading. "What do you mean, bye?" asked Joan. "You're coming with us."

"No, I'm not," answered Megan.

"Now, look, miss...."

"Go ahead! Spank me! Ground me!" Megan was up on her knees. She threw her book across the room. "I don't care what you do to me!" Suddenly she burst into tears and threw herself back down on the bed, sobbing.

"Megan, what's the matter, honey?"

Megan sobbed through her tears. "You don't even know, do you? You just don't care about me. Or Eric. You don't even care about Daddy. All you care about is that stupid museum and collecting a bunch of dumb, dead stuff!" Her little body shook with crying.

Joan sat down on the bed and took Megan up in her arms. "I care about all of you, baby. I can't tell you how much I care."

Megan allowed Joan to rock her, but remained stiff and angry. She had green eyes flecked with gold like her father, and they flashed up at Joan. "Why can't you be like other mothers, and spend time with your kids?" she frowned.

"I hate to say this, but I have a plane to catch," said Joan. "Ride with me to the airport, and I'll try to explain it to you."

Joan and Megan sat in the back seat of the car. Eric was forced, much to his delight, to ride up front.

"When I was about your age," said Joan, "my Aunt Dorothy took me to the Metropolitan Museum in New York. I had never seen so many beautiful things, or such a wonderful place, in may life. She bought me a catalog, and I took it home. I looked at it, day after day. I memorized everything in it. Ever since then, I've wanted to be a part of a museum like that. I want to show people things that they'll never forget, things that will change them.

"When your father and I decided to have children, we knew that it wouldn't be easy. Your father has given up a lot to spend extra time with you when I'm busy at work. You know, I think you're really lucky. A lot of kids never see their dads. You've got a wonderful father, and you get to spend a lot of time with him.

"I know I've had to miss out on being with you as much as I'd like, but I cherish the time I've had with you and your brother, and I would do the same things over again, if I had the chance. Always remember, wherever I am, wherever you are, we're a family, and I'll always be proud and happy to be your mother."

They dropped Joan off at the United Red Cap station. Joan hugged Megan and Eric, and promised to send them cards from Shanghai. Paul put his arms around Joan, kissed her and said, "I'll always be proud and happy to be your husband."

5. BANAUE

The big car rolled to a stop, its tires crackling in the gravel. Rudy turned off the key and set the parking brake. "Mum, sir, it's Banaue. We're here."

Paul looked out the window. It was still raining, pounding hard on the sidewalk next to the car. There was a polite knock at the car door, and then the door was opened. Two tiny young women welcomed them out of the car and under the giant umbrellas they were carrying. They wore modern versions of the *tapis*, the long Ifugao women's skirt, in narrow stripes of red, yellow, green and black. "Welcome, ma'am. Welcome, sir. We're so glad you had no trouble with the road and the rain. We were starting to worry when it grew dark."

The rain thundered on the umbrellas and poured off their edges like spillways of a fountain as they were led up the thick plank steps and under the broad eaves of the Banaue Terrace Hotel. It was a long, low, modern structure built at one end of town on the edge of the plateau. It was simply but strikingly built of wood and stone. The broad, open-beamed lobby was dominated by a large stone fireplace crackling with pine logs. The polished wood floor gleamed in the flickering light of the fire.

Their hostesses asked them to be seated in wide, comfortable chairs near the fire. A tray with cold bottles of San Miguel Beer and baskets of pork rinds and peanut crackers arrived. The concierge brought them check-in forms to fill out, but please, no hurry. After they had rested a while would be fine. It was only a formality. He strutted off, his elbows flapping like a banty rooster's wings.

They finished their beers and filled out the forms. As they rose to take them to the reservations counter, the concierge came bustling back to them. Thanking them for troubling themselves with the forms, he assured them that their room was ready, and their luggage was already in the room. Rudy was in his room having his dinner. The dining room was available for their dinner, or it would be happily served in their room, whichever they chose. They were to think of the hotel as their home while they were here in Banaue. After all, they were almost the only guests right now. No one comes to Banaue during the rainy season. It is the worst time. But, please, no offense was intended. They were here at last, and they were welcome to stay as long as they wished.

Should they need anything at all, they need only to ask. If they needed more towels, the answer would be Yes. A magazine or a book, Yes. If a massage was desired, Yes again. Whatever they were to ask him, his answer would be Yes.

As they walked down the hall to their room, Paul laughed, "What a character for my notebook! The concierge of concierges. The ultimate yes-man." Joan giggled and put her hand over his mouth. They had a light supper in their room, climbed between the goose down comforters on their king-sized bed, and read themselves to sleep.

* * *

"Joan, wake up! Look where we are!" Paul pulled the drapes back from the wide, floor-to-ceiling window in their room. The morning sun streamed in. He opened the sliding glass door and stepped out onto their narrow balcony. Joan slipped on her robe and followed him.

Stretching out below them the steep ravines and flanks of a dozen mountains were covered with huge steps--"the stairways of the gods," as the Ifugao called them—the Banaue rice terraces. The sun, rising beyond the mountains, reflected in the water-filled terraces, turning them brilliant gold.

Paul had read the story of the rice terraces, begun by Ifugao ancestors more than 2,000 years ago and now reaching thousands of feet up many of the mountains throughout the Cordillera. Of them all, those at Banaue were said to be the most spectacular. He had seen photos of this eighth wonder of the world, layer after layer of stone and clay dikes, each thirty to a hundred feet tall, sculpted around the mountainside and meticulously planned with brooks and canals running from top to bottom, irrigating all the paddies. Flat stones protruding from the walls provided steps for climbing up and down the dikes. There were other renowned structures, like the Great Wall of China and the pyramids of Egypt and Mexico, but they had been built with forced labor and much grief and death. The rice terraces were a living, growing collaboration developed by a community over thousands of years, structures built with simple hand tools and a rare vision for the common good.

Nothing he had read or seen had prepared him for this sight. A thousand feet below, he could make out the tiny specks of people working in their fields. He put his arm around Joan. "In all of those dictionaries, there's not one word to describe this." She smiled and hugged him back.

They took breakfast on the hotel's covered terrace, offering them another spectacular view of the mountains and their amazing constructions. The sun was higher now, and the terraces glowed with the unimaginably bright green of young rice shoots, especially vivid against the dark rock of the terrace walls and the mountain faces themselves.

Their waiter returned to pour more coffee and handed Joan a small piece of paper. "Excuse me, but there is someone of importance in our lobby. He would like to pay his respects."

Joan looked at the paper. Neatly printed on it was: *Teopisto Gumangan, Mayor, Banaue, Ifugao, Republic of the Philippines.* "Please," she said to waiter. "Show him to our table. We'd be honored." As the waiter left, she whispered to Paul, "It's obvious that the senator's been at work for us. It's the Mayor of Banaue."

Across the room a group of half a dozen Ifugao men approached them. They wore Western style slacks and sport shirts open at the collar, the tails hanging outside the pants. They were all small, brown men with lined, open faces. As Paul started to get up from his chair, the leader extended his hand and said, "Please, do not disturb yourself. I am Teopisto Gumangan, mayor of Banaue. We are honored by your visit." He shook hands with Joan, then Paul. "Please call me Teo. And allow me to introduce my deputies of health, finance, education, administration and security."

He pronounced the word, "finance," as if it started with a "p." There is no "f" sound in the Ifugao language, Paul remembered. They pronounce the name for themselves as "Ipugao."

Grinning with enthusiasm, the five men each shook hands with Joan and Paul, then pulled up nearby chairs, forming something of a circle around them. Coffee was served, and each man added sugar, normally two or three spoons. Paul watched as the deputy of security added six, then stirred the coffee carefully. His name was Valerio Pawid, and he seemed to be the oldest of the six. Paul had noticed that the others treated him with some deference, calling him *Lakay* Pawid, a term reserved for elders. He was the first of the deputies to shake hands and the first to sit. His face and hands were no more brown than the others, but the creases were deeper, the texture of the skin rougher, the stoop of his back slightly more noticeable.

The mayor was quizzing Joan on their itinerary, "And I am sure you would like to visit some of the nearby villages? If the weather allows, you must go to Batad. I have an aunt there, and there are several families with items handed down for many generations. They will be happy to loan them for your exhibition, I am sure. The mountains may be dangerous to some, but with our help, we intend to keep you safe. And if you visit Batad, you must see Cambulo and Patpat. Luis, here, has a cousin in Patpat...."

So Joan had hit the jackpot. Her plans had intrigued Boy and Vicky. Boy had made a few phone calls, to all the right people in Baguio and Banaue. Every one of these men had relatives throughout Ifugao. And each was anxious for his family to arrange for the loan of finer items than the next.

"The rain, it usually comes in the afternoon and evening," Teo continued. "Today, we will introduce you to the people here in Banaue-- our friends and families. Tomorrow morning, if you'd like, you'll be taken on a tour of the rice terraces. Then, the next day, you'll visit Batad." He pushed his chair back and stood up. "Now, we must go and make the arrangements. Someone will call for you after lunch. Wear simple clothing." Joan and Paul shook hands again with the six of them, and, with many smiles and bows, they left.

Paul looked at Joan and smiled, "I'm exhausted. And we haven't even met their wives yet."

* * *

That afternoon about two, the deputy mayors of health and finance called for them. When they reached the front door of the hotel, the girls who had welcomed them the night before presented them with a pair of heavy-duty umbrellas. They began skirting the mud puddles on the road through Banaue, and Mariano (Sonny) Lumauig and Eduardo (Duarding) Meimban pointed out highlights of the little town. They passed the post office and the municipal hall, a square, two-story clapboard building. Above the second-floor windows and centered on the building's facade three-foot-high letters announced, "BANAUE MUNICIPAL HALL." A short way farther north was the Good Shepherd Clinic, a Protestant mission establishment and the only source of health care for miles. Beyond that, the Tourist Information Center, closed now during the rainy season. Just ahead was the town's market.

"We will meet the mayor at his family's home," said Duarding, and they turned off the road and started down a much traveled footpath. A hundred yards down the path they came to a traditional Ifugao house. It was raised four feet off the ground by four corner timbers with barrier blocks, designed to keep rats from climbing farther. The four-sided, thatched roof looked like a large pyramid extending beyond the windowless wooden walls nearly to the level of the floor. Woven openwork baskets that looked something like tea cozies or large bells hung from the floor of the house; each one was a safe haven for a family chicken during the night. As they ducked under the eave, Paul saw that a wooden ladder reached from the dark doorway down to the ground. At Sonny's smiling invitation, Joan climbed the ladder, and Paul followed. Next to the door, prominently displayed, was the skull of a pig, sacrificed for the health and safety of those living in the house.

As Paul entered the house, the mayor appeared, smiling and shaking his hand, "Welcome to our home. Please, sit." He motioned to a space to Joan and Paul's left. Paul sat down cross-legged on woven mats and glanced at Joan. She was enthralled by everything around her, and hardly noticed him. Paul rubbed his eyes, burning slightly from the smoke in the air, and counted thirteen, no, fourteen other people in the large, central room. Some of them also sat cross-legged, but many of them bent, their legs and feet jackknifed into a low, squatting position. Sonny and Duarding had followed them in and were seated on either side of Joan and Paul.

"Welcome, all," began the mayor. "We are privileged to have so many people whom we respect in our home. And we are pleased to take this opportunity to welcome Paul and Joan Webster to our community. We are honored by this visit, and we wish to celebrate it with our oldest *tapuy*."

The elderly woman next to Teo handed him a large, Chinese porcelain jar, beautifully painted with chrysanthemums and dragons. It had a lid and handles woven of split rattan peel. Duarding leaned close to Paul and whispered, "That's Teo's mother with the tapuy. Tapuy is rice wine. This tapuy is the finest, made from rice harvested at the full moon, boiled, then stored with a little sugar in an earthenware pot. Teo's family has used that jar for hundreds of years."

As Teo and his mother proceeded with the ritual of opening the tapuy, blessing the carved wooden dipper and preparing the cups for their guests, Paul examined the house, now that his eyes had adjusted to the dim light and the smoke.

The high, slanted ceiling formed a peak at the center of the roof. A framework of four tie beams and a central cross-beam supported two queenposts that rose to either side of the smokehole at the peak. It was designed to suck out the smoke from the smudgy fire that burned slowly, banked back in the fireplace below, but the air in the house was thick with smoke. On each wall, two or three rows of heavy shelves ran the length of the room. Across the room from him, one of the shelves was supported by two tall wooden figures, simply but elegantly carved with lances and shields. Another shelf was held by the skull and horns of a *carabao*, and two shelves had rows of animals--dogs, pigs, carabaos-- carved on the undersides of the shelves, their snouts, horns and tails serving as hangers for clothing and baskets. On the shelves were wooden storage boxes and baskets holding the family's household items. Paul knew that this traditional home was full of the kinds of things that Joan had come to collect. Teo tasted the wine, swirled it around in his mouth like a wine steward at a three-star restaurant, swallowed, and grinned with delight at all. "It is a fine wine, and I am proud to pour it for our guests."

Duarding leaned over and said, "The wine ages at least six months. But until it is tasted, there is no way of knowing if it is sweet and good, or sour and undrinkable."

Cups were filled, passed around, and lifted. Teo raised his highest of all and said, "Let us all drink to the good fortune of our visitors."

The wine was smooth and sweeter than sake. Everyone drank, and the house was filled with conversation and laughter. Teo was a good host; he made sure that everyone's cup stayed full. He took Joan over to meet his mother and seated her in his spot so they could talk. Sonny laughed and elbowed Paul. "Your wife sits in the mayor's place. That is an honor reserved for special people only. I think you are married to an important one, eh?"

"It's as he says," said the deputy mayor of security, squatting down on his haunches in front of them.

"Lakay Pawid," said Sonny, raising his cup, "to your health, and your family's also." The three men sipped their wine.

"Mr. Webster..."

"Paul."

"Paul, tomorrow morning, if you will be ready early, I would find pleasure in taking you and your wife to the rice terraces."

"That would be great, Lakay Pawid..."

"Please, call me Val."

"Somehow Val doesn't seem respectful of your status."

"My status with my own people is as old as the terraces. With you and Joan, well, all new things from the outside world are not necessarily bad." He stood up. "Oh, and tomorrow morning, wear clothes suitable for climbing." He joined the mayor for a minute, then left the house.

* * *

The next morning was brilliantly clear. Paul scooped a spoonful of soft white flesh from the strange grayish fruit in his dish. It was called

85

atis, or custard apple, and it looked something like a hand grenade. "Honey, taste this," he said, offering Joan a spoonful.

She smacked her lips. "Oh, that's good! But you know me. I can't pass up a really good papaya. And this one is perfect!" she said, squeezing more lime onto it.

The sun had risen far enough to reach the terraces at the bottom of the valley. With the heat of the sun, mist began to rise from them. The air seemed filled with magic. They ate their breakfast, then, just as they finished their second cup of coffee, Val arrived. He wore a short-sleeved white shirt as he had the day before, but this morning, instead of slacks, he wore a traditional Ifugao man's G-string. The long strip of woven cotton was held in place by a narrow sash. Its wide stripes of red and black were accented with yellow and white. The long fringe in front and back hung nearly to his knees. His legs and feet were bare.

"Good morning," he said. "I trust you slept well? You must excuse my appearance today, but I have climbed the terraces for so many years that I cannot get used to your Western pants and shoes when I am out there."

"You certainly don't need to apologize," said Joan, getting up from her chair. "We feel fortunate that someone with your knowledge is willing to entertain a couple of tourists."

Paul excused himself and returned to their room to get his daypack and camera. When he rejoined them in the lobby, Val stopped at the front door and picked up a large, woven bamboo backpack. He slipped it onto his back. "I have packed a few things, in case we are hungry later."

They walked north on the road for a short distance, then Val turned onto a path leading east, toward the terraces. "Before we reach the terraces, I will show you the source of our name," he said, stopping in front of a small version of an Ifugao house. He opened the door and led them inside. "This is an Ifugao granary," he said. In the dim light, Paul could see that the building was filled with all manner of baskets, piled high in neat rows.

Val removed the lid from one of the baskets and reached in. He held out his hand to Paul and Joan and dropped a few large grains of white rice into their hands. "This is *ipugo*," he said. "It means, 'from the hills,' and it is the rice we prefer above all others. It has nourished us for centuries, and it is the word we call ourselves."

Several small carved figures stood here and there in the granary. They were human figures, either standing or sitting with their knees up and their arms crossed on their knees. "And these?" Joan asked.

"Those are *bulul*. They protect our rice, and help ensure that the next harvest will be successful. Certain bulul have special powers which can even miraculously multiply the rice after it is stored in the granary." Val stepped to the side wall and gently stroked the arm of one of the figures. "This one has been in my family's granary since my grandfather was young."

He led them outside and secured the door. "Bulul are carved only from narra wood. They are always carved in pairs, a male and a female. And the rituals that accompany their carving are elaborate and expensive. Not every Ifugao family can afford to honor them and receive their protection."

"Will there be any way to borrow some of the bulul for our exhibit?" asked Joan.

"I'm sure there will be those who will be happy to share them."

They continued down the trail to the edge of the uppermost terrace on this slope, turned south and skirted it to its farthest edge. The wall of the terrace jutted out about 20 feet, then curved north to parallel the mountain slope. Val led them out the narrow path worn into the top of the wall. On the left, the glassy surface of the rice paddy was a foot lower than the path. To their right was a nearly sheer drop of seventy or eighty feet to the next terrace below.

Val stopped and pointed down the mountain. Joan joined him, shielding her eyes from the morning sun, as Paul snapped their photo. "This is *payon di a-ammod*, the fields of our ancestors. Down there you see people working," he pointed several terraces below them. "We will climb down, and you will see what they are doing." He started along the path, then paused and turned to Joan, "This is something you wish to do? I understand that these heights can be frightening."

Joan looked back at Paul, and he nodded. "No, Val. It's all right. I know I'm nervous, but it's fascinating. We'll be careful."

They started down the steps built into the terrace wall. Paul marveled at the way the wall was built. The large stones were placed so perfectly that the wall was nearly smooth except for the flat rocks protruding as steps. A mortar of clay held the entire construction together. They reached the base of the wall, followed the path around the next terrace level and started down again. He looked ahead, past Joan, at their guide. Val's bare feet were so accustomed to climbing these rocky walls they had become nearly prehensile. They curved and grasped, adjusting to the terrain met with each step. His legs were slightly bowed and, even at his age, looked strong and powerful.

At the fifth level, they stopped for a rest. The sun was warm on their faces and the still water in the paddy calmed him. A small carp swam by, its back disturbing the glassy surface.

"What is that shrub growing on some of the walls?" asked Joan.

"It is called *dongla*," answered Val. He squatted down, opened a small woven pouch on his sash and pulled out a short pipe and tobacco. "In Manila, they call it tea plant. It is sacred to the Ifugao. Its roots strengthen the terrace walls, and its red leaves are used in the headdresses of our warriors during the *Himong*, the war dance ceremony."

"Speaking of war dances," asked Paul, "how long ago did the Ifugao stop hunting heads?"

"They still do," answered Val, tamping the tobacco into the pipe's bowl. "It's true that once head hunting was a common occurrence and an everyday part of our men's lives. Today, we have learned to live in peace with the other highland tribes, but there are still occasions when outrage demands retribution."

"What kind of occasion could that be?" exclaimed Joan.

Val lit his pipe and puffed on it silently for a moment. "In 1977, an Ifugao youth was hit and killed by a bus. The village council decided that the bus driver or a member of his family must die, and soon after that a member of the village took the driver's head. Only two or three years ago, several Ifugao passengers died in another bus accident. The relatives of the dead sharpened their head axes when the bus company failed to admit any fault. As a result, no bus driver would enter Ifugao territory, and local jeepneys were the only transportation available until the bus company finally made reparation for the deaths."

It was a simple, terrible system. An eye for an eye, a death for a death. But somehow, sitting here on this silent mountainside, Paul could understand the reasoning behind this kind of law that Val was talking about. It was far removed from the courts and attorneys and penal codes of the States, but even here they had plea bargaining. Taking a head in revenge was all wrapped up in loss of face, not just loss of life. The bus company admitted responsibility for the accident rather than lose a driver. Paul had read that in recent years, differences like this were often settled with the payment of carabao or pigs.

Far down the mountain, he could see three carabao being driven across a paddy, their hooves turning and plowing the rice stalks into the muddy soil. The beasts were broad and dark, their massive horns silhouetted against the shiny water of the terrace. "Val, those carabao down there. How do they get them up to these terraces?"

"They don't. Carabao can only be used on the lower, flatter terraces. All these terraces up here we work completely by hand, with hoes and our feet." He snuffed out his pipe with the calloused tip of a finger and slipped it into its pouch. "We'd best be going," he said, shouldering his pack.

The mountain slope was more gradual here, and these terrace walls were only thirty or forty feet high. Paul watched Joan step carefully but surely from ledge to ledge. She was at ease here, he thought. She was as comfortable here as she was hosting a corporate fund-raiser in San Francisco. He had heard stories from Emory Barclay's travels, and he could see the same intensity in Joan. The thrill of discovery would continue to drive her, as it had Emory.

As they climbed down the terrace wall above the work party, Paul could see that it was an entire family, from older children to grandparents. They were spread in a line across the paddy up to their knees in water. Each carried a handful of young rice plants. Bent at the waist, they moved slowly down the paddy, reaching under the water and plunging each plant by hand into the mud.

Val waved, and the oldest man, grayer and more weathered than Val, straightened up and waved back. He wore nothing but a G-string, and his body was dark and wiry. He called to the youngsters minding the store of young plants stacked at the edge of the terrace. One of them waded out to take his place, and he crossed over to Val and stepped out of the water, shaking his hand warmly. Val spoke briefly in Ifugao, and the patriarch grinned, his toothless mouth open and his eyes slits in the deeply creased face.

"Joan and Paul," said Val, "I'd like you to meet Charles Tumapang. Lakay Tumapang, this is Joan Webster, and this is Paul Webster." The old man pumped their hands energetically, smiling and bowing. "Lakay Tumapang's English is not too good," said Val, "but he is happy you are here to watch his family." Val pulled out his tobacco, and the other man warmly accepted the symbol of respect, squatting down to fill his pipe.

Val pointed out to the Tumapang family in the rice paddy. "Today they are transplanting the small rice shoots," he said. "About two months ago, they chose the best seed rice from their granary, and when the weather and the gods said the time was right, Lakay Tumapang's wife planted the seed rice in one of their paddies."

At the sound of his name, the weathered little man nodded to Val, who smiled and nodded back.

"While the ipugo, the rice, grew, they prepared the soil in their other terraces, turning it with hoes and leveling it by stamping it with their feet. Now that the rains have come, it is time to transplant the small shoots."

"Then they'll harvest it next year?" asked Joan. Paul was hunkered down low to the ground, taking a low angle shot of the row of planters.

"No," answered Val. "Now that we have chemical fertilizers, we get two crops a year at this altitude. This crop is a small one. The main crop is planted in three months' time. Terraces above 4,000 feet only get one crop, because of the cooler weather."

"You mentioned the weather and the gods. There's a god for growing rice?"

"Rice is so important to the Ifugao, we actually have many gods who are important to our crops," said Val. "*Wigan* is one of the major gods of *Daya*, the Upstream Region. He watches over the terraces, and many call him the god of good harvest. Yesterday, Lakay Tumapang and his family sacrificed a pig to *Ampual*, the chief god of the fourth Skyworld. He has power to make the rice transplanting successful."

The old man looked up at Val and grinned, "Ampual, yes, and Jesus also."

Val smiled. "You see, we take no chances when it concerns our ipugo."

The sun was high in the sky by now, and a thin cloud cover was starting to build. Val opened his pack and produced a thermos of strong, dark tea and a package of sweet rice cakes. Their host accepted a cup of tea, but declined the rice. Paul was really starting to develop a taste for rice, in all its many forms, and Val encouraged him to take more cakes, which he did, until they were gone.

"We should head back," announced Val. "The rain will come soon, and we have a good climb ahead of us."

They shook hands with the old man and waved to his family, who waved back without interrupting their planting. As they walked along the terrace wall one level up, Paul looked back down at the Tumapang family. Their patriarch was back in the water, planting with the rest of them. Families around the world who toil together like this, thought Paul, share a bond that the rest of us will never know.

* * *

Back at the hotel, as Paul and Joan were finishing their lunch, the concierge bustled up to their table. "I hope everything is satisfactory. Have you any complaints at all?"

"We couldn't be happier," answered Joan.

"Well, just let me know if you need anything at all. And, there is someone here with a message for you." He glanced up for them and indicated a young man standing at the doorway. "He is from the mayor's office, and he says that the mayor regrets to inform you that he will not be able to meet with you until later today. He hopes that will not be an inconvenience."

"Later today will be fine," said Joan.

The concierge nodded to the messenger, who left with his answer. "Please let me know if you need anything," said the concierge. His elbows flapped slightly. "Anything at all," he said, looking back over his shoulder as he returned to his perch in the lobby.

"Free time," said Joan. "I guess I'll work on my notes now, while the hike down the terraces is fresh in my mind."

Paul finished his beer. "I'm so stuffed from having lunch after eating all those rice cakes, I feel like taking a nap."

"Well, why don't you?" said Joan. "I'll wake you when I get back from the mayor's office."

"But first I've got to get a shot of that great sky. Look at the way the sun is shining down through those clouds onto the terraces," he said. "It doesn't look real. It looks like a painting."

He unzipped his day pack and rummaged through its contents. "Where on...? Damn! My camera! I must have left it.... Shit! It's sitting on a rock where we took that break on the way back up! I'd better go get it before the rain starts."

"That wasn't too far," said Joan. "I'll hike down with you."

Joan stopped at the hotel desk, and the concierge beamed with hospitality. "Please tell our driver that Mr. Webster and I have to go retrieve his camera down the mountain."

"But madam, we can send a boy to get it for you. It will be raining soon."

"Thank you, but Mr. Webster wants to take some pictures," she said, and they left the hotel.

The precipitous steps on the terraces were feeling more familiar, and they climbed quickly down. Sure enough, the camera was exactly where Paul thought he had left it, four terraces down the mountainside. But by the time they got there, the light had changed, and the photogenic sky had disappeared. They started back up along with the first few spatters of rain.

As Paul followed Joan up the rocky steps, he admired the way her khaki shorts fit her. "Hey, beautiful," he called. "I'd follow you up any mountain."

She turned and laughed as she reached the next terrace. "Let me follow you for a while. I want the good view for a change."

As they reached the next to last terrace, the rain began to come down hard. They hurried around the rim of the paddy, and stopped at the base of the last terrace. They were both soaked to the skin. Joan's hair hung clinging to her wet shirt. Paul put his arms around her, "Just like in the movies. The couple gets caught in the rain, and throws caution to the wind."

He pulled her to him and kissed her. Joan twined her fingers in his wet hair, as he held her tight. He could feel her warmth through their cold, wet shirts.

"Oh, baby, I want you," she whispered.

He put his hand on her breast; he could feel her heart beating.

"Not here in the mud, silly," she said. "I meant in our hotel room."

He let her go reluctantly. "Follow me," he said, and he started back up the mountain.

"Be careful," she called. "It's slippery."

He hurried ahead, feeling at one with everything around him: this country, the mountain, the rain, the woman he loved. He was sure-footed as a goat. The rain worried Joan, and she climbed more cautiously. He looked back down the rock wall and called, "C'mon, wonderful."

He reached the top of the terrace, climbed onto the edge of the paddy and hiked around to its end. When he stopped to wait for Joan, the thunder started. He hadn't seen any lightning, he thought. Then he realized, the thunder was coming from all around him, from the ground. He started to run back for Joan, but the top of the terrace began to shake, and he slipped and fell to his knees. The rocks under him came to life, moving terribly. He turned back and scrambled toward solid ground just in time to see the end of the terrace separate itself from the mountainside. The path under him broke away, and the placid rice paddy became a torrent. The water hit him and swept him off the mountain.

6. GOOD SHEPHERD

Joan slipped on the stone step and fell hard against the terrace wall, scraping her hands on the rock face. Don't be foolish, she thought. Love is grand, but not at any price. She called ahead to Paul to be careful, then saw him disappear onto the walk at the top and breathed a sigh of relief. The rain pounded on her, running down her face and neck. She'd never been so wet, she thought, outside of a shower.

As she climbed to the next step, she felt the earthquake. She knew she had to get off this ledge. She turned and carefully climbed back down to the foot of the wall and the security of solid ground. The ground shook hard, and she ducked up against the wall of the terrace, fearful of falling rocks, then looked up, wondering where Paul was.

She saw the rocky face at the other end of the terrace start to come apart. First a few rocks broke free, then the whole wall started to crumble, then a waterfall...

"Paulll!" she shrieked in horror, as she saw him twisting above in midair, riding the deluge down. The water pushed him far out off the mountain. He landed in the rice paddy ten yards from her with a horrible splash, and the wall above broke into a chute of rubble, rumbling down until it churned past Paul, ripping away part of this paddy's wall.

Joan leaped into the water, pushing herself through the mud as fast as she could move. As the water began to race out of the paddy, she felt the current dragging her, pulling her along. Paul's body started to move. The current was taking him! She lunged ahead and reached him, lifting his face from the muddy water. She braced herself against the water's pull, holding his limp body until the paddy drained itself, leaving them lying there in the mud and the rain.

"Help! Somebody!" she screamed. "Help us!"

The mountain was still now, quiet under the driving rain and the pounding of her heart. Joan put her hand to Paul's chest, and tears of relief filled her eyes as she felt his heart, still beating strong. "Oh, darling," she wept, wiping mud and blood from his face. She looked up the mountainside and shouted again for help, hoping desperately to be heard over the noise of the rain, which fell harder than ever, stinging her face.

"Mum!" Rudy appeared above her, looking down from the top of the wall.

"Thank God!" she cried. "Rudy! Paul has fallen! He needs a stretcher!"

"Wait there, mum," answered Rudy. "I will get help," and he turned and ran toward town.

Joan looked down at Paul's still face. "You're going to be all right, baby," she whispered. "Oh, God, you've got to be all right!" She shivered with the cold and slumped down, her body racked by sobs.

Presently, she heard voices. Then she saw Rudy and three other men climbing cautiously down the track of the slide. With the southern end of the terrace gone, there were no built-in ledges now. The lead man dug the sides of his feet into the muddy earth, carefully prodding and tamping as he went. Suddenly, a cluster of soil and rocks broke loose, bouncing past Joan and Paul down the mountain.

"Joan, are you all right?" It was Val, standing on the ledge above her.

"I'm all right, Val, but Paul fell from up there. He landed on his back here in the paddy. He's unconscious."

Val began to lower a stretcher down from above. One of the men on the slide track slipped and slid a few feet. "Be careful!" yelled Val. "We want no more injuries!"

The four men reached Joan. Rudy gently took Joan's shoulder. "Come on, mum. Let us get him on the stretcher."

Joan stood up, suddenly feeling slightly dazed. As the men carefully rolled Paul and slid the stretcher under him, more ropes came down the rock face.

"Bening," called Val, to one of the men. "Take the end of the rope on your left and tie it around the lady's waist."

"Joan, I want you to start climbing up the path of the slide. We will pull you up. You will be all right."

She hesitated, looking back at Paul.

"Don't worry about Paul. We will take good care of him."

Bening tied the rope securely around her waist, "Go ahead now, mum. We will follow with your husband, eh?"

She grabbed the rope in front of her. It was wet and slippery, but she held on tight and began the ascent, putting her feet in the steps dug by the rescue party. Three men above her pulled her up as she climbed. As she reached the top, she was amazed to see what must have been the entire village, standing in groups along the path in respectful silence. A few of them held banana leaves or umbrellas, but most stood unprotected, soaked by the pouring rain.

Teo, his mother, and his wife joined her and helped her untie the rope. "Ahh, me," said Teo, "we are so sorry about what has happened.

Happily, you are okay. And they will take your husband to the Good Shepherd Clinic, where hopefully he will get well soon."

Joan smiled at them and turned back to see the rescue team inching up the slope with Paul. Four ropes had been tied to his stretcher, and each rope was being monitored by a pair of men at the top.

"*Alyog* is angry. This one must be made happy again," said Teo's mother, putting her arm around Joan's waist. She looked up into Joan's reddened eyes. "He made the earth shake, and he made your husband fall. We will find out what upsets him, and make peace, for your husband's sake, and for the sake of our home."

The stretcher bearers reached the crest and stopped, while the rope teams untied the ropes. Then Rudy and one other man took the stretcher and headed up the path for town. As they reached Joan, she fell in beside the stretcher, wanting to touch Paul, but afraid to injure him. A young woman approached the opposite side of the stretcher to hold a large umbrella over Paul's face and body. Joan glanced back at Rudy; he smiled reassuringly at her. She was glad he was here.

The clinic was expecting them, and, as they entered the front door of the two-story, wood frame building, a slim, young man with a lowland accent met them. Under his white jacket, he wore a beige polo shirt, with turquoise slacks and tasseled loafers. His glossy black hair was freshly trimmed. Joan could see the narrow tan line behind his ear. He looked like he should be playing golf at John Hay, except for the tongue depressors in his pocket and the stethoscope hanging around his neck.

"Take him to Room Three," he said to Rudy and his partner. "Follow this nurse here. And just put the stretcher carefully on the examining table. Don't take him off of it. Millie? Vital signs, stat."

The nurse nodded and hurried down the hall, leading the stretcher bearers.

The doctor turned to Joan, "Mrs. Webster? I am Florio Sanchez. Tell me exactly what happened, please."

"He fell about seventy feet, Doctor," answered Joan. "He landed on his back in a rice paddy."

"How much water?"

"It was about a foot deep."

"Okay," he said. "You're welcome to wait here while I examine him, or I can have someone take you back to your hotel."

"I'll wait."

"You should get out of those wet clothes. Perhaps..."

"I'll get the lady some dry clothes from the hotel," said Rudy, returning to the reception room.

"Good," said Dr. Sanchez, and he hurried to Room Three.

"I'll go to the hotel now, mum," said Rudy.

"Thank you, Rudy. The concierge can have one of the maids get some clothes from our room. All I need are jeans and a sweater."

"Right away, mum."

"Oh, and Rudy?"

"Yes, mum?"

"Take the time to put on some dry clothes yourself, and get two umbrellas from the concierge."

Half an hour later, he returned with a plastic bag emblazoned with a Singapore Airlines logo, and Joan took it into the women's room to change. She looked in the mirror and gasped in amazement. She didn't recognize herself, she was so muddy. She pulled off her wet clothes and washed the mud from her face and hands, then rolled up her wet shirt and used it to wipe the worst of the mud from her arms and legs.

She bent over to pick up the bag just as the floor started to quiver. It was just an aftershock and lasted only a few seconds, but when it ended, Joan slumped down on the toilet, her whole body shaking. She sat there for a long time, limp from exertion and fear, staring at the floor through eyes blurred with tears. Finally, she took a deep breath, got up and stepped back to the sink. The cool water felt good, soothing, like lotion on a sunburn.

She opened the bag of clothes. As she had requested, a pair of her jeans was in the bag. There was also a black cashmere sweater, part of an evening ensemble that featured a floral design done in silver sequins. There was no underwear, so Joan pulled the sweater and jeans over the damp things she was wearing. The maid had also included a pair of red high heels. Joan left those in the bag with her wet shirt and shorts and put her wet sneakers back on. She dried her hair with some paper towels and went back to the reception room.

Rudy was sitting on the olive green vinyl couch, looking at a brochure entitled, "Christ Loves the Little Children." He started to get up when Joan walked in, but she motioned him to keep his seat.

"You don't have to wait here with me, Rudy," she said, sitting down in the orange armchair next to the couch.

"Oh, but I do, mum. The senator sent me along to help you and Mr. Webster. I could not foresee the earthquake and the accident, but I am here to do everything I can for you."

A nurse's aide brought them cups of hot tea, which they gratefully accepted. Joan was anxious to know of Paul's condition, but the aide knew only that Dr. Sanchez had asked her to bring them tea.

Joan sipped the hot tea, and felt the tension inside of her uncoiling, in spite of her fears for Paul. She looked at Rudy. He sat attentively, sipping his tea, studiously avoiding looking at Joan, except when she spoke to him. He had a professional and powerful presence, and she was glad he was there: a staunch ally.

"Rudy," she asked, "how did you find us on the terraces?"

"Don't you remember, mum? You had the concierge tell me you had gone to get Mr. Webster's camera?"

"Oh, yes. I had forgotten."

"When I felt the earthquake I feared for your safety, and came looking for you."

She studied the polished wood floor. The words, "I feared for your safety," brought back the vision of the accident. She stifled the urge to cry. She looked back at Rudy. She wanted to throw herself into the arms of this brown man. In his brown slacks and beige shirt. Wearing brown shoes and socks and drinking brown tea. This man would hold her and comfort her like her own father never could. "Now, now, Janing," he would say, "Rudy's sure everything will be all right. Rudy will make sure no one hurts Janing." His big, broad hands would stroke her back, and she would go to sleep in his arms, safe and happy.

"Mrs. Webster."

Joan looked up. It was Dr. Sanchez. "Paul...?"

"He's badly injured, but I think there is no permanent damage," he said. "A stable burst fracture of the twelfth thoracic vertebra. There doesn't seem to be any neurological damage; his lower extremities seem to indicate no loss of sensation. And his right leg--the femur--is broken. It's a spiral fracture--we'll have to put him in traction. With Christ's help, he should heal completely, but we won't know for sure until he regains consciousness."

"He's still unconscious?"

"Yes, he's also suffered a severe concussion. It's hard to estimate how long he'll be unconscious."

"What about the blood?"

"A nasty bump on the head, but just a superficial cut. Probably hit by a rock. He also bit his lip when he landed. But our major concerns are his back and his leg. He's very lucky he was moved so carefully. As it is, he'll be with us quite some time, before it's safe to move him again."

"Can I see him?"

"Of course. And then I'd like you to go back to your hotel, take a shower and take this." He handed her a small, blue pill. "Then, go to bed. Come see your husband in the morning. In the meantime, if there is any change, we'll send someone for you."

"I can't leave him here and go to bed."

"For his sake, and yours, I think you should. You've gone through a terrible ordeal, and you're suffering from exposure yourself. Please do as I say, Mrs. Webster. There's nothing more that you can do now, except pray that his injuries are no worse than we think they are. He could be unconscious for days. We can only wait and pray."

* * *

104

Joan woke just before dawn. She rolled over to snuggle against Paul. His side of the bed was empty, and reality flooded back into her brain. She rolled back, looking up at the dark ceiling but seeing nothing. Tears filled her open eyes and slid down her cheeks; she could feel the warmth as they ran into her ears. She stretched her arms out and spread her legs wide under the down coverlet. She couldn't fill the spacious bed. She lay there for a long time, watching through the tearful blur as Paul fell toward her, his body twisting in the air. He hit the surface of the rice paddy and still more muddy water splashed into her eyes.

When she woke again, her eyes were glued shut. She rubbed them to get them open. It was light outside. She got up and pulled on her robe, went to the window and pulled back the drape. The morning sun shone above the Cordilleras. The terraces glistened in its light; all except the three closest. They were empty and dark. The young rice shoots stood naked and unprotected in their muddy bottoms.

The slide had broken down their walls and connected them with a long scar of rocky rubble. But the slope bustled with the activity of an anthill. A large group of villagers was already hard at work, digging into the edge of the slide, sorting rock from earth, continuing the job of building and rebuilding that had occupied the Ifugao for centuries.

Joan dressed, had a hurried roll and cup of coffee, and headed for the door.

"I hope your husband is better today, madam," said the concierge.

"Thank you..., I'm sorry, I don't even know your name," said Joan.

"Please call me Manny, madam."

"Thank you, Manny."

The sun was warm, and the sharp scent of pine smoke drifted from the hotel's chimney. She headed up the road, toward the clinic.

"Excuse me, mum." It was the young woman who had held the umbrella over Paul yesterday.

"Yes, what is it?" asked Joan.

"There is something it is important that you see," she answered.

"But I have to go to the clinic, to check on my husband."

"Oh, mum, please." She began to cry. "I'm a good girl, and you must see this, before my parents become angry with me."

"All right, but please hurry."

The girl led her down the trail to the terraces, but left the trail at the top of the slope and turned south, skirting the rim of the fractured earth. At the far end of the top of the slide's wake, she stopped, and climbed down across the freshly exposed earth a few yards. A pile of heavy, mud-caked timbers lay on the ground, exposed when the grassy knoll above the terrace had been ripped apart.

"I saw these old boards here," she said. "And I found this."

The timbers had slid a few feet with the falling earth, exposing a hole in the ground about ten feet deep. It was some six feet square and reinforced with more timbers. At the bottom, the opening turned and continued out of sight. Reaching out of the adjoining tunnel into this shaft was a human skeleton. The front of its skull had been pierced by something about the size of a bullet.

Joan staggered with the shock of this discovery, and looked up at the girl. "Why didn't you tell your parents? Why did you come to me?" she asked.

"I was afraid they would be angry, mum," she said. "I didn't mean to offend this ghost." She began to cry again.

Joan put her arm around the girl and led her away from the macabre sight. "No one will be angry," she said. "I'll talk to Lakay Pawid, and we will take care of it."

"Oh, thank you, mum."

When they reached the road, Joan again assured the girl that everything would be all right. The girl turned toward home, and Joan headed back up to the Good Shepherd Clinic, thinking to herself, I could use a Good Shepherd. First Paul, and now this. What she had seen didn't fit with the Ifugao burial rites she had studied. Their dead were interred seated on chairs. This was definitely an open tunnel, not a grave, and that skeleton had been climbing into that shaft from somewhere else.

As she approached the clinic, Joan heard a curious, keening chant and saw a group of nine or ten village elders near the front porch of the clinic near a grove of pine trees. They all wore traditional clothing, the men in G-strings and loosely wound cloth turbans, the women in brightly colored tapis and elaborate hairdos and jewelry. Two of the women sported large necklaces of triangular pieces of mother of pearl woven together with split rattan. One of them was the mayor's mother.

One man squatted to one side, tapping out a simple rhythm with his fingertips on a small brass gong. The rest performed a slow, shuffling dance as they chanted, alternating stanzas as a chorus with the solo chants of their leader, a small, wizened man wearing a necklace of boars' tusks.

Joan walked quietly past them and up onto the porch of the clinic. They scarcely noticed her, and she realized they were in some kind of a trance.

A young, barefoot woman from a nearby village shared the couch with a boy of five. She wore blue jeans and a sleeveless blouse. Around her neck was a woven red cord, strung with small, brass *lingling-o*, the phallic broken circles that symbolized fertility to the Cordillera people. The boy wore shorts. His Smurf T-shirt was nearly as grimy as the cast on his right arm. From the way he squirmed in his seat, Joan figured they were here to have the cast removed.

Rudy, wearing the same clothes he had on the day before, was sitting in the orange chair.

"Rudy, have you been here all night?" exclaimed Joan.

"Yes, but mum, someone had to be ready to fetch you if things changed," he replied.

"You're wonderful," she smiled. "But, please, I'm here now. Go back to the hotel and have some breakfast and get some rest."

The nurse, Millie, came down the hall into the waiting room. "Oh, he's eaten breakfast. He's also eaten my lunch." She smiled at Joan and said, "How do you like our entertainment?"

"What is it?" asked Joan.

"I am not from the highlands, but I understand it is a ceremony supposed to bring good health to Mr. Webster. They have been there since last evening. Doctor hasn't been able to get them to leave."

"How is Paul?"

"There is no change in his condition, ma'am. He is stable, but still unconscious. Doctor is away from the clinic for a short time. He said you are welcome to go to your husband's room."

Joan saw to it that Rudy left, then went to Paul's room. The well-worn wooden floor in the hall shone with last evening's coat of wax. The door to Paul's room was open. Joan walked across to the high hospital bed and looked down at her husband. He looked the same as he had the day before, except for the fact that he needed a shave. His wavy brown hair curled against the white pillowcase, and his face was darkly tanned from the days in Manila. The crisp white sheet was turned down far enough to reveal a light blue dressing gown. His right leg was elevated, attached to a series of pulleys and cables. His forehead was bandaged, and Joan could see stitches in his lower lip. She bent over and kissed his stubbly cheek, then sat down in the straight chair next to the bed.

The morning light cast a bright reflection off the room's varnished knotty pine paneling .White lace curtains at the open window fluttered from a soft breeze. The air was fresh, the scent of pine trees reaching in here from outside. A small, framed picture of Jesus hung on the wall over the bed. Except for the IV bottle hanging next to the bed, the room felt more like a mountain lodge than a hospital room. There was something healthy and naturally medicinal about it.

She put her hand on Paul's shoulder and sat for a long time, feeling his warmth through the fabric of the hospital gown. She focused herself, willing him to wake up, mentally pushing the thought down her arm and through her fingertips and into his body. The sounds of the ceremony outside drifted hypnotically through the open window. But Paul did not respond to her hand or the chant; he lay there quietly sleeping.

The sun moved higher, and the light dappling the wood floor shrank and then disappeared. A fly buzzed angrily, trapped between the windowpane and the curtain. It fretted its way across the glass, competing with the chanting, then escaped out the open window. Joan stroked Paul's head, running her fingers through his hair. He liked the feel of that so much, she thought. It always turned him on when they made love.

Then the fear started building in her again. What if the doctor was wrong? What had he said? "We won't know for sure until he regains consciousness." Would they ever make love again? Would Paul wake up paralyzed, to spend the rest of his life in a wheelchair? Would he ever wake up, or just lie in a coma until he died?

"Don't even think it!" she said out loud. But she couldn't shake herself loose from the thought. She knew she couldn't let her imagination run away with her, but it stuck to her, burning her like a piece of dry ice.

"Sweetheart," she cried, and she laid her head on the edge of the bed. The tears rolled down her cheeks and stained the white sheet. Her closed eyes saw the terrace come apart again, and he was falling again, clutching at the air with his fingers, hitting the surface of the paddy with a sickening smack. He slowly sank beneath the water, and she splashed across the paddy to reach him. She reached into the muddy water and pulled him up, and choked in horror as she saw it: she was holding a skeleton! In its skull was a hole the size of a bullet. She let go of it in disgust, and it sank back into the water, the young rice shoots threading their way between its bleached ribs.

"Mrs. Webster...."

Joan lifted her head and looked toward the door. Dr. Sanchez was standing in the doorway. Today, the doctor's jacket was accompanied by a royal blue polo shirt and cream linen slacks. She sat up and wiped her eyes. "I'm sorry. I'm just so worried," she said.

"No need for apologies. We all share your concerns; he was in our prayers at services this morning. But he is doing well. Patients who have suffered concussions like this can remain unconscious for days, weeks even." He entered the room and put his hand on her shoulder, "But his heart and respiration are good, he is in no pain right now, and his injuries are mending."

He stepped around her and looked down at Paul, then reached out, gently raised Paul's eyelids with his fingertips, and looked intently at Paul's eyes, "With our care, and the graciousness of Jesus Christ, he'll be OK. Still, we understand your fears. We'll all rest easier when he regains consciousness."

"I feel so helpless," said Joan. "I wish there was something I could do."

"You're doing just fine."

"Doctor, there is something else that worries me. One of the local girls showed me before I arrived here this morning. The earthquake broke open a shaft on the edge of the mountain. There's a skeleton in it."

"Happily, my work is not concerned with skeletons," he said. "I suggest you report it to Deputy Mayor Pawid."

"That's what I told her I would do," said Joan. "The girl was afraid she had offended a ghost."

"That's the kind of thinking that makes our job here so difficult. When people believe that illness is caused by some displeased spirit...if only they would just accept Christ's blessings and come here to the clinic...," he paused. "At any rate, I just came from the Municipal Hall. Mr. Pawid was in his office. Why don't you go take care of that. We'll send someone if Mr. Webster awakens. It's a small town--we'll be able to find you."

"Oh, and doctor, our driver Rudy--please don't let him sit and wait here at the clinic. He was here all night. I think he feels responsible for Paul's accident."

"Men like Rudy don't take their responsibilities lightly," he answered. "We won't encourage it, but I don't think he knows what else to do." He turned to leave, then paused, "And I think my nurse has caught his eye."

As she left the clinic, Joan stopped and watched the chant. The participants barely noticed her, and continued the interminable, shuffling dance. The leader was involved in a solo section, accompanied only by the tapping of the gong. His chest and upper arms were covered with faded tattoos of human figures, scorpions and centipedes. I wish I wasn't so distracted, thought Joan. This ceremony is definitely material for the exhibition. As she left, the stanza ended, and the chorus took up the next section. She wondered if they thought it was Paul who had offended the spirits.

* * *

Valerio Pawid sat behind the gray metal desk in his office in the Municipal Hall. Each of the deputy mayors of Banaue had an office here, but Val, in charge of security, and Duarding, the deputy in charge of finance, were the only ones to use them full time. Most of the others were really storage rooms, full of file cabinets and little else. Val's position was essentially Banaue chief of police, although Banaue had no police force, and the nearest jail was twenty kilometers south in Lagawe, the provincial capital. Val's authority in the community came from the high esteem held for his family and the many years he had been a respected elder, and his role was often as not that of mediator in respect to property disputes. The Ifugao laws regarding property, especially ownership of rice terraces, were strict and specific, but when a question did arise, Lakay Valerio Pawid determined the outcome of the matter.

He stood up when Joan arrived. "Good morning, Joan. Our prayers are with you and Paul," he motioned for her to sit down.

"Thank you, Val," she said, sitting down in the straight-backed oak chair. The chair reminded her of her school days; she felt like she had been sent to the principal's office.

She looked at Val. In his long-sleeved *barong Tagalog*, the dress shirt of the Philippines, he barely resembled the Ifugao tribal leader who had led them down the rice terraces just twenty-four hours ago.

"What can I do for you this morning?" he asked.

"First of all, how was the rest of the town affected by the earthquake. Were there any other casualties?

"Thankfully nothing severe. There was some damage to several buildings, but your husband was the only one unlucky enough to be injured."

Joan thought to herself, please, please, make my husband whole again! "Tell me about the ceremony at the clinic," she said.

"The mayor sponsored that," replied Val. "You are given much respect. That ceremony is the *alim*, performed only when persons of high rank are ill. The *mombaki* and *mamah-o*, the priests and priestesses, are led by a chief mombaki, the *mombagol*. They retell the stories of the lives of the gods from the four Skyworlds. The Ifugao believe that there are six worlds: four in the sky, one on Earth, and one below. There are many gods to ask favor of, and the request lasts an entire night and day, and requires the sacrifice of as many as nine pigs."

"I thought the mayor might have had something to do with it," said Joan. "I'll have to thank him."

"Most of our young people are not interested in the stories of the old gods. And more and more of our people are converting to Christianity. There may not be many more alims performed."

"I'm sorry to hear that," said Joan. "The same thing happened with the Native American cultures in the U.S. By the time the new generations of Native Americans realized the importance of keeping many of the old ideas alive, it was too late. Many priceless things were lost: language, ideas, skills and property."

"That is why we welcome you and your project with open arms," said Val. "The more we document the ancient beliefs, and the more people who learn of our traditional arts and crafts, the easier it will be to hold these things as part of us."

"But the real reason I'm here, Val," said Joan, "is I promised one of the girls in the village. She's found an open mine shaft or tunnel that the earthquake broke open. There's a skeleton in it."

7. KIWIL

"We'll need a ladder," said Val, "and some light." He stood up and turned his head, looking down the slope behind him, a gesture of self-preservation more instinctive than practiced.

"Have you any idea what it is?" asked Joan.

"None," he replied. "I've never seen anything like it. It certainly wasn't dug by the Ifugao." He glanced up at the sky. "We'd best hurry. The rain will come soon." He took Joan by the arm, and they carefully crossed the broken earth to the end of the path that hung suspended at the edge of the slide like some cruel practical joke.

"I'll get the equipment we need," said Val. "Get Rudy, and we'll meet here in twenty minutes."

Joan went back to the hotel and knocked at Rudy's door. After the second knock, the door opened a few inches, and Rudy peered out. His hair was rumpled from sleep.

"Rudy, I'm sorry to wake you, but we need your help."

"Is Mr. Webster...?"

"He's fine, Rudy, but hurry just the same."

"Of course, mum," he said, stifling a yawn.

"Meet me in the lobby in ten minutes," said Joan, "and wear clothes you won't mind getting dirty."

She went to her room and changed into jeans. She finished tying her sneakers and stood up, looking out the window. The sky was darkening, and the mountains looked angry. She rummaged through her suitcase, found the mini-camera Paul had given her, and stuck it into her pocket.

* * *

Joan and Rudy reached the path and headed toward the terraces. Up ahead, Val stood waiting with a boy. When they reached them, Joan realized that the boy wore a mustache. He was a very small man, less than five feet tall. He was wearing an Ifugao backpack.

"Joan, Rudy," said Val, "this is my deputy, Luis Gahidan."

The little man smiled broadly and shook their hands.

"We call him Kiwil, or Magic Charm, because he's so small and quick that he can disappear, right before your eyes."

Kiwil laughed heartily at this, a joke he had heard most of his life, and said, "I do not disappear, but they say I do. Well, maybe I do sometimes, eh!"

As they climbed across the torn mountainside, Val looked at Joan and said, "Why did you change? You'll not need to climb down."

"Yes, I do," she answered. "I have to see what's there. I have to solve this mystery for myself."

"Well...," he wavered.

"I'm going with you, Val. There's nothing more to say."

They reached the shaft, and Val lowered the ladder into it.

Kiwil looked down at the skeleton reaching from the side tunnel and climbed down the ladder. While the others climbed down to join him, he took off his backpack and pulled out four flashlights. He carefully sidestepped the skeleton, crossing himself and saying, "Please forgive me, sir. We do not wish to disturb your rest, eh."

The side tunnel sloped steeply downhill. It was about five feet high and nearly as wide, and reinforced with heavy timbers. Kiwil flashed the light into the shaft while the rest stood impatiently behind him. "I can see a few feet ahead only, then it is dark, eh," he said. "I must go ahead only." He walked ahead into the tunnel, testing his footing as he went. The floor of the tunnel was solid and rocky, and rutted with peculiar, parallel grooves running lengthwise down the tunnel. A water channel six inches deep had been dug at one side of the shaft. It was wet from the recent rain, but otherwise the tunnel was dry.

Twenty yards in, the tunnel turned to the left, toward the mountain. Kiwil looked back and called out, "It seems sturdy enough, Lakay Pawid. You can come along, eh."

Joan and Rudy ducked down and followed Val into the tunnel. Hunched over, it was not difficult to walk, crablike, although it sloped down at quite an angle. Joan flashed her light overhead. The tunnel had been carved into the heart of the mountain and heavily reinforced. Someone, whoever dug it, had wanted to make sure it would stand the test of mountain monsoons and temblors. Joan had been inside gold mines in the California gold country, and she was sure that this shaft was newer than those--the wooden posts and beams seemed almost fresh.

They turned the corner, and the light from the open shaft disappeared. Except for the light from their flashlights it was pitch black. They could be a thousand feet into the mountain, and it would be no darker than this. The reinforcing timbers and the grooves in the floor stopped here. Ahead of them stretched an eight-foot wide crack in the mountain that reached up twenty feet like a Gothic arch. Joan stopped and stood up straight, stretching her back and looking up and down the shaft with awe. The floor was solid rock and smooth except for a small underground rivulet that emerged from the rock at one side and rushed gurgling down the incline.

Ahead of them, Kiwil's light stopped. "Lakay Pawid!" he shouted. "It is here, eh! This is truly magic!"

Val hurried ahead, and Joan stumbled down the slope trying to keep up with him. She caught her balance without falling and regained the rhythm of her shuffle down the incline.

"Careful, mum," Rudy said from behind her. "It is steeper at this place."

They caught up with Kiwil and Val and stopped in amazement. The four of them stood at the edge of a vast, underground cavern. Their lights barely reached the roof above. The river spread to a width of three feet, turned to the left, and flowed into a pool as large as a good-sized rice paddy. The water was as smooth as glass and shone brilliant turquoise in the light of their torches. A border of sparkling, white crystals encrusted the edge of the pool. In front of them, a beautifully built wooden bridge arched gracefully across the stream. Joan instantly recognized the classic Japanese design.

They crossed the bridge and reached the floor of the cavern. It was nearly level, and stretched beyond the range of their flashlights. On their right, a large area lay deep in drifts of bat guano. Val played his light over it. "We're not alone," he said, looking up toward the roof of the cave. His voice echoed back from the walls of the cavern ahead of them, and a soft rustling started overhead, then quieted.

They moved to the left, staying on bare rock, the four of them hushed with awe, and nervous at the thought of thousands of furry little bodies filling the air.

Kiwil's flashlight was the brightest, and it picked out the shape ahead first: it was a *torii*, a traditional Japanese wooden gate. Two posts twenty feet apart reached thirty feet up into the gloom at the center of the cave. They were connected by two horizontal wooden beams, the uppermost cut diagonally at the ends. The gate was painted vermilion, and white *kanji* characters decorated both posts. On either side of the gate, a tall, bamboo fence stretched fifty yards in each direction.

"It's a Shinto sanctuary," whispered Joan, "built to protect something valuable from evil spirits." She could make out some of the *kanji* and was surprised to see the name, *Tsukuyomi*, the Shinto goddess of darkness and the moon. Most Shinto shrines were built to honor *Amaterasu*, goddess of the heavens and light, or *Susano'o*, god of the oceans, but then, thought Joan, most Shinto shrines aren't built inside a mountain. The Shinto religion honors nature, not the underworld.

Just beyond the gate, Kiwil stopped. In the light of his flashlight, five more skeletons lay, stark white against the dark stone, twisted in a macabre heap on the ground. The other three joined him, adding their lights to his. The holes in two of the skulls' foreheads looked just like the one at the entrance to the tunnel.

Joan couldn't help wondering who would desecrate a sacred site like this with murder, most likely of local workers enslaved by the occupiers until they were no longer needed. Shinto priests went to great lengths to ensure the purity of a shrine, and blood and death were especially polluting. She raised her flashlight, penetrating the darkness beyond the skeletons. There stood row after row of wooden packing crates, each neatly labeled in black paint with Japanese characters. She recognized some of the characters: *gin* (silver), *kagu* (furniture), *e* (paintings), *nunoji* (fabric).

Rudy stood staring, astonished at what he saw. He looked back at Joan. "It's true!" he exclaimed. "It's Yamashita's treasure!"

His shout bounced off the far wall of the cave and came reverberating back. Right behind it came the explosion. It sounded like an explosion, but in reality, it was the beating of thousands of little wings. The startled bats dropped down from the cavern's roof and thundered through the cave, filling its space like water from a burst pipe. Joan shrieked and threw herself to the ground as dozens of flapping shadows brushed by her, the wind from their wings blowing on her face and bare arms.

The brown, furry storm passed them and circled at the lower end of the cave, then flew back above them, near the roof of the cavern. Joan aimed her flashlight up into the living cloud as the bats returned to their perches and began settling themselves for sleep after the intruders' noisy interruption.

She looked at the others; they had all searched for shelter on the ground, as well. Kiwil crouched, nearly hidden, behind the pile of bones.

"Val," Joan whispered, shining her light in his face, "you're bleeding!" Blood sprang from a cut on his cheek.

"One of them hit me," he said. "It must be a scratch from its claw."

"We'd better get out of here and have Dr. Sanchez take a look at you," she said.

"Yes," he agreed, "you're right. There is plenty of time to come back here."

They retraced their steps to the bridge, quietly, none of them wanting to deal with another flurry of frightened bats.

* * *

Joan knew that, in spite of his rashness, Rudy was right. They *had* found Yamashita's treasure. It couldn't be anything else. One of the most famous modern stories of hidden treasure, thousands of people had searched for it for more than forty years.

During their occupation of The Philippines from 1942 to 1945, the Japanese had systematically stripped the country and its citizens of their most prized possessions: gold, silver, paintings, artwork, ancient Chinese porcelain and ceramics, the artifacts of three hundred years of Catholic dominance, priceless pieces from Muslim Mindanao, modern works from private collections, anything a conquering army might consider valuable.

At the same time, priceless treasures from the rest of occupied southeast Asia--Burma, Siam, Indonesia, Malaya, Indochina--were gathered and shipped north, to the Japanese clearing house in the Philippines.

When the tide turned against the Japanese, and General Tomoyuki Yamashita was sent to command the occupying forces, the allies cut off the naval supply line the Japanese had enjoyed until then. They also cut off any exit. Yamashita retreated with his troops into the Cordilleras and dug in, defending himself against the allies for months. Somewhere along that trail of ultimate defeat, went the legend, Yamashita had buried the entire treasure of occupation. When the Americans tried and executed him, the secret went with him. Some said it was worth billions of dollars in 1945; at today's values, who could guess?

In the Sixties and Seventies, a second story spread around the Philippines: President Ferdinand Marcos had found the treasure, and this was the explanation for his incredible wealth. Joan was sure that that story had been planted by Marcos himself and the CIA, since most people believed that Marcos' money came from siphoning off billions of dollars of American aid.

* * *

Joan reached the open shaft, stepped around the bony warning and looked up into the sky. It was raining again, but the water felt cool and welcome on her face. The floor of the shaft was wet and slippery, and rain water coursed down the tunnel's ditch to feed the underground pool below.

One by one, they climbed the ladder out of the shaft, then stood and looked at each other. Suddenly, as if cued by some stage manager in the wings, they all began to shout and laugh. Throwing his arms around Joan, Val kissed her on the cheek. Rudy collapsed on the ground, holding his sides with mirth, and Kiwil jumped up and down, yelping with excitement.

" Kiwil," laughed Joan, "you really are a magic charm!"

"Ahh," giggled the little man, "but you haven't even seen me disappear and reappear yet."

Val reached out for Rudy and helped him up off the ground, and the four of them took each other's hands. It didn't seem the least bit strange to Joan that she was dancing in the rain with three men on a quake-torn mountainside while her husband lay unconscious a few hundred yards away.

8. ILEUS

He was drowning. The sun was high in the sky, but vague, obscured by several feet of water. He held his breath until he thought his lungs would burst. His body felt like lead, heavy and useless; he somehow couldn't bring himself to raise his arms and swim to the surface. He had to breathe, he knew. Finally, his body frozen with fear, he knew he would drown. With a rush, he exhaled the old air, prepared to gulp the killing, calming water into his lungs. He inhaled...new air!

He blinked his eyes in amazement, and tried to focus on the sun. It gradually resolved itself into the light from a lamp. Awake now, he realized he was lying in a bed in a pine-paneled room. He started to raise himself, and a terrible pain shot through his back. He looked down; his right leg was pulled up, attached to a stainless steel post that extended from the foot of the bed. He looked at his leg and wondered what was wrong with it, and he began to feel the deep throb of pain in his thigh. He started to cry out for help, thought better of it, and lay there, moving his eyes right and left, taking in as much of the situation as his peripheral vision would allow: Pine walls...wooden frame window...trees and rain outside...gooseneck lamp on wall above bed...picture of Jesus blessing children...IV bag on stand. So, he was in a hospital? What kind of hospital was this? It felt like a Christian fishing lodge. What had he been doing? What day was this? What was that dream about drowning?

"Oh, you are awake! Praise be to God!"

A small brown face looked down at him. A very pretty face with deep, dark eyes. Her teeth flashed white as she smiled at him. Her black hair was trimmed very short; the white collar of her dress opened to a thin gold chain and small cross on her long, slender neck. A Filipina Audrey Hepburn.

"What...?"

"Just let me get Doctor," she said. "He'll answer all your questions." She turned and hurried from the room.

Paul stared after her, the afterglow of her neat, white uniform filling the blank rectangle of the open doorway. Beyond the door he could see only a piece of wall of what seemed to be a hallway with more pine paneling.

A few moments later, a slender young man in a crisp, white doctor's jacket stepped quickly into the room, followed by the vision of a nurse. "Mr. Webster," he said, smiling, "we're delighted to see that you're awake. I am Florio Sanchez. Welcome to Good Shepherd Clinic."

He leaned close and looked into Paul's eyes. "Tell me, do you remember why you're here?"

"No. I woke up from a dream. I thought I was drowning."

"Not unusual," said the doctor. "The shock and the concussion are playing with your memory."

"Concussion?"

"You've been unconscious for more than twenty-four hours," he replied, taking Paul's arm and checking his pulse. "Millie, temperature and blood pressure, please."

The nurse shook down a thermometer and placed it in Paul's mouth. He attempted to say, "Hello, Millie," but with the thermometer it came out, "Mmmm mmm."

She wrapped the deflated cuff around his arm and pumped it up, put the stethoscope on the inside of his arm and released the pressure.

"You had a nasty fall on our mountain," the doctor said, uncovering Paul's unelevated foot. "Your back and your leg are broken, but I can see by your reflexes that there's no damage to the nerves. Can you feel that?"

"Mmm mmmm," answered Paul. Yes, he thought to himself. That sounded familiar. He could picture climbing a mountain in the rain.

The nurse removed the thermometer.

Paul looked up at her; she smiled at him, and suddenly he remembered! "Doctor! My wife! Joan was on the mountain, too! Is she all right?"

"Yes, she's just fine. We've sent someone to find her. She'll be extremely happy to see you. She's been very worried about you. We all have." He continued checking Paul's legs and feet for sensation. "You're looking just fine, but I'm afraid you're going to have to spend some time with us, until these fractures heal. The leg has a spiral fracture, and frankly, I'm more worried about it than I am your back. We don't have the facilities here to move you. You're very lucky, you know. Landing in the water of the rice paddy probably saved your life."

Paul closed his eyes. He could see the water rushing at him again, feel the sickening sensation of falling, then, nothing.

"Do you feel any pain or discomfort?" asked the doctor.

He opened his eyes again and looked at the ceiling, "I moved when I woke up, and there was a shooting pain in my back. There's a deep throbbing in my leg, and my head hurts a little."

"Yes, you probably took a rock in the forehead during your fall. Let us know if the pain gets too uncomfortable. You'll heal faster without it."

"And, doctor? I'm starting to feel a little nausea."

"Of course, Mr. Webster," said the doctor. "That's the initial symptom of *ileus*. It's a condition caused by your body's reaction to the trauma of your broken bones. You'll experience nausea and bloating for several days. You won't feel hunger, and we won't feed you anything. You'll get liquid nutrition only from the IV."

"Paul!"

Joan stood in the doorway of his room. Her hair hung, wet and dripping on her shoulders; her shirt and jeans were muddy and soaked through. "You're awake!" she cried, crossing to him and caressing his whiskered cheeks. She pressed her wet mouth against his, kissing him again and again. Paul took her head in his hands. The water from her hair dripped onto his face and ran down his neck.

"Mrs. Webster," said Dr. Sanchez, "you're soaking wet!" He motioned to the nurse, and they started for the door. "No matter, we'll leave you two alone. Just remember, Mr. Webster, you're badly hurt. Please remember to stay quiet. And Millie? Get Mrs. Webster a towel."

"Darling," she said. "Are you really all right?" She pulled back to look at him and brushed a smear of mud from his nose.

"The doctor seems to think I'll mend up OK. But I guess I won't be doing any more swan dives for a while."

" Don't even joke about it! When I saw you fall, I thought you were dead!" she whispered, then kissed him again, stroking his head.

He brushed a wet coil of hair from her face and looked up at her. "Thank God you weren't hurt," he said, "but what's going on? You look like you've been swimming!"

She sat down in the chair next to him. "I was sitting here with you this morning," she said. "The sun was streaming in the window, and I felt so desolate. Was it only this morning? Yesterday was the worst day of my life, and today is the best! You're here with me, and you're going to get better, and I just discovered an amazing treasure!"

She took his hand and stroked it. "The quake broke open a huge cavern under the rice terraces," she chattered, excited as a little girl with a new puppy. "Val and Rudy and a man named Kiwil--that means "magic"--and I went down into the cave and found the treasure. That's why I'm all wet and muddy and..., honey, you won't believe it! It's the treasure the Japanese hid at the end of the Second World War! It's huge! It's immense! It'll be the most important discovery since King Tut's tomb!"

Paul lay there, dumbfounded, looking at his wife in amazement. "A treasure? Under the rice terraces?" he finally asked.

"A whole Japanese underground shrine!" she exclaimed. "A beautiful bridge over an underground river! Hundreds of crates of gold and jewelry and paintings and..., I don't know what all! We'll have to hire a staff to even catalog it all. Val says that the roads won't be able to handle the convoy of trucks we will need to move it until after the rainy season, so we'll have to work right here in the cave. We didn't have time to even open anything, because Val got bit by a bat, and..."

"A bat?"

"Well, it's really just a scratch. He's in the other room waiting to have the doctor check it, but I'm sure it's nothing. But we'll have to put up nets or something, so that we can document everything without having thousands of bats diving on us all the time."

"It sounds like you've got this all worked out," said Paul.

"Well, not everything," she replied. "It'll take a lot of planning. We'll have to let the Philippine government know, of course, and the press, too. But first we need to make sure that it's all secure. It's probably worth billions! But you're here, anyway. And I want to be with you. So, I'll stay here and bring in some of my staff and go to work."

Paul didn't know what to say. This was certainly not the reunion he had expected. But what a break for Joan, to discover something like this. This would surely give her a respected place in museumology. "The most important discovery since King Tut." Wasn't that what she had said? This was big time! Maybe he could write the story....

"Pardon, Mr. and Mrs. Webster," interrupted the nurse. "Doctor says that Mr. Webster needs to get some rest, and Mrs. Webster needs dry clothes again."

She smiled at them and handed Joan a towel. What a smile, thought Paul, angelic, an appropriate look for an angel of mercy. "It is good that you are happy. We are happy for you also. Maybe Mrs. Webster could come back again this evening to visit," she said. "But not too late only."

* * *

For the next few days, Paul slid in and out of consciousness. When he was awake, his surroundings were blurred, either by the pain or the medication. The medication worked, not by relieving the pain, but by distancing him from it. He could feel the pain, but he could step aside and view it as an outsider, almost as if he were consoling someone else for their pain. The blur became routine, the routine reassuring. In spite of his nausea and the constrictions in his gut, they kept fluid and pain killer running through him, dripping out of the IV bag, down through the needle in his wrist, out the catheter and into another plastic bag attached to the foot of the bed.

Every day, two or three people he had met from the town would spend half an hour or an hour sitting in his room. Teo, Sonny, and the others seemed to be taking turns spending time with him. They rarely spoke, but smiled and occasionally commented on how much better he seemed, how the weather was improving, how happy they were he had come to Banaue. Not, of course, happy he had fallen, but happy at their opportunity to meet such fine people as he and Mrs. Webster. He learned later that this was their way of paying tribute, as important to their social well being as the alim ceremony.

Twice daily, Dr. Sanchez took a long and careful look at him, checking and rechecking his reflexes and his awareness of sensation. Once daily, the nurse and an aide carefully sponged him down and rubbed lotion into his back. And once a day, Joan came to see him, in the late afternoon, after it had started to rain. She never came in dripping wet again; she changed after the hours spent in the cavern of the treasure and used one of the large umbrellas from the hotel.

While she was there, she would shave him and tell him about the events of the day in the cave. They had erected a fence and a guardhouse around the opening to the tunnel. Val had sentries posted, but, as he said, they would do little good if someone were intent on stealing the treasure. The story spread around Banaue was that the fence had been put up to protect residents from danger--that the earthquake had undermined the hillside and that it might collapse at any time. Right now, the bad weather and the difficulty in removing so great an amount of material were the major factors keeping the treasure safe.

They had contacted Senator Vital, and he was arranging a meeting between Joan and President Corazon Aquino herself! Rudy would drive her out via the long eastern route through Nueva Vizcaya next week. In the meantime, they had erected nets around the treasure to keep the bats at bay and were compiling a list of the contents marked on each crate. Joan's training in Japanese was very helpful. They had even opened a few crates, and their early discoveries had been as remarkable as expected.

Everything in the crates was carefully wrapped. It was obvious that the treasure had been packed for an ocean voyage, until the allies severed the shipping link between Luzon and Japan. One of the first crates they opened was filled with treasures of the Catholic religion in the Philippines, such as polychromed *santos* and gold reliquaries. Another contained Chinese porcelain, some of it twelve hundred years old. Joan was certain now that the treasure was worth many billions of dollars.

Every day, Joan would talk and Paul would listen, although his powers of concentration were weak, and occasionally he would find himself watching the curtain fluttering at the window and attempting to control the pain in his leg by willing the throb to transfer itself into the lace. Sometimes he would hold a contest, trying to determine whether the leg or the back or the knots in his stomach hurt the most. The winner varied until, at about five o'clock, Millie would come in and inject his next dose of pain killer into the IV. Millie, the angel of mercy blessing him with a cessation of pain. In a few minutes, he would drift off. When he woke two or three hours later, Joan would be gone, and he would look at the ceiling and wonder who else had lain in this bed looking at the ceiling as they recuperated or died. How many broken bones, how many cases of pneumonia and dysentery, how many bullet wounds had healed in this room. He would glance down at his leg, elevated crazily toward the ceiling, and feel himself floating feet first into the air, sailing out the door and down the hall, that hall that so mysteriously led nowhere as far as his vision was concerned and led everywhere, because rationally he knew that it was not just a pine-paneled closet, as it appeared from his vantage point. He wondered how far he would float until he came to the nurses' station. What was it like? Was it just an old desk and a wooden school chair, or was it a polished counter with shelves full of tongue depressors and sterile gauze? Did the night nurse, Cece, catch a few winks there, or was she busy with paperwork and cleaning duties when she wasn't checking on him? The glow of her white uniform dazzled him, and he covered his eyes with his hand. "Mr. Webster," she scolded, "Doctor said you're not to float out of your bed anymore." He retreated headfirst down the hall to his room with something like an airborne backstroke, sank into his bed and watched as the cables and pulleys reattached themselves to his leg, pulling up on the metal pins in his knee and hoisting his leg into the air. He looked back up at the ceiling, listening to the rain outside. The ceiling melted into a lake that rose up and struck him like a fist, and he fell off the mountain again.

* * *

On Wednesday morning, six days after the fall, Paul was awakened by the sound of his own stomach rumbling. The sun streamed into his room through the open window, and the fluttering of the lace curtains reminded him of summer mornings in Kansas. He remembered great stacks of pancakes with butter from the churn and maple syrup. Glasses of cold milk, fresh and frothy. When he was little his mother had told him those bubbles on top were money. And he remembered the thick-cut, hard-smoked bacon the Remlingers up at the junction of Teaberry Road and Route 36 had given his dad for helping them in a case with a Topeka meat packer.

His mouth watered, and he watched the door for a minute or two, waiting impatiently for someone to walk by, then called out, "Millie!"

The nurse came into his room almost instantly. "Yes, Mr. Webster?"

"Millie, I'm starving. Do you think I could have some breakfast?"

"Well, Mr. Webster, praise be to God! You're getting better!" She started for the door. "I'll just see what Doctor will allow you to eat."

It was only a soft-boiled egg, some dry toast and tea, but it was a feast to Paul. He finished the tea awkwardly, sipping it through a straw which didn't want to stay in the thick, white mug. When he finished, Millie took the mug from him and brushed some crumbs from his dressing gown. Paul could feel the warmth of her hand on his chest. He lay back and licked his lips, savoring the last traces of egg yolk, then wiped his mouth with his napkin. "Is Dr. Sanchez around, Millie?"

"He had to go into town for a little while," answered the nurse. "I'll tell him you'd like to see him when he gets back. But for now, please rest. You're not well yet." She put the napkin on the tray and left.

He watched her leave the room and wondered if she was more beautiful from the front or the back, deciding to do further research. He looked up at the now familiar ceiling. It was made with pine lumber, like the walls, but was painted white. Resin from knotholes bled through the paint in several places. A fly stood upside down on the ceiling halfway between the bed and the window, absolutely still and silent. Paul lay quietly, too, enjoying the warm satisfaction of the tea and the food in his stomach combining with the easy glow of the drug dripping from the IV.

How strange, he thought, that this place could seem so comforting. He felt at home here, in this place where his broken body was mending.

* * *

He had never had a serious illness or accident before, but Paul could remember his anxiety when going to a clinic in San Francisco for a very minor surgery.

He had pulled off his shirt and put on the white, poncho-like cover-up that the nurse had given him. The nurse prompted him to a stool in the corner of the examination room. "Go ahead and read your book. I'll be a few minutes getting things ready for the doctor," she said.

He had brought a copy of Graham Greene's *A Burnt-out Case* with him, and he opened the book and dove into its world of lepers and tse tse flies and the oppressive heat of central Africa. He read of the leper named Deo Gratias, cured of the disease after losing all his fingers and toes. He thought to himself of the upcoming surgery, the doctor removing a benign but tender and irritating growth from the upper edge of his ear. He could see himself in the mirror after the bandages came off, the top half of his ear gone.

The doctor would say, "We had to take more cartilage than we'd planned on."

He could hear the nurse on the phone a week later, "Doctor wants you to come in as soon as it's convenient. There's a problem with the biopsy."

Six months and several visits later, he would look in the mirror again, after the last of the bandages were removed. The sight would make him swoon with terror--a hideous version of Deo Gratias, with all his appendages removed: nose, ears, fingers, toes, penis. A complete stub of a man--a leadless, eraserless pencil.

"Good morning," said the doctor brightly as she entered the room. She wore the standard white coat and had enough gray streaking through her shoulder length brown hair to elicit respect. "Now, what we're going to do this morning is give you some novocaine, so you won't feel a thing. We'll remove the growth and a little of the cartilage at its base, then stitch the skin together. You'll have a small scar, and the curve of the top of your ear will be slightly different, but hardly noticeable."

He lay down on the examination table, and the doctor used the foot pad to raise the table. She gently turned his head to the left and swabbed the region around his ear. "You'll feel a small pinprick," she said. He lay quietly as she injected the anesthetic. She peeled the backing off a small, flexible sheet of plastic, cut a small hole and stretched the plastic over his ear, pressing the adhesive down to secure it. "Is that comfortable?"

He replied that it was, and crossed his feet, trying to relax. He felt the doctor's fingers manipulating his ear. No pain, just some movement and small sounds, then pressure. He knew the pressure was to stop the bleeding, but he saw nothing except the ceiling and wall to his left and the edge of the plastic sheet above his right eye. He heard the snip of surgical shears nipping small bites of cartilage, then more pressure. He held his breath and could feel sweat running sideways across his back.

"Five mil nylon," the doctor told the nurse. The pull on his ear as the doctor stitched up the incision seemed oddly familiar, and he remembered his mother when he was young, listening to the radio with the darning basket next to her on the sofa. Why did his socks always have holes in them? Now that he was grown, he never put holes in his toes or heels. Was it a function of his age? Or were they just manufacturing better socks now? Somehow he couldn't believe the latter was the reason.

"All done," said the doctor. "You shouldn't feel any pain when the anesthetic wears off, but if you do, you can take some Tylenol. Make an appointment out front to come in next Thursday or Friday to have the stitches removed." She left the room while the nurse finished applying the bandage.

The nurse smiled at him as he sat up. "Well, you'll never have to worry about being mistaken for Mr. Spock."

* * *

When Paul woke up, it was afternoon, and the sun had moved above the clinic and out of range of his window. Dr. Sanchez was standing by the bed looking pleased with himself.

"So the ileus has passed," he said. "Next thing you know you'll be running up and down the hall." He winked at Paul, sharing the joke.

"But, seriously, I thank God that you are mending so well. Soon, your sojourn here will be nothing but a memory."

"How long will I really have to stay chained to this bed?" asked Paul.

"Ten, twelve weeks," answered the doctor. "You remember, I told you both fractures are serious, but if allowed to heal properly, you'll be as good as new when you leave here."

Ten weeks, thought Paul to himself. That's two-and-a-half months--a long time to lie flat on your back, staring at the ceiling. "As long as I have to stay here, can you ask my wife to bring me my laptop computer? And could you get me some books to read?"

"I'm sure I can get some books for you, but how you'll be able to use the computer while lying on your back is another problem. But I'll give it some thought. We're only here to help you make the best of your situation," he smiled again at Paul. "With God's help, of course."

* * *

Joan arrived at three that afternoon. She reached over and kissed him. Her mouth was soft, and Paul recognized the fragrance she was wearing. It was the Chanel that he had gotten her a few years ago. There was something very sexy about it; he had never been able to figure out why he found it so irresistible, but it never failed to turn him on. He remembered the day he bought it--a cool, foggy summer's day in late August. He was shopping for Joan's birthday, her fortieth. He had decided to help her celebrate this much feared and much maligned event by buying her nothing but items that were glamorous and sexy and expensive. For the first time in his life, he was shopping in Saks Fifth Avenue--he couldn't remember why, but he had never been in the store before. The woman working at the perfume counter was strikingly beautiful and perhaps ten years older than Paul. Her black hair was pulled back into a severely tight bun, and the brilliant white crepe blouse made her olive skin seem even darker. It seemed to him that she would be completely at home on the afterdeck of some fabulous yacht or greeting guests on the patio of a Mediterranean villa high up in the hills above a clustered white town tumbling down to the azure sea below.

He explained to her his shopping objectives, and she asked him to describe Joan. After a few minutes of description, she interrupted him and said, "I think I know the right perfume for your wife. And I think it will be the right perfume for you as well." She opened a square, bevel cut glass bottle and dabbed the stopper to her wrist, just below the cuff of her blouse. She showed him what was available in the scent--perfume, and cologne, of course, but also bath powder and body lotion, soap and facial cleanser, hand lotion and showering gel.

"The fragrance needs to blend with the chemistry of the skin for a few minutes before it achieves its true essence," she said, and she reached across the counter and held her wrist out to him, the slender hand bent back in a gesture that seemed to Paul completely trusting and intimate. He bowed his head and breathed in, her hand so close that it blurred before his eyes. The perfume was flowery but not sweet, and Paul was enraptured.

"A woman needs a wardrobe of scent," she said. "When she dresses, she should wear one scent and only one scent. The fragrances of her bath should not fight with the fragrance of her perfume."

And it occurred to Paul, what an elegant, sexy gift--a whole basket filled with one fragrance, in all of its myriad variations. He spent several hundred dollars and left the store dizzy with his success.

Joan loved the gift, and the Chanel had become her special fragrance. Paul never tired of its scent on his wife, and he hadn't thought of the day of its purchase for years.

"...I'll be leaving the day after tomorrow."

Paul looked up. Joan was sitting in the chair next to the bed. He hadn't heard what she had been talking about until, "...I'll be leaving the day after tomorrow."

"Honey, I'm sorry. I was drifting again," he explained.

"I could tell, baby," said Joan. "I've watched you drift in and out for days now. I just keep talking. I guess the aftershock of your accident and the excitement of my discovery have me all mixed up. Just sitting with you and talking helps a lot, even if I know you're not really hearing what I'm saying.

"I hate to leave you at all, but tomorrow we'll finish copying down the contents marked on all the boxes, and Friday Rudy'll drive me back to Manila, where I'll meet with President Aquino. I shouldn't be gone long. If everything goes well, I'll get her approval, call the museum and have Rosie and Michael fly to Manila to help me hire the beginnings of a cataloguing crew. We should be back up here by Thursday or Friday next week."

Paul looked at his wife. Her soft hair spilled onto the shoulders of her navy silk blouse. It shone with hints of gold and copper, just slightly more blonde than the varnished wall behind her. But that was nothing compared to the way her eyes sparkled at the prospect of taking this treasure and showing it to the world.

He had always admired the way she could take a complicated project, instantly dissect it into manageable chunks, put together a team to produce and complete all those disparate pieces, and then manage the whole thing while developing other, equally complex projects. But today, he wished she could forget the whole thing and just take him in her arms, pull all the needles and catheters out of him and make love to him, slow and soft and delicious, all of her just for him. He felt like whimpering and pouting. He felt like a six-year-old whose mommy was going on a trip. He felt like he was being abandoned. But he knew that his thinking was distorted. He clenched his fists under the sheet and thought to himself: it's all just an effect of the drug dripping into me.

* * *

The next morning, just after breakfast, Joan appeared with a tiny, brown man whose smile was as wide as his face.

"This is Kiwil, darling," she said. "Kiwil, this is my husband, Paul." Paul held out his left hand and winced at the little man's viselike grip.

"Ahh, Mr. Webster," grinned Kiwil. "I am so sorry. I sometimes forget not to be so strong, eh. When I was a boy, all the children made fun of me I was so small. It made me very angry." He crossed his arms and scowled, acting out his story. "I worked very hard to be stronger than anyone in my village, even though I was the smallest one. I succeed at this, and now everyone is afraid of Kiwil, eh. Hee hee hee!" He held his arms around himself, lost in mirth and very happy at his story's outcome.

Joan laughed along with Kiwil. "Paul, Dr. Sanchez said you wanted to use your computer. I talked to Val and Kiwil about it, and Kiwil is going to build a frame for it so you'll be able to use it while lying in bed. Kiwil needs to take some measurements." She smiled at Kiwil.

"It will be a few seconds only," said Kiwil, "and I will be careful not to cause you discomfort, eh." He took out a small tape measure and began measuring the widths of the bed and of Paul's chest, the height of Paul's chest above the mattress, the length of Paul's upper arm, the height of Paul's hand when bent back at the elbow.

"That is comfortable for you, eh?" he asked.

"While I'm gone, Kiwil will look in on you. He'll take good care of you. Remember, I told you his name means Magic Charm? Well, he *is* magic. He can do just about anything!"

Kiwil smiled and put the tape measure back in his pocket, "Sometimes I know I am not really magic, eh. But sometimes, who can know only?"

9. CORY

Early Friday morning, the crunch of the gravel drive in front of the clinic signaled the arrival of the big limo. It rolled softly to a stop, and Rudy jumped out and opened the back door for Joan before she could open it herself.

"I'll just be a minute, Rudy," said Joan, and she crossed the drive and climbed the stairs to the clinic. She exchanged smiles with Millie in the reception area and turned down the hall to Paul's room.

Paul was finishing his breakfast. Good morning, lover," said Joan. She took the glass from him and picked up the napkin and wiped his mouth, then bent down and kissed him. He tasted good, of egg yolk and mango, and she wished she could slip her clothes off and slide into bed next to him.

"God, I wish you weren't going," he said.

"It'll be just for a few days," she said.

"But the days are so long already, and without your visits, they'll seem even longer."

"Maybe these will help." She pulled two books from her purse. They were the books he had brought with him to Banaue, Deighton's *London Match* and a Maigret mystery.

"Well, at least a little," he said. "I've almost finished the Deighton, and the other is so small it won't take very long."

"I can bring you more books when I come back," said Joan. "What should I look for?"

"That'd be great," said Paul. "How about some Clavell? For once, I actually have plenty of time to read."

142

"I'll see what I can find."

"The gift shop at the Inter-Con in Makati has a pretty good selection."

She looked down at him ruefully, feeling like she was leaving him unprotected and homeless. "Who's going to shave you while I'm gone?" she asked, stroking his cheek.

"No one," he answered. "I'm going to quit shaving and grow a beard. As long as I'm trapped at the end of the world, I may as well look the part." He reached up and held her hand tight against his face, then turned and kissed her palm.

"I guess I'd better go, Paul," she said, her eyes brimming with tears.

He drew her down to him and held her close. She could feel the steadiness of his heart through the sheet. "I'll be OK," he said. "Remember? I have Kiwil taking care of me. You be careful."

"I've got Rudy to look out for me." She gently pulled herself away, kissed him once more and stood up.

"Bye, baby," she said and hurried from the room, before she could lose her resolve.

He shouted down the hall after her, "Say hi to Cory for me."

Millie was still working at the front desk. Joan paused and, seeing a box of tissues on the desk, asked for one. Millie slid the box toward her.

"Take good care of him," said Joan, dabbing at her eyes with the tissue.

"Mr. Webster will be fine," said Millie. "Look how he's improved already. With God's grace, he'll just rest here a few weeks and then leave us as good as new."

"I know that," said Joan. "I keep telling myself that everything will be all right. I just don't understand the terrible fear--I can't seem to shake it. Somehow, I feel that I'm still in danger of losing him."

"Just take care of your business. We'll all be here when you return," Millie said.

Joan nodded and started for the door.

"Go with God, Mrs. Webster," said Millie, "and Mrs. Webster?"

"Yes?"

"Give my best to Rudy."

* * *

Late the same night the Mercedes turned left where President Elpidio Quirino Avenue met Roxas Boulevard. The tires splashed through a few puddles, but the heat of an August evening in Manila had already evaporated most of the downpour they had driven through an hour ago. A few blocks ahead on the right, the Cultural Center of the Philippines loomed up from a flat peninsula of reclaimed land jutting into Manila Bay. Imelda Marcos had sponsored this splendid piece of modern architecture, pushing the contractors with a deadline so tight that several workers died building her tribute "to the people of all the islands of The Philippines."

At the end of the peninsula, a few blocks beyond the cultural center buildings, the limousine turned into the elegant entrance of the Westin Philippine Plaza. This time, even Rudy was not fast enough to beat the doorman who opened the car door for Joan. The night manager stood just behind him, smiling as Joan stepped from the car.

"Mrs. Webster, welcome to the Philippine Plaza! The senator advised us of your arrival, and your room is ready. You must be tired after your long drive," he continued. "I would be happy to send some hot tea to your room, unless, of course, you would prefer something else."

"Tea would be fine, thank you," said Joan. "And do you have a room ready for my driver as well?"

"That is not necessary, mum," said Rudy. "I'll drive back to the senator's compound and sleep in my own room. I'll pick you up here in the morning. When will you need me?"

"I'm not sure yet, but I'll call Vicky in the morning," said Joan. "Good night, Rudy, and thank you for all you've done."

"It was little enough. Good night, mum."

* * *

After the bellman delivered her luggage, Joan unzipped the garment bag and hung up its contents in the closet--the wrinkles would hang out by morning. There was a knock at the door. It was a young man from room service with her tea. He wheeled the cart into the room. "Is there anything else you need, mum?" he asked.

"No, thank you," answered Joan. She tipped him, closed the door as he left and poured herself a cup of tea. She felt distracted, tired but not sleepy, excited but ill at ease. The suite was beautifully decorated with modern Philippine ikat fabrics, bleached wood and split bamboo. The plush pale rose carpeting in the living room and bedroom gave way to pale rose marble in the bathroom and dressing room. She took a shower, toweled off and slipped on the blue silk robe Paul had given her for her birthday the year before. The carpet felt wonderful under her bare feet.

She took a sip of tea; it was tepid. She padded into the bathroom and dumped it in the sink, then came back to the cart, poured herself a hot cup, stepped to the picture window and pulled back the curtain.

Her suite was high up on the north side of the hotel and looked out across Manila Bay to the dazzling lights of the city. At the base of the peninsula, the boats in the Manila Yacht Club sat quietly, protected by the stone breakwater that extended out into the bay. Just beyond, the bright lights of Roxas Boulevard ran north along the edge of the bay to the dark section that was Rizal Park. Past the park and the old fortified town of Intramuros stretched the lights of Chinatown and Quiapo. Even farther was Quezon City, and she knew, far beyond that, in the dark and hazy distance, loomed the Gran Cordillera Central. There, in a tiny village called Banaue, her husband lay sleeping, his broken bones slowly mending. And beneath him, deep inside the mountain, was a treasure that would make Joan Webster a name known around the world. She sipped her tea, looking at that distant darkness, and smiled as she thought about how Emory Barclay would have applauded her discovery.

* * *

"Welcome back to Manila," said Senator Bonifacio Vital, smiling and pressing her hand between his two hands. They were large and soft, and enveloped her hand like a warm, dry bath. "We're so glad to have you with us again," he smiled. "We were shocked to hear about Paul's accident. I understand, though, that he is healing nicely."

"He seems to be," said Joan. "Everyone in Banaue has been so helpful, and Dr. Sanchez at the clinic has done a wonderful job with him."

"Dr. Sanchez is an excellent doctor," said the senator. "His evangelism can be a little tiring at times, but definitely...an excellent doctor." He picked a dark thread from his barong Tagalog. "But the other news," he continued. "You've found Yamashita's treasure? Can it be true?"

West of them, out in the bay, a dayboat pitched in the wake of a large Bertram, its windshield catching the morning sun and flashing it into the limo like a signal from a distant sentry. The senator turned abruptly at the flash and gazed out the window for a few seconds, rolling the thread into a ball between his thumb and forefinger. Joan glanced ahead, saw Rudy smiling at her in the rear view mirror, and smiled back.

She turned back to her companion in the rear seat. "Oh, yes, it's true, Senator..."

"Boy. Call me Boy, Joan," he said.

"All right, then, Boy, it's a treasure so large, I have trouble believing it myself. Hundreds of crates full of the most priceless objects from all over southeast Asia. All carefully placed inside the mountain and guarded by a Shinto shrine."

Vital shook his head in disbelief.

"But tell me about President Aquino," said Joan. "I've never talked with a president before. What should I call her?"

"She's an old, dear friend, and very easy to talk to. You'll like her, and she'll like you--you're both very straightforward women. Oh, but don't call her Madame President. She doesn't like the word Madame. She thinks Imelda tarnished that word."

* * *

The richest family in Tarlac province, north of Manila, is the Cojuangco family. Huge sugar and rice plantations, the largest brewery in the Philippines, banks, major corporate and real estate investments grew from a simple rice mill and sugar mill opened in the 19th century by a family of immigrants from Fujian province in China. In 1933, Jose and Demetria Cojuangco had their fourth child, Corazon Sumulong, baptized into the Roman Catholic church. As a girl, Cory attended a series of exclusive convent schools. She was delicate and studious, a very proper young girl, and class valedictorian at her sixth grade graduation in Manila.

Cory's introverted nature was unlike that of most of her family. Her father was a member of Congress, her mother's father had run for Vice President of the Philippines, and two uncles were a Senator and a Congressmember. Politics was in the blood of the Cojuangcos and the Sumulongs.

In 1946, at the end of the Japanese occupation, the Cojuangcos moved to the United States, Cory's father taking a position as president of a bank in New York. Cory continued her studies at Ravenhill Academy in Philadelphia and later at Notre Dame Convent School in New York. After graduating from Mount St. Vincent College in 1953, Cory returned to the Philippines to attend law school, where she met and married Benigno "Ninoy" Aquino. The Aquinos were the other prominent family in Tarlac, and his union with Cory was a definite step up in Ninoy's drive for power, with the Presidency as his long-range goal.

But Ninoy's political dreams, in spite of his family's wealth, were intrinsically tied to helping the people of the Philippines, to improving the quality of life for the 70 percent of the population that lived in poverty. He ran for and was elected mayor of the little town of Concepcion, forcing his shy wife out of her shell and into a carabao cart to show that she was one of the people, too.

Ninoy had studied politics and the law, and he understood that many of the positions taken by the Communists and the NPA were truly intended to better the lives of the peasant farmers and to bring about land reform and a shift from oligarchy to a truer democracy. As he gained power, he took the time to meet with many rebel groups, forging coalitions that would bring the people to his side some day in the future. Ninoy's boldness and his convictions gradually became Cory's, too, as she bore four daughters, kept house, and listened to soap operas on a transistor radio.

Her existence was buoyed up by her devout Catholic beliefs, but her Christian devotion was sorely tested when Ninoy, at 34, the youngest Senator ever in Philippine history, was thrown into prison by Marcos. Cory became Ninoy's link with the outside world, as she listened to him for hours and hours across the years of incarceration, learning his political strategies by heart.

Finally, more than seven-and-a-half years later, Marcos released an ailing Ninoy and granted him permission to travel to the U.S. for heart surgery. Cory, Ninoy and the children settled in Boston for what she calls the happiest years of her adult life. But in 1983, just three years later, Ninoy decided to ignore the death sentence trumped up against him in the Philippines. The greatest goal in his life had been to overthrow Marcos, and he was determined to accomplish the feat, one way or another. He stepped off the plane in Manila and was assassinated by Marcos' soldiers.

The widow of a martyr, Cory resisted efforts to place her at the head of the opposition party to run against Marcos in 1986, but eventually realized that the person who had the best chance of beating Marcos had to be completely different from him. She was that person--a woman and a widow who had suffered under his oppression. She formed a coalition with Salvador Laurel and hit the campaign trail. Everywhere she went, thousands of her followers listened to her prayers and her memories of Ninoy, and their chants of "Cory! Cory! Cory!" filled the air.

A few hours after the polling booths closed, hearing the reports of cheating and tampering with ballot boxes by Marcos supporters, she took the upper hand and declared herself victorious. Turning down an American proposal at a compromise, she was adamant, "Do not threaten Cory Aquino, because I am not alone."

Thousands of her supporters proved this no empty statement by lying down in front of AFP tanks in the streets of Manila. The "people power" revolution forced Marcos to flee the country, and Cory became the first female president of The Philippines.

In the four years since her election, she has dealt with attempted military coups, restructured her cabinet, and struggled with the massive problems of poverty, rebel unrest and foreign debt--all legacies of the Marcos dynasty.

* * *

They drove through the gates, entering the grounds of Malacañan Palace. There was a crowd on the front steps of the imposing stone mansion that had been home to nineteen Spanish executives, fourteen American governor-generals and nine Filipino presidents.

"Tourists lining up to see the palace," said Boy. "Cory has proven to be good to her word. During her campaign, she promised to give the presidency back to the people. One of her first acts as president was to open the palace to the people. Her offices are in that small building to the right, the old guest house. The palace itself is only used for cabinet meetings, state dinners and official functions."

The sentries beyond the palace drive waved them ahead as they drove up to the two-story Executive Building. Rudy jumped out and opened Boy's door, then, as if by telepathy, stayed where he was while Boy walked around to open Joan's. Joan felt the reassuring squeeze of Boy's hand on her arm as he led her up the stairs. It was obvious to her that he was a frequent visitor by the way he was received by the President's staff. They were ushered into a small drawing room paneled with narra wood but furnished in a style reminiscent of other rooms she had seen in Washington, D.C. A member of the President's staff brought a silver tray with teapot, cups and saucers of English bone china in a pattern that reminded Joan of the set that Mrs. Mencken had used.

The door opened, and the President came in, petite and trim in a navy blue linen dress edged with white piping. Joan had agonized over what to wear, and she had nearly worn its twin. She made a silent prayer

151

of thanks that she had worn the light blue silk suit instead. Cory closed the door behind her and greeted Boy warmly, then turned to Joan.

"Cory," said Boy, "I'd like you to meet Joan Webster."

"I'm honored to meet you, President Aquino," said Joan.

"Please, call me Cory," smiled the President. "If that's all right with you, Joan." She sat down on the couch with Boy and poured herself some tea, then looked at Joan. Her dark eyes were intense with concentration. "Boy tells me you've unearthed a problem."

Joan stopped short, her teacup poised in midair. On the drive down from Banaue she had imagined all sorts of agendas and rehearsed possible approaches to support her position, but this was one question she was totally unprepared for. She glanced at Boy, but he just gave her a small smile, the standard Filipino response to any embarrassment. "A problem, Pres...er, Cory? I don't understand."

"What would you say the treasure is worth, Joan?"

"We've only opened a few of the crates, but based on what I've seen so far, much of the treasure is priceless, with immeasurable religious or historical value...."

"But what if the whole lot were auctioned off, what would it be worth?"

"Well, conservatively, at least several billion dollars. American dollars."

"That's what I gathered from what Boy has told me," said Cory. She sipped her tea, then stared into the dark fluid in the cup. "Several *billion* dollars. Do you have any idea how much money that is to our country, Joan? Last year's total exports amounted to nearly 150 billion pesos.

That's about seven billion dollars." She looked up at Joan. "Two-thirds of our people live in poverty. Your treasure could fill a lot of hungry bellies."

"Yes, I agree," interrupted Joan. "But I don't understand why this discovery is a problem."

"You've probably heard that I'm a very religious person," answered Cory. "This treasure has forced me to spend many hours searching my soul and seeking guidance from Our Father. I suppose each of us has to cope with temptation at one time or another. One of my greatest temptations has been the idea of never telling the press about the treasure; instead, just quietly selling it off and putting *all* the money to good use. But I know that's short-sighted, virtually impossible. I also know I could not live with myself if I committed such a crime.

"The treasure was stolen from all over Asia, and taken only fifty years ago. It will be possible to find many of the rightful owners, and we must do our best to return as much of the treasure as we can. What's left can be used to create seed money for loans with the Asian Development Bank or some such organization, to help the entire region, not just the Philippines."

Joan looked at this small woman. She had read of Cory's devotion to God, and her sincere efforts to rebuild this troubled nation. "In order to accomplish that," she said, "many thousands of items need to be identified, catalogued and held in safekeeping. Let me bring a couple of my people over from San Francisco to help set up a staff to handle all of that. They worked with me on the Emory Barclay collection, and they're highly qualified.

"But you mentioned that these items were stolen fifty years ago. Next year, the U.S. will be observing the fiftieth anniversary of Pearl

Harbor. Let us choose five hundred pieces--the best, most important items of all--and let us build a traveling exhibition to commemorate and honor all of the lives lost in the Pacific war. I want to take this around the world to remind people what happened. So much attention is given the Holocaust in Europe, and it's true that that was a crime against humanity that should never be forgotten. But the world should not forget what happened in The Philippines, or Malaya, or the rest of Asia, in those days. I'm flattered that you shared with me the turmoil you've gone through. This exhibition can deliver the message that The Philippines is a place inhabited by remarkable people. You have given up some cash; in return, you will win the respect of the whole world."

* * *

The waiter pressed his serving spoon along the backbone of the sea bass, and the sides of the fish fell away from the skeleton, steaming and fragrant with ginger and scallions. He served up a plate of the delicate white filet for Joan, then broke the head away from the carcass and served it to Boy. As Boy began to pick apart the head with delight, Joan picked up a morsel with her chopsticks; it was the best fish she had ever eaten.

Boy was elated over Joan's meeting with Cory, and of Cory's agreement with Joan to create a traveling goodwill exhibit. He had insisted on taking her to his favorite Hong Kong style seafood restaurant in Makati. He signaled the waiter and asked for two more Tsing Tao beers. "Ordinarily I drink San Miguel, of course," he explained. "We do what we can to support the Philippine economy, but with Chinese food, I much prefer Tsing Tao."

"This fish is delicious," said Joan.

"When you are in Hong Kong, you will find it on the menu under the name *garoupa*, but it is *lapu-lapu* here in the Philippines, to my mind the tastiest fish in the world." He pulled the fish's cheek apart, separating the white flesh with his chopsticks. "I truly enjoy bringing Westerners here." He looked up at Joan and smiled. "I never have to argue over who gets the head."

* * *

Rudy was waiting for them outside the restaurant. Boy got in after Joan, waving to the doorman at the restaurant.

"Oh, that was a lot of food!" exclaimed Joan. "I won't be hungry for a week."

"Well, maybe just a small snack at our house this afternoon for *merienda*," offered Boy. "Vicky is looking forward to seeing you. She's very excited about your finding the treasure. There will also be a few people there who you should meet. They'll be able to assist you in building your curating team."

"You and Vicky have been such a help. I can't thank you enough."

"You really should be staying with us. We have so much room, and Rudy will be handy for you when I leave for the conference in Djakarta tomorrow."

"I'll only be in Manila for a few days. Perhaps next time."

"At any rate, we're happy to do what we can. It's a pleasure to help with something that will bring so much good to our country," said Boy. He looked out the window at the traffic. "It's interesting that Cory was tempted to use the treasure just for the Philippines. That same thought had crossed my mind."

The car stood still, trapped in the midday gridlock barely moving west from Makati. Outside, pedestrians wilted in the heat and humidity as dark clouds rolled in from the east, filled with the afternoon rain. Inside the limo, Joan rubbed her bare arms; the air conditioner made it chilly. She looked at the crowd outside the car. Across the street, two young men dressed in punk black were pushing and shoving each other, and their companions were trying to pull them apart. Joan hoped that the treasure would indeed bring only good for the Philippines. As Kiwil would say, "With treasures, who can know only?"

10. LORING

The laptop computer hung suspended above him, trapped in mid-air by an ingenious frame of split rattan and bamboo. With his arms comfortably resting on his stomach, Paul had merely to raise his fingers to find the keyboard. Kiwil stood next to the bed, adjusting the legs of the frame that straddled Paul's body, his eyes happy slits as he chuckled at Paul's incredulity and at his own workmanship.

"Kiwil, this is wonderful!" said Paul. "Would you plug it in so I can see how the screen works?"

"Of course, I will be happy to plug it in, eh," said Kiwil, as he unwound the cord. "I have seen TV in the lowlands. This is like a small TV only?"

"Some others are more like TV. This one just shows words. I use it for writing." Paul flipped the power on, and waited for the screen to light up.

"I hope it will keep your thoughts away from your injuries while you are here in the clinic."

"It certainly will help," said Paul. The prompt showed on the screen, and he typed "WP" and pushed the enter key. "Here, take a look, Kiwil."

The little man bent forward slightly and frowned at the screen as Paul pressed F5, and the screen lighted up with its list of WordPerfect documents. "How many pages are inside, eh?" he asked.

"It will store thousands of pages."

"Much better to carry around than all those heavy books," decided Kiwil. "If you are content, I must go now. Lakay Pawid is waiting for me. I will come here later only."

"Thanks again, Kiwil," called Paul after him. "Say hello to Val for me."

He scanned down the directory and saw an unfamiliar entry. ILOVEYOU.WPD was dated just three days before. He highlighted it and pushed F1 to retrieve it. The screen was filled with:

August 17, 1:35 am

Darling Paul,

I'm sitting here on my spacious bed in my beautiful empty room wishing you were here making love to me. I still have trouble believing all that has happened since we arrived in Banaue. Every night I go to sleep, only to wake up after seeing you fall off the mountain again. I woke up ten minutes ago screaming and crying, thinking that I'd lost you. I guess the terror of it will fade with time, at least I hope it will.

You've been very patient with me during our visits at the clinic. I know that I tend to rattle on about the treasure, but it does help to keep my mind occupied and my thoughts away from your terrible injuries. I know you'll be fine sooner than we even think. You've already improved so much. But the treasure does give me something to think about, and it is a fabulous opportunity for me to give something important to the world. This discovery is so amazing; I can't even begin to tell you what it means. It's so far beyond anything I ever expected of life. I only wish Emory were here to share it.

I'm leaving Banaue this morning. I guess I'll be in Manila when you read this. (I hope you find it. I didn't realize how many files you have in this thing.) But wherever I am, my thoughts and my heart are with you. I'll always love you.

Joan

Paul scrolled back to the beginning of the letter and started to read it again. He dozed off during his third reading and dreamed that Joan came into the room while he slept. She picked up the laptop in its frame and set it on the table next to the bed, then leaned over and looked at his sleeping face, bent down, kissed him softly and left the room.

* * *

The next day, Paul was eating lunch and trying to drink his red punch without spilling it all over himself when Millie poked her head in the door.

"Millie, did you move my laptop after I fell asleep?"

"I hope I didn't break anything, Mr. Webster."

"Not at all," he smiled. "I just wanted to thank you. And please call me Paul."

"Very well, Paul," Millie said, blushing. "you have a visitor. It is Lakay Bulahao. Is it all right?"

"Sure, he can have a laugh watching me eat."

Millie disappeared, and a few moments later, the head of Emmanuel Bulahao appeared. It extended around the door jamb as if someone were holding it on a stick. There was something rather rodentlike about the narrow face and small mouth.

"Excuse me, sir," said the head, "but I see you are busy. I'd best come back another time." And it disappeared.

"Wait!" shouted Paul. "Come back!"

The head reappeared. "Mr. Webster," it said, pausing to glance about the room, "It is I, Emmanuel Bulahao."

With a jerk, the right half of Emmanuel Bulahao became visible.

"But please, call me Bingo, Mr. Webster. Emmanuel is much too formal."

"Come in, then, Bingo. But you must call me Paul." Bingo! thought Paul. He wondered what little Emmanuel had done to inspire that nickname.

Bingo timidly stepped into the room and stood just inside the doorway. "Please excuse this interruption. Go on with your lunch."

"Thanks, but I was nearly done anyway. Have you ever tried to eat lying down?"

"Not once, sir. But if you recommend it..."

"Anything but!"

Bingo held up a rattan backpack he was carrying and stepped towards Paul. He moved strangely, erratically, in a way that matched the body to the face. Paul remembered watching him that night at Teo's house.

"Then, perhaps a good book, instead?" He smiled. Now he was on familiar ground. "Lakay Pawid told me you were in need of books to read. You see, since I am Deputy Mayor of Education, it is very often that I have books. Some old, some new." He brandished the backpack. "Lakay Pawid said you should have some books, so here I am."

He dug into the backpack and produced a sheaf of booklets. "These should provide much food for thought. They are from our Iglesia ni Cristo, and they tell of the good works of Jesus Christ, our Lord." He started to pile them on Paul's food tray, thought better of it, and stacked them on the chair next to the bed.

Next, Bingo pulled out three faded paperbacks. "These books, they were left at the Happy Mountain Hotel by guests. They are called *Dark Desire, Throne of Passion* and *Once More, My Darling*. I have not read them, but the reviews on the back covers are very encouraging." He stacked them on top of the religious texts and gave a little bow to Paul, who bit the inside of his cheek to keep from smiling.

Somewhere down the hall someone dropped a metal tray, and the crash echoed through the building. Bingo's shoulders jerked up protectively, and he spun around toward the door. It seemed to Paul as if he were sniffing the air, searching for the scent of danger. He turned back to Paul. "It is nothing," he reported, smiling with chagrin, "nothing to be worried about," and he busied himself with what was still in the backpack.

"And now I have some excellent texts," he announced, bringing out two well-worn books, one a plain red cover, the other black and orange. He held up the red, and paused, playing his audience with finesse. "Mr. Webster, are you an accountant?" he asked.

"No," said Paul, "I'm a writer."

"Well, good. Then this book should be of interest to you. It is *Accounting Principles*, a fine edition we use at the school." He smiled and pulled the book back a few inches, ready to reel in his catch. "If you were an accountant, I'm afraid it would be of little interest, since it is a very basic text. But as a writer, it will be a completely new subject to you, and I am sure you will find it interesting." He placed the book triumphantly on the growing pile.

"The second is our favorite book of Philippine history, entitled *History of the Filipino People*. It is read by all of our senior students, and I recommend it highly." Bingo topped the pile of books with the history and smiled at Paul. "I can only hope that your period of healing here at the clinic will be more pleasant with the time spent reading these books."

"I'm sure that will be the case," said Paul, scratching the stubble on his cheek. "Thank you very much for your efforts, Bingo."

"I am pleased to be of service, Paul," said Bingo, with a conspiratorial wink. He picked up his backpack, repeated his jerky bow and darted out the door.

* * *

". . . *our soldiers here and there resort to horrible measures with the natives. Captains and lieutenants are sometimes judges, sheriffs and executioners. . . 'I don't want any more prisoners sent to Manila,' was the verbal order from the Governor-General three months ago. . . It is now the custom to avenge the death of an American soldier by burning to the ground all the houses, and killing right and left the natives who are only 'suspects'.*"

"Oh, I see you are being indoctrinated."

Paul looked up from the book he was reading. Dr. Sanchez stood at the door to his room, crisp in turquoise and navy under his white lab coat.

"What do you mean?"

"That book, spoonfed to all our students, is so slanted toward American interests, it's a mockery."

162

"But I just finished reading about the struggle between the Philippines and the U.S. in 1898," said Paul. "He certainly doesn't paint a pretty picture of the American interests there."

"How could he? And slur his own countrymen?" The doctor pulled up the chair and sat down next to Paul's bed. "But read on, and you'll see the praise building year after year for the U.S.--the heroes of World War II, the fathers of democracy, even the protectors of Cory's new deal. It doesn't talk about the ways that the U.S. finished what Spain started. Building an oligarchy tailored to the interests of the rich and the powerful. America let big business interests strip the Philippines for their own profits, and now agriculture is on the wane, many of our islands are eroding away after the loss of their forests, and poverty is worse than ever!"

This was a side of the doctor Paul had not seen before.

"You sound as if you've been studying politics, not medicine," said Paul, scratching his chin.

"No, I was not a student of politics, only perhaps a student of those who were. I was in medical school at the University of the Philippines during the days of martial law, which Marcos had declared to maintain his dictatorship and make it easier to liquidate his enemies. Read the chapter about martial law in your book. It makes Marcos sound like a saint.

"I spent time in southern Luzon as an intern, treating the peasant farmers in the region. They had no money, no way to pay for medicine. Friends of mine experienced the same problems in the cities. It became very clear that the great majority of our people were victims of a system that rewarded only the privileged few. No matter how hard they worked, there was no way out of poverty for most of them.

"I saw the NPA, the New People's Army, at work in the provinces, punishing criminals, protecting the weak, preaching equality and working for land reform. They promoted communism, it's true. The pure ideologies of Mao. Some of them were overzealous. There were incidents of needless violence and atrocities on both sides, but the NPA was fighting for the people, the Philippine Constabulary was supporting Marcos and his rich cronies, as well as American interests and the CIA.

"I very nearly joined the NPA; some of my friends did. A few years earlier, hope had been stirred up by Ninoy Aquino, who was willing to talk to all sides, including the communists, and was committed to ousting Marcos and helping all our people. But by the time I got to college, Ninoy was in prison for crimes he never committed.

"Martial law gave Marcos greater powers than ever, and he sent the PC, his army, out to neutralize the NPA. They were very thorough; they killed and imprisoned hundreds of NPA cadres and sympathizers. And along the way, they raped and murdered hundreds of innocent bystanders, they looted and burned entire *barangays,* villages that they suspected of harboring the NPA.

"Two of my best friends were shot and killed, another was imprisoned without a trial for six years until he was pardoned by Cory. Those three were all doctors--guilty of nothing but working in NPA barangays treating the sick and injured, helping peasant women live through childbirth, teaching farmers ways to deal with malnutrition. That was their crime."

He paused, staring past Paul at the open window. Paul could see the pain of vivid memories in his eyes.

"But you work here at the clinic for Americans."

"Don't misunderstand," continued the doctor. "I'm not anti-American. I'm only against the wealthy taking advantage of a situation and subjugating millions of people to maintain their power and status. Sure, the missionaries who built this clinic want to bring the word of God to the Ifugao. But they also want to give the Ifugao ways to improve their lives. That's why I'm here--I wanted to help in a way that would be legally sanctioned by the government, no matter how corrupt. But even working here was not always as safe as you would think. During martial law, the PC murdered many priests--anyone who worked openly for the betterment of the peasants was at risk, whether they belonged to the Communist party or not. And, of course, a lot of crimes were committed by the PC and blamed on the NPA--it seems that if anything bad happens in the Philippines, it's the fault of the NPA. That's why so many citizens will tell you that they're no better than thugs or bandits. The press has a favorite scapegoat, and you know the Americans hate anything that has to do with communism, although they don't really understand the way communism works here in the Philippines.

"Now that Cory is president, the worst of the corruption and atrocities are history, but she still represents that small group of families who virtually own the islands. Although, I must admit, she has shown that she's willing to make concessions. She seems to be working at measures that will eventually lead to true land reform, not some useless propaganda like Marcos created--read the book, read all about his wonderful land reform projects--it's a pack of lies!"

165

"So the NPA is painted by the press as the cause of all of the Philippines' problems?"

"To a great extent, yes. For the media, it's far easier to deal with one great villain, rather than dozens, as there are in reality. Of course, since Cory's election and the ousting of Marcos, it's also become popular to blame all our ills on him."

Paul turned to the index of his book and looked up NPA. "But, Doctor..."

"Call me Loring, Paul."

"Loring, there are only two references in this entire book to the NPA."

"There are two ways to report NPA activities. One is to exaggerate the number of cadres and the incidents of violence. The other is to pretend that the organization hardly exists--to minimize its importance."

Paul put the book down. "So who's writing the truth? Can you get me any books that tell the real story?"

"There's very little available, but I'll see what I can do," he said, getting up to leave.

"Thanks. And thanks for being candid with me."

"Do me a favor, Paul," said Loring. "Don't mention what I said, not to anyone, not even your wife. Some people in this country don't appreciate candor."

That evening, Millie came in to see if he needed anything before going to sleep.

"I'm curious, Millie. What do you know about the NPA?"

She looked just as if she'd seen a ghost. Suddenly, her face became a mask of tragedy, and tears started streaming down her face. She buried her head in Paul's chest, and sobbed uncontrollably. Paul stroked her hair, not knowing what to say.

"Millie, I'm sorry. I didn't mean to upset you."

She raised her head from his chest and looked down at him, tears still clinging to her long eyelashes.

"You dear man, you have no idea," and she bent down and gave him a long, sweet kiss.

He put his hand on the back of her neck, savoring the miracle of the feeling until she pulled away and stood up.

"I had no right to do that. I'm sorry, Paul."

"You had every right. I want you to be happy, Millie."

"Good night, Paul. Sleep with Jesus' love."

11. JEREMIAH

"Rosie! Come take a look at this," called Joan.

Rosie Giovanni was the senior curator of the museum's Chinese collection.

She had just arrived from San Francisco with Michael Hamada, the museum's lead photographer, and driven to Banaue with Joan, three other Asian art specialists and a small truckload of equipment that was now installed in the Yamashita cave.

Val had to close off all the upper rice terraces, explaining to the people of

Banaue that the ground adjacent was still dangerous and liable to collapse at any time. Work on the upper terraces was halted until further notice. He disliked making up excuses like this, but agreed that the treasure was worth the white lie.

Rosie crossed from the table she was working at. Her great shock of permed gray hair was pulled through the back of a Giants baseball cap. It flowed out behind her like a physical manifestation of her aura; it created the effect of motion, and motion was Rosie's game. She loved to run. And dance. And when she wasn't moving, she was still moving. She tapped her foot, or swung her leg, or nodded her head to whatever music was playing. Energy, in the form of motion, fairly seeped out of her pores. In spite of her gray hair, Rosie seemed quite young--ageless, Joan thought. She was happy to have Rosie with her in Banaue. Her knowledge made her indispensable, and Joan loved running with her early every morning since they had gotten here.

"Ohhhh, Joan!" she whispered and did a little dance of triumph. "That's

exquisite! It's such an elaborate piece of Yaozhou, it must have been a commission or a gift for someone very important."

"I know. It's so beautiful, it probably deserves to be in the traveling show."

Rosie took a deep breath, carefully picked up the six-inch bowl and turned

it in her hands, admiring it from other angles. "I think it's a winner, for sure, but you know, it's so different from any Yaozhou I've seen, I think you ought to date it."

"You're right, especially if it's going to be in the show, it would be good to

know more about it."

Like the other items, it had been wrapped neatly in scraps of cloth and tied with string. Joan had untied the package, and watched the cloth slide off a small bowl. The bowl was unlike anything she'd ever seen. She recognized the style and the period. It was Chinese porcelain and was carved with a common gray and green peony motif, probably from the 11th or early 12th century, the Northern Song period; it was called Yaozhou ware and was a popular style for everyday tableware during the period. But this piece was carved with uncommonly elaborate peony and leaf motifs inside and out, and was shaped in a very unusual cusped style, more like some of the metalware from the period than ceramics, and Joan had immediately called Rosie to confirm what she saw.

Rosie went back to her workspace, and Joan took out a small

drill and drilled a tiny hole in the base, putting the grindings into a small plastic bag and filling out the information blanks printed on it.

Later, they would send the grindings to a laboratory at Oxford University that would date the piece with precise accuracy by measuring the ceramic's thermal luminescence.

* * *

They had debated over simply frightening off or even exterminating the bat colony, but Joan argued that the bats had been here long before even the Japanese discovered the cave, and would be here long after they removed Yamashita's treasure.

The workroom was forty feet across. It was nothing more than a large wood and bamboo frame covered with netting and woven grass mats. It loomed from behind the torii and the boxes of treasure like part of a Disney adventure ride. A small generator provided electricity for the lights, the computers and the cameras in the workroom. One quarter of the room was Michael Hamada's still photography studio, covered in an extra layer of mats to keep the flashes from startling the bats. The rest was a working space filled with tables and chairs, a small chemistry lab and piles of books and portable file boxes.

Joan returned to the business at hand, lay the Yaozhou vessel upside down on the cloth and carefully printed a catalog number on the bottom, using a crowquill pen and India ink, which wouldn't harm the piece. She entered a brief description into the computer and saved it to disc, then bundled up the porcelain and moved it to the line waiting to be photographed.

It was slow work. With six of them working ten-hour shifts, they had done the preliminary cataloguing for less than a tenth of the collection, and they had been at it for more than a week.

She took out the next package. It was a set of four small nesting bowls. Sometimes this work felt like drudgery, but then she was handling such beautiful things, and, with this treasure, there was always the thrill of discovery when something like the Yaozhou bowl was unwrapped. She had to leave the day after tomorrow for San Francisco. The museum commission had called; the news of the treasure had leaked, but the paper with the story was holding it as a favor. They wanted Joan back to meet the press with them. She was amazed they'd been able to keep the news from leaking as long as they had.

Tomorrow. And she hadn't told Paul. What was wrong with her? She certainly loved him, but something in her made her hesitate when she wanted to be close to him. He seemed unperturbed, lying there in his bed, waiting to heal. She had brought several books back from Manila, including a couple of Philippine history books that Val had called her about. He seemed content for now, reading, taking notes on the laptop, sleeping, seeing her for their daily hour of conversation. But there seemed to be a growing distance between them. It felt to her like she had become extraneous. Whenever Millie entered the room, Paul couldn't keep his eyes off her. Well, after all, thought Joan, when she is in the room, it's always because there's some procedure or other that she's performing.

Paul had said that he was thinking about working on a project when he got out of the clinic and that he might stay on for a while in the Cordillera. Joan was pleased that in bringing him here, even with the horrible accident, he had found something or some place that inspired him. Enough of this needless worry, she vowed. I have to tell him this evening that I have to make the trip. After all, with so much happening, it's to be expected that I need to meet with the museum staff and the media. She finished entering her notes on the four little bowls and moved them to the line for Michael's photography. This crate was going faster than some of the others, since she and Rosie were both experts on Chinese ceramics.

* * *

"I have to leave on Thursday for San Francisco," said Joan, as she rubbed Paul's shoulders.

"When's Thursday? I have no idea what day it is."

"Oh, you're right," she smiled. "You don't even have 'big paper day' to keep you connected with the calendar."

"Well, there are some church bells that must mean Sunday, but I've lost track of when I last heard those."

"Anyway, today is Tuesday. I have to leave tomorrow to catch a flight Thursday morning. The museum commission called, and the media knows about the treasure, but is holding the announcement, thanks to Joe Abruzzi, our commission president's pull."

"You should be there for the announcement," agreed Paul. "This is your baby. You should be there to get the credit."

"For being in the right place at the wrong time, in the worst of circumstances."

"It matters not. You found it. You knew what it was. Grab the glory." He squeezed her hand. "I'll be well soon, and you'll still have the treasure."

That wasn't so hard, she thought, as she stroked his new beard.

He put his hands on hers. "I hope it softens up, when it gets a little longer. It's pretty prickly now."

"You were made for a beard," she said, moving around to the side of bed, bending over and kissing him on the mouth. "I'll be back sooner than you know," she paused, chuckling, "so make sure you leave Millie alone."

* * *

The 747 taxied to a stop, and the open mouth of the jetway reached out to meet the curve of the fuselage. Joan unbuckled her seatbelt, stood up and stretched her arms in the roomy First Class cabin behind the cockpit on the upper deck. She picked up her briefcase and swung its strap over her shoulder. As she reached the bottom of the circular staircase on the main deck, the flight attendant handed her the wardrobe bag she had carried on. The leather was cold from hanging for hours next to the jet's skin at 38,000 feet.

"Thanks, James," she said. "I'll see you on the flight back to Manila in a few days."

"Have a good stay, Dr. Webster, and congratulations!"

As Joan headed toward Customs, she passed the duty free store and airport gift shop. The headline in the L.A. Times read, "PACIFIC TREASURE COMING TO L.A." USA Today announced,

"GREATEST TREASURE EVER WILL TOUR U.S." The National Enquirer shouted, "IMELDA'S PSYCHIC SAYS TREASURE IS HOAX." Well, it's all public now, she thought. Joe's weight with the press hadn't held, after all. She had talked to him from Manila, and the news was out. He had gotten her on the Jeremiah Mills Show for the following day to kick off the blitz, so she'd flown directly to L.A. and would fly up to San Francisco after the show.

Outside Customs, a young woman stood holding a sign that read, "Webster." She spotted Joan and hurried over. "Dr. Webster? I'm Naomi Winters. I work for Jeremiah Mills. I have a car waiting outside to take you to your hotel."

Naomi Winters was young and black and beautiful, a shade taller than Joan. She had fine features and a long, elegant Ethiopian neck, and her accent matched her looks--her English was crisp and precise. She found a Red Cap and turned Joan's luggage over to him, then led Joan through the sliding doors toward a white Cadillac limo.

" We've booked you at the Universal City Hilton--it's so handy to the studio. Jeremiah is so glad you agreed to appear on his show--everybody's talking about the treasure, and we're the first ones to get you. Oprah was just green. You'll be great on TV--you're even prettier than I had heard."

The chauffeur opened the door for them while the luggage was loaded into the trunk.

"If you don't mind, Dr. Webster, could we make a little stop at the studio before we go to the hotel? Jeremiah is dying to meet you. Would you like something to drink? There's a refrigerator right here. Evian? Iced tea? A glass of wine?"

"Iced tea would be perfect, Naomi. And please call me Joan. Dr. Webster makes me sound even older than I am."

"I'm sorry," laughed Naomi, pouring the tea from its ice cold pitcher. "You're not old!"

"Next to you, I am."

* * *

"Dr. Webster, what a pleasure!"

Jeremiah Mills was tall and handsome, with skin the color of a cafe latte. His grey silk suit was custom tailored and showed off his muscular body with just a hint of tightness. He looked like a football player, which, in fact, was what had gotten him where he was. He had grown up in south central L.A., a street kid with an uncanny ability to catch a ball and run. A college scholarship to USC gave him the chance to move up, and he had taken it with gusto. He made the NCAA All-American list his junior year, and his future looked bright, when a Husky middle linebacker took him down and tore up his knee, ending his chance at a pro career.

Two years later, physical therapy and voice lessons landed him a spot with NBC Sports. His skill as an announcer, along with his mocha good looks and a way with people eventually led to a morning talk show which was in its fourth year of syndication. It was a live show, with just a 15-second window of opportunity for bleeping out the F-word and other unusable material. Jeremiah had developed a reputation for using that live format to create an atmosphere that, to the delight of an audience addicted to sleaze, put his guests on the defensive and milked their embarrassment.

Joan was angry that he'd buffaloed Joe into signing her up for the show, but she'd accepted the challenge to defend herself, and museums in general, because he had intimated to Joe that she'd gotten where she was with her good looks, and not much else. How dare he call her a bimbo, she thought. So she'd decided to take him on. Now she wasn't so sure she'd made the right decision.

"How do you do, Mr. Mills?" Joan took the offered hand. It was warm and held hers firmly.

"So polite!" He grinned at Naomi, who smiled at his little joke. "Please, it's Jeremiah to my friends, and I do hope we'll become great friends!"

"Then call me Joan, Jeremiah."

"Naomi, would you check in with Roger? He wants to go over some details on tomorrow's show with you."

As Naomi excused herself, Jeremiah went to the bar in the corner of the spacious office and filled a glass from an Evian bottle, then added ice with a pair of silver tongs. "Evian, Joan?" He held out the glass to her. "Or something stronger?"

"Thank you, no. I had something on the ride out here."

He sipped the ice water and motioned to the leather couch in the sitting area at one side of the room.

"I'm afraid I've gotten off to a bad start with you, Joan. My conversations with Joe Abruzzi seem to have put you on the defensive."

"I'm not used to people suggesting that I don't know what I'm doing," replied Joan.

"Well, that's just what I mean. We're really excited that you're appearing on our little show. You could have picked from any of the networks. The whole country is buzzing about your treasure--you're big news, you know."

"I'd just like the opportunity to set the record straight and to get the promotion of the treasure off to a good start."

"And that's exactly what we want you to do. And to show you there are no bad feelings, let me buy you dinner tonight."

Jeremiah pulled out a gold cigarette case, snapped it open and offered it to Joan. When she declined, he asked, "Do you mind?" and lit one for himself.

"Well, I am pretty tired from the flight. I thought I would get to bed early."

"And so you shall. Just a little early dinner, then we'll whisk you back to your hotel." He leaned back in the couch and blew the smoke to the side, away from Joan.

"Well, all right. I suppose I could get a little sleep this afternoon."

"Great! I'll pick you up at seven."

* * *

The phone in her room rang at five minutes to seven. Jeremiah was in the lobby, whenever she was ready, no hurry. They drove downtown, and the traffic was heavy, so they had time for martinis from an icy silver shaker. Jeremiah was friendly and talkative, pulling details from Joan about the treasure: How they found it, how it came to be there, how much it was worth; and about herself: How she liked the Philippines, how her meetings with President Aquino went, how Joan had gotten into the museum business, how Joan met Emory Barclay, and so on. The restaurant, Nicola, was even better than its reputation. Of course, they knew Jeremiah and were delighted to see him, and, of course, they were shown to one of the best tables in the place--in the more intimate dining room. The pan-fried monkfish was delectable and the second bottle of wine even better than the first. Jeremiah told her of the tough neighborhoods he grew up in, and the rich ones he frequented now. As they left the restaurant, she felt his hand on her bare back.

The balmy September night air was fragrant with fall-blooming gardenias. Joan walked around the back of the limo as the chauffeur waited for her at the open door . When Joan got into the car, Jeremiah was already there next to her, pouring another glass of wine. The driver shut the door, and Joan glanced forward, noticing that the privacy screen behind the driver's seat was up.

"More wine?" Jeremiah suggested, offering her a glass of red wine. His body swayed as the limo left the curb, and the wine lunged dangerously close to the rim of the glass.

"Thank you, but I think I've had enough for tonight. I have to be fresh for the show tomorrow morning."

"Oh, you'll be fresh," he said, downing a third of the glass. He turned toward her, his face brimming with studied excitement. "You want to be fresh in the morning? I'll tell you how to be fresh in the morning." He paused for another swallow, winking conspiratorially at her.

"I know your secret," he said, mysteriously. "You and your husband haven't made love for some time." He smiled, pleased with himself, and finished the wine.

"You're not making sense," said Joan.

"Of course I am," he pronounced. "You've been married a long time. You're used to getting it all the time. You must be starving right now." He reached over and put his hand on her shoulder. "How about a little snack here in the car?"

He dropped the wine glass on the floor and lunged forward, knocking Joan back onto the seat and falling on her.

"Jeremiah!" shouted Joan. "Stop it!"

His mouth brushed against hers, and the smell of wine and saliva sickened her. He grabbed at her breast with his right hand, and Joan balled up her fist and slugged him on the ear.

"Oww!" he cried, backing away and cupping his ear tenderly. "I was just having a little fun."

"Well, I wasn't." She pulled herself up and backed against the door. "I think you'd better tell the chauffeur to take me to my hotel."

He signaled the driver, and the limo turned left. They sat in silence as the big car headed north on 101.

As they pulled into the entrance drive of the hotel, Joan opened the door of the limo and started to get out.

"Wait, Joan. Let me apologize." Jeremiah reached after her, grabbing her hand. "I'm sorry. I know I was out of line. You're a very attractive woman, and I just got carried away."

"Apology accepted," said Joan, extracting her hand from his.

"OK," he said, smiling. "Get a good rest. I'll see you in the morning? OK?"

"OK," she said, forcing a return smile. "In the morning."

* * *

"But, what do you think, folks?" asked Jeremiah, screwing up his face in mock puzzlement. "Do we want to make this just a little more interesting?"

"Yeesss!" shouted the audience, urged on by the teleprompter screens.

"Well, okay then!" said Jeremiah, turning to Joan. "Joan, we've got an old friend of yours here I know you're just dying to see." He spun back to the audience. "John Terry used to work with Joan at the Museum of Asian Art, and he just happens to be here this morning. Folks, welcome John Terry."

John Terry stepped through the curtains. Joan hadn't seen him for 15 years, since he left the museum in a fit of temper after Emory had willed the curatorship of his collection to her. He was a little grayer, but otherwise looked the same. She had heard that he had been working in Orange County.

He shook hands with Jeremiah, who led him around to the couch. Joan reached up to shake his hand and was pointedly ignored.

"My, my," said Jeremiah. "Don't you have anything to say to *Ms.* Webster, John?"

"I do, indeed," answered Terry. He turned and melted butter with his voice. "Hello, Joan. I have only one question for you. Who did you have to sleep with to get *this* treasure?"

The audience roared with delight, Joan felt the heat of embarrassment and anger flush across her face, and the director cut to camera two for a close-up of Joan. She looked at Jeremiah, who was feigning shock at about the level of a first-year drama student. She stood up and walked toward the audience, and the boom mike operator swung back to follow her.

"Mr. Terry wants to know whom I slept with. Fifteen years ago, I was given Mr. Terry's job, and he accused me of the same thing then." She spun to face Terry. "You've never been able to accept the fact that a woman could do a better job than you. I did, and that's the only reason I was given that promotion!"

Terry stared at the floor in silence, unable to meet Joan's gaze.

"As for *Mister Mills*..."

Jeremiah frantically signaled the floor director to go to commercial. The floor director spoke softly into his headset, "Camera Two, stay with her."

"John Terry is here this morning trying to discredit me because I wouldn't sleep with Jeremiah Mills last night!"

She walked past Camera Two and up the center aisle, through the audience. The director nodded to Camera Three, and the two side cameras followed her. The audience rose, sending her out the door with thunderous applause and cheering that was still going on when they came back from the commercial break.

* * *

"God damn it, Joan! How could you be so stupid?" Joe Abruzzi slammed a copy of the LA Times Calendar section onto the polished granite desktop, and Joan winced at the impact. The headline read, "BEAUTY AND THE BEAST. WHAT PRICE ART?" Employees in the corporate offices of Joe's construction company scurried past on the other side of the smoked glass trying not to show they had noticed their boss' anger. The fog was beginning to lift outside the office's highrise window, and in the distance, Joan could just make out Coit Tower atop its hill.

After the Jeremiah Mills debacle, Joan had flown up to San Francisco. Joe's administrative assistant had left a message on her answering machine cordially informing her that Mr. Abruzzi would very much like to meet with her the next morning at nine o'clock.

Joan glanced at the brass ship's clock on the credenza behind Joe's desk. It said 9:02.

She looked back at Joe. "Look, Joe, I'm sorry, but Jeremiah was hinting that I didn't know what I was doing, and..."

"And he was right!" shouted Joe. "When I agreed to serve as president of the museum commission last year, I did it because I wanted to give something back to the city. I didn't do it so I could spend my time backfilling after your PR gaffes!"

"Joe, I..."

"Look, you know you do a great job. That's the problem." He leaned back in his chair and ran his hands through his thick gray hair. "You've led such a charmed life, you think you can do anything. Even

182

beat Jeremiah Mills at his own game. I'm sorry I agreed that you should do the spot, but you should have seen what was coming the night before.

"If you hadn't walked off that set the way you did--if you had stayed to try and battle it out--they'd have made you look like a gorgeous fool.

"There's just too much at stake here, Joan. The Yamashita treasure will bring millions of dollars with it, but more important, it'll bring millions of new bodies into museums across the country. New eyes looking at Asian art. We can't blow this, Joan. We have too much of a reputation as appealing only to dilettantes, of being too elitist. How are we going to compete with movies and TV? We don't even have dinosaurs that we can throw around like the natural history museums do."

He picked up the mug of steaming coffee on the desk in front of him and took a careful sip, watching Joan intently over the rim of the mug. "I think you'd better get back to the mountains and bring that treasure of yours home."

* * *

When Joan got back to her hotel, there was a message for her that had been left at the front desk. It was from Norman Diakhate:

"Wow! What a celebrity you've become! I'm back at Berkeley, this time on the teaching side. It'd be great to get together and talk about old times. And new times."

Norman

* * *

"I haven't been thish drunk in a long time," said Joan, playing with the mixed nuts in the silver bowl on the bar.

"I think you're holding your own just fine," Norman answered.

"I can't 'splain it, Norman. Paul's right there in the clinic, an' I know he's healin'—gettin' better. An' I see him every day. But I feel thish huge gulf 'tween us."

"See, there's the difference between you and me, Joan," said Norman, sipping his Scotch and water. "I never noticed anything until Joyce decided to leave me."

"There isn't anythin' specific, 'cept that Paul feels more distant 'n usual. It could jus' be the injuries. But, y'know, I have a hunch he's fallen 'n love with his nurse, who's 'stremely pretty and sweet."

"All men fall in love with their nurses, Joan. I fell in love with two of them at once when I gave my appendix to science."

Joan picked up her martini glass, lifted it to her lips, and noticed it was empty.

"Bring the lady another martini, with extra olives, Roger. There's a good man," said Norman.

Joan laughed. "Lady, indeed! Why if it were up t' the likes o' the Jeremiah Mills o' the world, I'm nothin' but a bimbo. An' you know they're really right, huh, Norm?"

You are a lady, one of the greatest ladies I've ever known, drunk or sober, you're a queen in the parlor *and* the bedroom."

"Oh, y' got me there, darlin'. An' tonight, a queen in the bar room."

"Unfortunately, most of my recent drinking has been alone, weeping in my beer for my long, lost Joyce."

"How could she do that t' you, after all you've been through together? Tell me, what didja do t' make her change like that?"

"Nothing."

"Then, there's your problem," said Joan, picking up the olives she'd just gotten and putting them on her fingers. She leaned over to Norman, holding up an olived hand. "Wanna bite?"

Norman took her hand, took one finger in his mouth, sucked off the olive, and then began sucking her finger. "Mmmm, good."

"Naughty boy," giggled Joan. "Seriously, though…what was I saying?"

"That nothing is the problem."

"Right. You should know by now that you hafta keep doin' somethin', anythin'. You can't jus' float along and spec' your marriage t' survive."

"Joyce, I mean Joan, no offence."

"None taken."

"You're right. If I want to stop being a lonely boy, I need to go back and do something to win her back."

"There ya go, Norm." She drained her martini. "Wanna come up t' my room for a nightcap?"

* * *

"Hi, wonderful," said Paul. "You were right. You're back before I expected."

"Your beard's looking great," said Joan, bending down and kissing him. "How's the rest of you?"

185

"Doing pretty well. You'll notice they've raised the top half of the bed a notch. It sure makes eating easier. They took new X-rays two days ago. My back is healing nicely."

"How about your leg?"

"It's coming along a little more slowly. I guess it's a complicated break that will take some time to heal properly."

He took his wife's hand. "But the pain is much easier to handle now, so they've reduced the medication quite a bit. I'm not so doped up as I was. Loring, Dr. Sanchez, says seven, eight weeks, and I'll be out."

"Honey, that's great!"

"Of course, I'll be moving pretty slowly for a while."

"At least you'll be moving.""Oh, I saw Norman. He says to give you his best."

"Norman's in San Francisco?"

"He's at Berkeley for a year. Teaching African art."

"How's Joyce?"

"You won't believe it, but they split up," said Joan.

Paul turned in amazement. "After all these years?"

"I was dumbfounded," said Joan. "But Norman said Joyce turned into a different person after their son went off to college. Empty nest syndrome, I guess. She's in New York, working the market like she's being driven by a devil."

"So Norman's all alone?"

"He's completely shattered by it. And, he was shocked when he heard about you."

"Probably so shocked he couldn't wait to get you into bed."

Joan felt her face grow hot. Paul was such a Puritan. "That's really unkind, Paul."

"Unkind, maybe," said Paul. "But perceptive, right?"

She could hear his voice tightening with emotion. Damn! she thought. Why can't I find it in my heart to be devious with Paul. I know there are some things he just doesn't understand.

"Well, you know we don't keep secrets from each other. I brought the whole thing up so I could tell you."

"You did sleep with him!" Paul whispered through gritted teeth.

"Honey, he's an old, old friend."

"Friends don't sleep with friends," he sobbed.

God damn me and my big mouth, she thought. "We both needed some comforting. It doesn't mean anything."

She reached out to stroke his forehead. He pushed her hand away. "Paul! Don't get carried away with this. It doesn't mean anything!"

Paul covered his head with his arms, shutting her out. His body heaved with rage.

"Paul. Paul?" She put her hand on his arm.

He lashed out at her in frustration, near panic. "Get out of here! Go show off your treasure!"

She took a long, slow breath. Something inside of her stepped back. A deep sadness, strange but terrifyingly familiar, filled her body and told her to go. She got up and crossed to the door. "I'll come back when you're feeling better."

"Don't bother."

12. MILLIE

It was four in the morning, and Paul was being a baby. He lay on his back with his pillow over his face and wept into the pillowcase, which was already wet with tears. He was enraged, and bereft, and appallingly sad. Tied as he was to the bed, in his mind he was running blindly through the night, crashing through underbrush that whipped his body and his face. Then the brush ended. And he was falling again, but this time there was no second terrace to save him. Nothing but air. And freedom. Why couldn't I just have died, he wailed to himself. Joan doesn't need me. I'm just a stone around her neck. What in the hell good am I? I'll show her. I don't need her either. Millie is falling in love with me. I'm sure of it. She's always so kind and gentle. She seems more beautiful every day. I know only Millie has kissed me. And what a kiss, meant only for me. Besides, Millie's not the kind of woman to mess around with other guys. Joan is history. Someone from my past. No more.

When Paul woke up, he felt like the worst hangover he could remember. His head was a drum, and his body was sore. It was gray outside, and cool. He thought he was back in San Francisco, but he knew better. There was no going back.

He heard Millie in the hall before he saw her. Then, when she turned the corner into his room, the glow of her white uniform, her aura, filled the room with radiance. She smiled warmly at him.

"Good morning, Paul. I trust you slept well?" she asked, as she put his breakfast on the bedtray.

"Not really, Millie. But thanks for asking."

"Were you in pain? Should I ask the doctor to check on your medication?"

"No. No medication for this. I guess you could call it heart pain."

"Ah, I see. Yes, I know what you mean. That is, about heart pain. In times like this, you must ask Jesus to abide by you," she said. "Paul, I need to talk to you. About heart pain. I mean. I need to explain to you what happened the other day."

Paul tried to control his excitement. "About the sweetest kiss I've ever felt? "

"And why I reacted that way when you asked about the NPA. Since it happened, I've been building up my courage to tell you my story. I was once a cadre with an NPA platoon in Negros."

* * *

Millie was from Negros, in the Visayan Islands near the center of the Philippine archipelago. Her family, like most of the families in Negros Oriental, worked for one of the four families who owned virtually every inch of arable land in the region, all of it planted in sugar cane. They were dirt poor as were most sugar workers. There were days, she said, when the six members of her family shared no more than one cup of rice. Negros was primarily Roman Catholic, and when she was young, some of the local priests and nuns started a campaign to improve the conditions in the sugar industry, condemning the low wages and shantytown housing provided workers. They began organizing the workers, and a wave of strikes asking for a higher minimum wage resulted. One morning, armed guards hired by the sugar barons attacked the strikers, opening fire on them. The strikers were chased off the plantation, and several of them were killed.

The Church's efforts to solve problems by legal means were also a complete failure, as they were on many other islands. The *hacenderos*, the plantation owners, paid off the courts, and when the workers arrived at the courthouse after a day of traveling and not working, cases were postponed. Many victims simply dropped their cases when friends and family were threatened. Landowners' security guards held rein over the workers and their families. Extortion and rapes were common. Then, in 1972, when Millie was eight, Marcos declared martial law, and a terrible situation grew even worse. There were no legal means to defend themselves, and more workers and independent farmers talked about armed revolution. They were desperate times, and some of their friends' older children left the plantations to join the Communist Party of the Philippines and other rebel groups.

With martial law, not only local armed guards were a problem for the farmers. Marcos dramatically increased the size of his military, and, with little training, Philippine soldiers abused their rights. Indiscriminate drinking and corruption were rampant, and, with the orders from Manila to control any adversaries to the dictatorship, the torture and murder of suspected guerrillas was common. Even innocent civilians were executed if any link to the rebels was suspected. In some parts of the country, the AFP began burning entire villages and herding villagers into larger, village centers they could control.

The CPP and the New People's Army grew in ranks as citizens had fewer and fewer choices. By the late 1970's, thousands of rural Filipinos joined or assisted the rebels with food and shelter, and even sometimes wealthy families who were against the dictatorial powers that Marcos was using gave them money and weapons. Some, sickened by the abuses that were everywhere, even gave up a life of wealth and went to the jungles to fight for human rights.

In 1979, a year after Marcos was reelected in an election dominated by fraud, Millie's father came down with appendicitis and had to go to Bais City, the nearest city with a hospital where he could find a surgeon. Bais was twenty kilometers away, and Millie was to go with him and care for him. Luckily, a friend got them a ride on a carabao cart loaded with coconuts. The coconuts were uncomfortable, but her father was in such pain he never could have walked there. They bumped along for hours, listening to the nervous clucking of the chicken they were bringing for payment. The hen was tied with strips of cane, and she lay sideways on the load and was definitely distressed.

When they arrived in Bais, the waiting line was so long, her father took his number and lay down to wait, sending Millie out to buy a soda for a treat. Millie was 15, but this was only her second visit to Bais. She had been here when she was four, but didn't really remember much about it. Today, however, it was a new world to her—crowded and noisy with shops and bartering. Fish stared up from iced counters. Baskets of shrimp and steaming pots of noodles flooded by. She walked in a daze, soaking in all of the new sensations. The smell of the sea was so strange and wonderful. Boats of every size and shape bobbed in the calm harbor. The rows of buildings had signs in Cebuano, Ilonggo and English. She had gone to the plantation school and could read a little.

"You, girl. Don't you want to help save your country?" a tall young man cried out to her. He was speaking to two teenage boys and a middle-aged woman.

"What do you mean?"

"There are groups in Negros who have the well being of the people in their hearts, who aren't trying to steal and cheat the poor workers."

"My father and mother are workers."

"Then why aren't you already a cadre?"

"What's a cadre?" she asked.

"A cadre is a member of a group who is prepared to lead and to fight, if necessary, who will teach the people how to help themselves, who knows that everyone deserves to have an equal share of opportunity."

"Oh, I know what you mean. Some people at our plantation have left and joined the PCC."

"My brother joined the PCC," said the plump teenage boy who had already been standing there, listening to the tall young man. His body looked like a stack of the soft round rolls sold by every store in every barangay.

"Good for him. How about you?" said the young man. "Will you join the PCC? Or maybe our group--the New People's Army. Our name says who we are. We are the army of the people."

"But where is your gun, eh?" asked the teenager.

"Remember, I said to fight, if necessary," he answered. "We know that fighting with words and education is better than fighting with guns. Sometimes, though, there is no other way."

Millie looked at this tall young man. He was handsome, in a stringy sort of way. His face was narrow, and the bold shock of hair on top made it look narrower. He looked strong and lithe. But what made her continue looking were his eyes. They were so full of the conviction of his words, she knew she could believe him absolutely.

"People on the plantation talk of organizing. They talk about rebelling all the time," she added.

"But they don't, do they?" he smiled. "Here is the truth: People are happier complaining about their bad lot in life than they are courageous about fighting for their rights. Can you be courageous? Can you fight to help your family and others? Are you ready to help make the world a better place?"

The two teenagers whispered to each other.

"I'll talk to my brother," said the sweet roll boy. "Maybe he has a good job for me," and they walked on down the street, laughing and punching each other in the shoulders.

The woman who had been standing there silent all this time said, "I have to finish my shopping. Good luck to you son, and may God be with you."

The two of them stood there alone, looking at each other in the noisy midst of the afternoon market.

"What's your name, girl?"

"It's Millie, and you...?"

"You can call me Tony," he said. "Well? Are you ready to go to work for your family and your country?"

"My father is at the hospital waiting for surgery. I have to go attend to him."

"Right."

"No, it's true. He's in great pain," she looked away from his eyes, pausing. Their intensity frightened her, but it somehow strengthened her, as well. Looking up, she said, "Give me an address where I can find you."

* * *

Millie paused. The breeze fluttered the lace curtains in the window. "I have other patients to attend to," she said. "I'll tell you more when I bring your lunch."

"It's fascinating, Millie. I appreciate your sharing your life with me. And could you have someone bring me my computer, please?"

"Of course you know that someone is me."

"Of course I do. Thank you. What would I do without you?"

* * *

Millie walked back to the hospital barely noticing the clamor of the market that had so impressed her a few moments before. She saw instead Tony's eyes, urging her to help save her country. She had heard about the NPA. Hadn't everyone? They were responsible for murders and attacks all over the Philippines. The newspapers and President Marcos said so. But workers she knew told a different story: It was true, they said, that the NPA was guilty of regrettable acts, but most of the accusers were guilty themselves of far worse. It seemed that when something bad happened, the NPA was a very handy group to blame. She knew there

194

were members of the NPA who were doctors and lawyers and priests whose only crime was trying to help common people.

She found her father asleep on the lobby floor. The hen had finally settled down and was curled against his leg. The nurse at the front desk called number 46. Her father's number was 58. She sat down next to him to wait.

* * *

When her father was wheeled out of surgery, she rose from the chair in the hallway and followed the gurney to a room three doors down the hall. There were no beds in the room, but three other patients already there rested on their gurneys. The nurse assured her that he was fine, that he would rest tonight and probably be ready to go home in two or three days.

It was dark when Millie left the hospital. She stopped at a street cart and bought some rice with shrimp paste. She asked the vendor how to find Panay Street and walked north, following a street near the waterfront lined with shipping offices, then boat repair yards. A watchdog behind a chain link fence barked at her and clanged against the fence. The smell of the sea, mingled with diesel fuel, was strong and tangy. A cross street ahead looked more like living spaces and homes. An old woman squatted on her porch, smoking a short pipe. Yes, the woman said, this was called Panay, but there were neither signs nor numbers. Millie described Tony to the woman, and she smiled and replied, "Oh, yes. Dat one. I see him, eh. He very nice boy. He like to help old lady like me." She puffed on her pipe and pointed up the street to a two-story clapboard building.

"You see dat blue bildin? He around back. It be downstairs. You like him, girl?"

"We just met today," answered Millie, feeling her cheeks grow hot in the dark.

"He be there. You like him, I think," the woman smiled a toothless grin and patted Millie on the butt, urging her up the street.

Millie turned onto the narrow dirt walkway next to the building and walked past open windows redolent with the smell of pork adobo. Her heart pounded when she reached the space behind the building and saw the concrete stairway leading down to an open door. Soft light from inside threw a dim glow on the lower stairs. She went down the stairs and rapped her knuckles on the wall next to the doorway. Tony appeared at the door and, seeing Millie, smiled broadly.

He welcomed her into the one room and cleared a pile of books from the only chair. "I didn't think you'd come."

"I wasn't sure I would, either," said Millie, "but I kept thinking about your words. 'Save your country,' you said. And I know how bad things are, for most people."

"How is your father?"

"Thank God he's all right. He had the surgery and will be ready to go home soon."

"That's wonderful news. I mean that," he said, "in a somewhat selfish way. If your parents are OK, maybe you'll feel free to join us."

"You're right. I don't think I could leave my mother if my father weren't well also."

Tony pulled a pack of cigarettes from his pocket and offered one to Millie, which she declined. He took one out, and tapped the end of it on his thumbnail, looking at Millie all the while. "So what are you prepared to do, now?"

She looked back at him and knew for sure. "I'll have to go home as soon as my father's able. I want to tell my family and leave with their good wishes. Then I'll be back."

"I'm so happy to hear that," he said, still tapping the cigarette. "Something tells me you'll make a great cadre. Oh, and to make your mother comfortable, I want you to tell her that I will never take advantage of you, and that I will see that you are always treated with the respect you deserve."

* * *

A week later, Millie returned to Bais, and Tony found her a room with a family who supported the NPA activities in Negros. She did chores around the house and helped with the family's children, and she started attending NPA meetings and reading the piles of books and pamphlets Tony gave her, especially Mao's *Little Red Book*. It was the bible of the PCC and the NPA, and strict adherence to it, the NPA leaders said, would keep them on the straight and narrow path, avoiding the misbegotten practices taken up by other countries, including the Soviet Union.

Tony, she found, was ten years her senior. He had grown up in Negros, the son of an executive with a shipping firm. He had a comfortable childhood and was sent to Manila for prep school and college. In college, he learned of the need for land reform in the Philippines, and he related well to what he learned because of the poverty he had witnessed all his life in Negros. He became a leader of college resistance in Manila, especially fighting the outrages of the newly declared martial law. He was a strong supporter of Ninoy Aquino and campaigned for his release from prison.

After the fraudulent election of '78, he had been sent back to Negros to create an NPA network whose mission was to help improve the sugar workers' wages and living conditions. Since he knew the island and spoke Cebuano, he was an ideal choice. He was dedicated and tireless, and he had a way of convincing people of his sincerity and of the need for some kind of action, which Millie was all too familiar with. While many NPA cadres felt that armed resistance was the only way to break down the chains of dictatorship, Tony still believed in creating legal organizations to bring about change.

Within a year, with Millie and a handful of other recruits, he created a dozen legal fronts designed to reach out to the hacenderos, inform workers and individual sharecroppers, offer emergency medical aid, and coordinate the efforts of the church with the needs of the people. On paper, they were making remarkable strides, but the reality was, there were only a few of them working day and night, and much of their time was spent begging for food from friendly supporters. Martial law made much progress nearly impossible, and they had to be very careful not to anger local politicians or the military. In fact, the military routinely arrested people on suspicion of just about anything, and many of these were tortured or even executed. However, Tony said he saw changes ahead. In 1980, Marcos released Ninoy from prison because of his heart condition, and he and his family flew to Boston. This news buoyed up all the cadres, and for a time things seemed to improve. One of the hacenderos agreed to clean up the water source for his workers when several of them were stricken ill, and the local doctor diagnosed their water as the cause.

The following year, Tony attended a high level conference outside of Manila. With the highest security possible, leaders of the CPP, the NPA, and other rebel groups met to plan long-term strategy. Reports of Ninoy's improving health led many to believe that he could return to the Philippines and create a referendum for change, in spite of the trumped up charges that put a death sentence on him if he stepped foot back in his home country. Several NPA leaders, however, were dissatisfied with current progress being made and felt that armed resistance needed to be stepped up. They berated Tony for his peaceful resistance methods in Negros, but Tony argued that only through negotiation could they achieve a lasting change. He said the NPA had become a national movement, not with guns and killing, but by forging bonds with the people who would benefit most from change. They would prevail, he explained, with the weight of the people's support. It was true that Marcos was powerfully fighting against democratization, but his was a desperate, losing fight. Tony came back to Negros believing more strongly than ever that his methods were good.

* * *

On August 21, 1983, Ninoy Aquino's jet landed at the Manila International Airport. He stepped onto the runway and was gunned down by Philippine soldiers. This was the final outrage that would create an unstoppable movement that would, three years later, drive Marcos from the Philippines and bring Ninoy's widow to the Presidential palace. When news of the assassination reached Negros, Tony was devastated, more perhaps than most, because he so idolized Ninoy and focused his hopes for the future on his ultimate success.

"It's inconceivable!" he cried.

Millie and Tony and three other cadres were in the small office where much of their work got done. They had just heard the announcement on the radio, that Ninoy, indeed, was dead. Everyone in the room seemed numb with grief or dead. Millie was slumped on the floor, weeping inconsolably.

"Tell me it's not true! Tony, what will we do now?"

Tony sat on a metal folding chair, his eyes red from crying. She had never seen him cry before.

"I don't know. I can't think. My mind can't comprehend it," he lowered his head and his body shook with sobs.

"Everyone just go home. Be with your families. Please, just go."

Chairs scraped on the floor. Everyone got up, picked up their bags and books, and without a word, started filing out the door.

"Wait, Millie," he said. "You stay. Please stay."

She turned at looked at him. His eyes begged her to stay. He rose from the chair, and for the first time in four years, she went to him and threw her arms around him. They held each other for a long time, their mouths together at last.

"Ninoy's death kills half my heart," he whispered. "Stay with me. You're the other half."

"You know I've always loved you, Tony."

"I've known for a long time. But the time wasn't right," he kissed her on her wet eyes. "Marry me, Millie."

"Of course I will, darling."

* * *

The next morning Millie and Tony were married in a civil ceremony at the Bais City courthouse. Later, they had lunch with Father Agustin Algarme, a college chum of Tony's and now a priest at a local parish. Father Algarme gave their marriage his personal blessing and even picked up the tab. Their honeymoon was four days spent in Tony's tiny apartment, talking, making plans and making love. When they came back to the office they had a new determination to help bring down Marcos and his thugs in the military. The response to Ninoy's assassination was so strong throughout the country that they sensed that the groundswell would continue until a new, more honest government was created. The other NPA members in Bais were delighted at Millie and Tony's marriage, and their main comment was, what took them so long? The days and nights went by, and more people joined them to help take the message of hope out to the people. More assistance, more food and more money from those hearing them speak gratified them and gave them impetus. And now, even when there were setbacks, they had each other.

In April, word came to Bais that one of the hacenderos had decided to expand the cane fields into part of its less desirable lands that had, until now, been farmed by squatters. Some of the families had worked these hilly plots for decades, and a few meager villages had been established near the edges of the mountainous jungle. The hacendero had sent security guards into the region to relocate the squatters and ready the ground for the planting of sugar cane. This amounted to driving the people from their farms and villages with their modest belongings, then torching everything, including the homes and the fields, to burn it all down to bare earth ready for planting cane. Several cadres working with Tony and Millie had friends who lived in the area, and they had heard that some guards weren't allowing people enough time to take even their kitchen utensils or clothing with them. They were setting homes on fire while the frightened people were still trying to pack. Tony had met with the hacendero over the years, and he asked if the people could be given more time, but the hacendero just shrugged and said he couldn't control the actions of his men in the field. He was sure they had good reasons for the way they were working.

Tony, Millie and six others decided to hike up to the remaining villages to help the people move out and, if possible, buy them more time by reasoning with the guards. They got a lift from Bais to the edge of the plantation and hiked several miles on plantation roads and trails until they started hiking past charred fields. Occasionally, they would see a few burned household items or broken, blackened remains of houses. They reached a village, still intact, that amounted to half a dozen bamboo huts, a couple of fire rings, and several barking dogs. They kicked at the dogs as they walked into the clearing and were greeted by several villagers who were busily loading a carabao cart with pots and pans, packages tied with palm fronds and cardboard boxes stuffed with clothes. A young child carried another pot from one of the huts, and a woman squatted in the doorway of another hut suckling her baby. An old man, who was standing by the cart supervising, looked up and recognized one of the cadres. He grinned and approached the group, taking the stub of a cigar from his mouth. They had been given one day and one night to pack up and move. Better than some, he said. He had lived here most of his life, but now, it seemed, they must move away. Where would they go? He didn't know yet, but they would move from here. Maybe go to work at some plantation. Others had done that as well. No, they were all right. They didn't really need any help. He pointed southwest and said they might help a couple of villages there. He shook each of their hands with a powerful grip and waved and gave them God's blessing as they started down the trail.

Two miles to the south, they reached a similar situation, with villagers frantically packing their belongings. However, this village was poor, and had no carabao to haul anything away. The residents had made several bamboo stretchers and were busily tying loads of household items to them. Several rattan backpacks sat nearby, ready to go. The headman explained that they must leave in less than one hour, and they were running out of time. Tony and the others volunteered their services, and they all pitched in to help. A few minutes later, six men walked into the village. They were in uniforms of a sort, mainly khaki pants and shirts, but did not look anything like AFP soldiers. They all carried guns, and they didn't look friendly.

"So you are not gone yet, eh?" asked the leader, a large, middle-aged muscular man.

"I am sorry, boss. We will be gone soon," answered the headman. "We want no trouble."

"But you said you would be gone by now,"

"Can't you just give them a little more time?" asked Tony. "We just arrived, and we're helping them."

"And who are you, eh?"

"We're friends. We just want to help."

"I think mebbe you have already help enough," the leader said. He tilted his rifle up at the hip and shot Tony.

Blood shot out of Tony's forehead and his body fell back, jerking as two more bullets hit him in the chest. His body fell with a thud to the ground.

"Noooooooo!" screamed Millie, as she threw her body on his, feeling his still warmth and shaking with sobs.

* * *

Millie sat hunched over in the chair next to Paul's bed, her hands to her face as she wept.

"Now you know, Paul."

"Oh, Millie. I had no idea."

"Saying the words brings back all those terrible feelings. I knew it wouldn't be easy," she snuffled. She took a tissue from the box near the bed. "But from what Doctor told me, maybe I can help you make a difference by telling the true story."

"But what happened? I don't want to upset you any more, but..."

"It's all right now," she wiped her eyes with another tissue. "Well...everyone ran. No one had any way of fighting with these men and their guns. The villagers just ran into the jungle, leaving all their belongings. I guess they came back for them later. A couple of my friends helped me up and took me away. The guards just stood there and laughed. They shot their guns over our heads to scare us off. I was in such shock, I hardly remember the trip back to Bais. A friend gave me a Valium. I cried and cried. What else could I do? Tony was gone.

"The next day, two of the volunteers went back up and brought Tony home. He was buried in a quiet ceremony. His family was there, too. I had never seen them before. They rejected Tony when he joined the NPA. I didn't know what to do. I felt like Cory Aquino grieving for her man. But I knew I couldn't do what she was doing. A few days later, I went to see Father Algarme. He was so wonderful. He had gone to the police as soon as he heard about Tony's murder. There was an investigation, but somebody got paid off, and the case never went to trial.

"I met with Father Algarme a few times, and finally he suggested that I consider becoming a nurse. I didn't want to go back to what I had been doing, and I didn't want to stay in Negros. He had friends in Manila, and they got me into nursing school. I never went back."

* * *

Loring stepped into the room after Paul had finished dinner.

"How are you feeling?"

"I'm fine, thanks," answered Paul. "Except I can't believe what that wonderful young woman went through."

"I told you she knew about the NPA, at least, one side of the story. It's been hard for her, recovering from the loss of her husband, but she's doing very well, and with the grace of God, she'll continue to do so."

"I suppose it's fortunate that Tony was the only one harmed. The guards might have opened fire on everyone, even though they were all running away. She said two of her friends helped her get away, and that would definitely have slowed them down, if the guards had been shooting to kill."

"Is that what she said?" asked Loring. "Yes, I suppose that would have to be what she would say."

"What?" asked Paul.

"She only told you part of the story. The guards shot in the air and scared everyone off, everyone except Millie, who wouldn't leave Tony. The guards beat and raped her. When they were done with her, they dumped her half dead body in the jungle, where her friends found her the next day. Maybe she's lucky she lived. She will never be able to have a child. Her body is still covered with scars from the cigarette burns. For some reason, the animals who attacked her didn't disfigure her face; they thought it was funnier to use their cigarettes on her genitals."

13. NIGEL

"OK, we're all here," said Joan, as Michael Hamada pulled up a chair in the hotel coffee shop. It was nine o'clock at night, and they were all done for the day in the Batcave, as it had come to be known.

"I talked to Rudy and Val, and they think it'll be four more weeks before the roads are stable enough to withstand the weight and movement of several large trucks and twenty men. You all know that's what we feel it will take to haul the treasure to Manila."

Rosie's foot swung up and down, like a confused pendulum. "We have plenty of material to keep cataloguing. What's the difference, whether we do it in Manila or here? And we're only a quarter of the way through the crates."

"That's part of the problem," said Michael. "I'm not going to have enough film to last even two more weeks. There's so much more here than any of us estimated."

"We can send a car out to get more film, and to take the film you've already shot to the processing lab. But the real problem is this: Now that the media knows about the treasure, they all want to know where it is. We can only keep it quiet up here for just so long, and when they do find out, it'll be like a dam bursting. How'll we keep the treasure safe and secure with only a few guards if hundreds and hundreds of reporters and photographers and TV cameras descend upon Banaue?"

"Why aren't they here already?" asked Bam. Bam was Bam Tsung, an art dealer and Southeast Asian specialist with large galleries in Manila, Saigon and Singapore.

When Joan had come back with Rosie and Michael, they had brought Bam and two other art specialists with them. The others were Zarina Janardan, the curator of South Asian classical art at the Bombay Provincial Art Museum, and Lucia Cavastany, a professor at the University of the Philippines. Joan was delighted to find such a great team in Manila, and they in turn felt fortunate to have a part in rediscovering Asian treasures in such a way.

"There have been scouting parties out looking for the commotion such a find would create, but Val and the Mayor have managed to keep all the residents in check, and have even sent a couple of media scouts who visited Banaue off on wild goose chases."

"I don't like it," scowled Lucia. "This could be really dangerous. That treasure is worth more than a lot of countries. People have killed for a whole lot less."

"I know," answered Joan. "That's why this meeting is happening. If any of you feels the risk of continuing to work here is too great, just say so. We'll let you go."

"What about the Army?" asked Zarina, brushing her fingers through her wavy black hair and reattaching a slipping barrette. "Cory and the government know about this. Why can't they just send up a battalion of soldiers to guard the treasure and us?"

"If the Army brought in guards, the media would definitely arrive by the truckload. Which brings us back to where we were: The roads can't handle all that traffic, or there'll be even more slides, and, quite possibly, deaths."

"Well, if we're stuck here for four more weeks, "said Bam, waving in the waiter's direction, "at least let me buy everyone a gin and tonic."

Joan took a sip of tea. It was tepid, and she picked up the teapot and refilled her cup. She was sitting alone in the coffee shop at her regular table near the window that looked out toward the spectacular Cordillera view. But it was already about ten, and the lush forests and peaks were hidden in the night. She had just finished another late dinner. Alone. Nothing seemed right without Paul. It had been over a week since their fight. She had gone to the clinic every day, but the nurses said he didn't want to see her. And when she went into his room, he refused to talk to her. Twice she had seen tears running down his cheeks, but he wouldn't look at her, and no matter what she said, he tried not to respond, other than the tears. Damn him! Why couldn't he grow up and realize that at times she had needs that had nothing to do with loyalty or trust or love. Damn her, for expecting him to change after all these years. She felt sick. She wanted to run to the women's room and throw up the dinner she'd just finished. She wanted to be held in someone's arms. She wanted Paul....

Her waiter, Doming, approached her and handed her a business card. The owner of the card was a correspondent for The London Times named Nigel Barclay. She looked up at Doming, who stood waiting for an answer, and nodded her head.

Presently, a gentleman came in from the direction of the lobby. He was dressed all in white—wearing the linen suit so favored by British nationals in the tropics, white shirt, white bowtie dotted with small black diamonds. Even his hair was white, but his face and hands were bronzed from time in the sun. Joan stared in amazement as he came closer. He was the absolute image of Emory Barclay!

"Miss Webster, I presume?" he asked, following the question with a soft chuckle. "Finding you is definitely reminiscent of Stanley finding Livingstone. Please call me Nigel. May I join you?"

Joan motioned to the chair opposite her and finally said, "Forgive me for being speechless, but I feel like I'm seeing a ghost."

"Ah, yes. I do bear quite a resemblance to someone who I know was quite close to you. Well, Emory was some sort of uncle, or cousin, from the black sheep side of the family that migrated to the New World." He paused, then asked, "Do you mind if I order something? I'm quite parched. It's been a bloody long trip up here."

"Certainly." She waved at Doming.

"Might I have a San Miguel, my good fellow? And the lady will have…"

"Nothing, thank you. I'm fine with my tea."

"Very well, just a San Miguel, then." He smiled and resettled himself in the chair. "At any rate, I was talking about Emory Barclay. I actually met him once. It must have been in the late 50's. At a men's club in Hong Kong. I had just come out to work the Orient for the Times, so to speak. He was quite a fabulous character. It must've been an experience to work with him."

"Yes, it was. I learned everything from him. He was like a father to me."

"Well, yes, hmmm. And now, all these years later, you've become quite the celebrity yourself."

Joan looked at this unexpected replica and wondered if Nigel also shared any other qualities with Emory, besides his appearance. "And since you deal in celebrity, this meeting must seem most fortunate to you," she said.

"Yes, of course," he drank some of the beer that Doming had just poured for him. "but I must tell you that you needn't worry about me. I won't blow the whistle on you, as you Yanks say."

"You won't bring the media circus in on me and this tiny town?"

"No, certainly not. Wouldn't be considerate. And besides, my motives are not only altruistic. I suffer from a selfish streak, too. You see, Emory and you are both treasure hunters--he found treasure in art all his life, and you're following in his footsteps. The treasures I seek are the stories—all kinds of stories, exciting and soothing, happy and tragic. I, like Uncle Emory, have searched all over the world for them. This story is bloody important, and I'm sure that if I can help you, I can also keep this story as my own."

Nigel went on to tell Joan that he could blow so much smoke and create enough false leads to keep Banaue the quiet little town it was tonight. He was even prepared to send his photographer back to Manila with the news that Banaue was a dead end, and that he had gone on to Cagayan to follow up a better lead. In return, he wanted exclusive interviews with all the principals, he wanted free run of the place, and he wanted to see the treasure and take photos himself. He knew how to send his stories in to his paper so that they could not be traced. He would obtain The Times' guarantee that they would indicate their source seemed to be somewhere in Cagayan.

"Waiter, could I trouble you for another beer?" Nigel asked. "Well, Miss Webster, what do you think?"

"I think I'll join you in a beer. You seem to have me over a barrel, Mr. Barclay. And call me Joan, Nigel. There's just one thing—you'll have to shoot time exposures without a flash. The treasure's in a huge cavern full of bats."

"Full of bats, eh? How cheery. Thank you, Joan, and... By Gad! What added brilliance! We won't send them off to Cagayan, we'll send them to Ilocos Norte! The irony of it, Marcos dead only a year, and the fabled treasure he supposedly found, in a feeble attempt to cover the facts that America and the CIA were funding him, turns up in his own back yard. It's perfect! My colleagues will eat it up!"

"It is a nice touch," answered Joan, "and Ilocos Norte is even a little farther from Banaue."

"I'm sure both of us will profit from this partnership, and if I may be so bold, your news photos don't do you justice. You're much more attractive than I expected. But then, Uncle Emory always had an eye for the ladies."

* * *

Rosie and Joan splashed through a wet section of the little dirt road they favored for their early morning jogs. The sun was just high enough to pierce the jungle here and there, turning some of the puddles to liquid gold. Leaves in the sunlight on the far side of the road started to steam.

"Four days, and still no army of reporters," Rosie said, as she stretched out her stride to avoid a large puddle.

"Yes, Nigel seems to be doing his job. And from the Senator's reports, the public and the press are overwhelmed by the photos of the cave, 'from somewhere deep in the jungles of Ilocos Norte.'"

"I love that part of the story. Nigel deserves a medal for coming up with that."

"He may not be winning any medals," said Joan, "but he and his paper are making a fortune with their exclusive, then reselling the stories a day later to the rest of the world."

They reached the top of the slope and paused for a minute, blowing and cooling down a little as they looked out over this part of the forest.

Later, after showering and changing, they met in the coffee shop for fruit and coffee before another day of cataloguing in the cavern. As they were going out the door of the hotel, they met Nigel coming in. He wanted Joan's thoughts on his proposals for the next three articles for submission. He handed Joan a piece of paper with an outline of his ideas, which she read as he walked along with them. They turned down the path toward the cave entrance.

"Where are your guards, Joan?" asked Nigel.

Joan looked up just as Rosie screamed. The guards, four young men from Banaue, were there, scattered near the entrance. Each of their throats had been slashed.

"Oh, my Lord," exclaimed Nigel, and he ran to the prone bodies and dropped to his knees.

Joan was too stunned to move for a second, then she followed him.

"They're all dead," he said, then looked towards the entrance. "But what's down there?"

"Rosie," Joan whispered, "go get Val. Fast."

Rosie turned and headed back up the trail, kicking up dirt as she ran.

"The blood is quite dry, Joan. This must have happened during the middle of the night."

"But who would...."

"Who would do such a thing? I daresay the list is quite long. There's a lot of money down there."

"There must have been several of them to have subdued all the guards," she said.

"Well, it would take several strong men to steal much of the treasure, assuming that is the motive, which is a fairly safe assumption."

It seemed to take forever, but Rosie returned in just a few minutes with Val, Kiwil and two other men. They were all armed with guns or machetes.

"No, Doning," he sighed as he bent over one of the guards. "Your mother will have my head for this. The gods will see that someone pays."

After Val convinced Joan to wait there, he and the other three quietly entered the cave. They returned in about ten minutes.

He looked at Joan with sadness in his eyes. The lines on his face seemed deeper than ever. "I'm afraid there is another. They killed your photographer."

"Oh, God, no!" screamed Rosie. "Michael! Michael! Why did you have to go back there last night?"

Joan put her arms around Rosie and held her tight as both of them sobbed for their friend. Finally, they wiped their eyes and turned to Val.

"Take us down there," said Joan. "What else did these fiends do?"

Just then, Bam, Zarina and Lucia arrived, and joined in their grief when they were told what had happened. Then the entire group entered the cave.

The collection was definitely missing a lot of items. The thieves had been very smart and had taken many of the small, more portable items. They had also taken many of the files and photos, including film not yet processed. Joan knew it would be difficult to track many of the pieces without photos, but luckily, they hadn't thought to destroy the computer files.

One of Val's men had gone out and come back with a stretcher, and they left the cave with Michael and with hearts nearly too heavy to carry them up the stony slope. While they had been in the cave, others in the town had taken away the bodies of the guards, but the weeds were still dark with their blood.

Joan and Nigel returned to Val's office with him and collapsed, as best they could, in the school chairs.

"Who could have done something like this?" asked Joan.

Val's puzzled expression told her a lot, but he answered, "Not that many people know where the treasure's located, although someone in the area could have let it leak to another village. This seems to have been well planned, and there must have been seven or eight men, considering the things you said they took."

Nigel frowned, "How in the devil can we hope to keep a lid on this sort of thing?" he wondered. "Hiding a treasure is one thing, but murder and theft..."

"This will not go the police yet," said Val. "I want to call Senator Vital. He may have some ideas on what we should do. He has major connections with Philippine security forces, and he knows how delicate the situation is."

"At this point, doesn't it seem reasonable to just load up the rest of the treasure and truck it down to Manila?" asked Nigel. "I know the roads need work, but perhaps just one small truck making several trips?"

Val frowned. "I want to err on safety's side. We really must wait while they are being shored up. And I'm also worried about doing anything that might call attention to Banaue. We must keep a low profile. It will be difficult enough to manage our own people, especially now with tragedy visiting four of our families."

Joan and Nigel left Val in his office and walked down the dirt road toward the hotel.

"Nigel, you go on ahead. I'll talk to you later, but right now, I have to talk to my husband," said Joan, and she turned and headed toward the Good Shepherd Clinic.

She entered the clinic and walked down the hall and into Paul's room. He was writing something on the laptop. He looked up and frowned when he saw her.

"Get out."

"I'll leave in just a minute. I just came to tell you that someone entered the cave last night, murdered our four guards and our photographer, and stole a portion of the treasure," Joan's knuckles were white, holding onto the back of the chair in front of her to keep her balance.

"Right now, I feel like I've been kicked in the heart, and our estrangement makes it all the worse. I'm stuck here until the roads are in better shape, and we can start moving the treasure to Manila. I'll be working on trying to put the pieces back together, for all of the people involved. If you won't see me, or change your mind about us, I'll just have to learn to live with that. But I want you to know that I love you, and I always will."

Paul looked at her, and for the first time in what seemed like forever, he smiled, even if only with sympathy.

"I'm truly sorry about what's happened. Believe me, I don't wish you any ill," he paused, and then Joan could see him pull back again. "But I'm working on something new that's consuming me. The doctor says I'll be out of here in only seven or eight more days. When I get out, I need to go somewhere even farther into the mountains. I have to do this, to save my sanity."

He started to type again.

Joan stood for a moment, then turned to leave.

"Joan?"

She looked back. "Yes, Paul?"

"Be careful."

* * *

As the sun dropped into the jungle, dusk crawled up the terraces, and one by one the shadows reached them. The last of the sun's rays bounced off the collection of glasses filling the table at the bar as Joan finished her third martini. She put the glass back on the sweaty cocktail napkin. In less than a minute, Doming replaced it with a fresh napkin and a fresh drink. Early in the afternoon, the members of the treasure crew had filed into the bar, one by one, and with barely any conversation, a wake in Michael's memory started. Normally, Joan wasn't a martini drinker—she usually preferred wine, but Michael had loved a good martini on the rocks with lots of olives, and that became the drink of choice today. Manny had come by about an hour ago and whispered in her ear that the hotel would be happy to do anything her people needed, and that the drinks today were courtesy of the house. She had smiled in thanks and squeezed his hand, and he had left blushing. Rosie and Michael had been very close. Neither of them had any family, and during the six years since Michael had joined the museum staff, they'd become like brother and sister. She was taking his death very badly. She'd downed three martinis in a hurry, gotten sick, left early and gone to her room. Joan planned on checking on her later. Nigel had joined them about four o'clock, and his presence was welcomed by all. In the short time she had known him, Joan had never seen him so subdued. For all his adventures, he obviously hadn't gotten used to losses this close, although he had assuredly seen his share of death. Lucia had gotten busy the moment she'd returned to the hotel. She'd found a sewing machine in the hotel laundry, talked Bam into giving her a black shirt he had, and sewn up black arm bands for everyone.

"A fresh drink deserves a toast," said Bam. He lifted his glass to Joan. "*Tram phan tram*, 100 percent, for Michael. We'll all miss him."

"Hear hear."

"What he said," chimed in the others.

"May we join you?"

Joan turned to find Val and the mayor standing behind her.

"Of course, Val. Teo, it's so nice to see you, but I wish the circumstances were happier."

The mayor took Joan's hand and held it silently. Then they pulled up extra chairs and sat down, and the circle widened to include them.

"I finally reached the senator," said Val, "and he shares our sorrow. He thanked me for using caution in this situation and said he'd confer with the President tomorrow. He agreed that there weren't many who could have known of the treasure, but said, in his words, 'This stinks of the NPA.' I'm inclined to agree with him. He'll call us tomorrow, with their decision. He also warned that we all stay away from the cave until this matter is resolved."

Val looked at the mayor, who nervously leaned forward.

"Joan, if I may call you that, we have a very large favor to ask of you only," he paused and looked towards Val, then continued, "With these deaths in our village, many of us feel that certain spirits must be angry. We are preparing to start the *hudhud*. You will recall the alim, which was chanted to bring your husband back to good health. The hudhud is much like that, but even more important to us. It is our way of honoring the dead, and will take four days to perform. With your permission, we would like to include your friend's memory in our chants. Is there any way that you could grant us this honor? We feel that your presence in Banaue," he nodded to include everyone, "will remain an important part of our heritage."

Joan looked around the table, and saw the sadness of the others brightened by this respect.

"Rosie was closest to him," she said, "but I think I can speak for her, as well as the rest of us, but mostly I speak for Michael, who has joined your young men somewhere else. We are grateful for the honor you bestow upon him, and us."

* * *

The next morning, Rosie's hangover was so bad that she begged off running, so Joan just did an abbreviated run of a couple of miles, then returned to the hotel and showered. She had nothing to do. No work, since the cave was off limits. She missed her babies, half way around the world in college. She'd see both of them next time she went back to the states. And she couldn't even spend time talking to Paul about these latest events, or about the events he was planning. What was he planning? He had mentioned that when he got out of the clinic, he was going farther into the jungle. What for? She wished she could talk to him. Find out. Hear his voice. Hold him in her arms. Kiss his warm mouth. Feel the bristles of his beard.

She left the hotel and walked toward the clinic anyway. She wouldn't try to see him, but she would know that he was there. As she approached the clinic, she could here the chanting farther ahead and walked on to see the hudhud, which had evidently started. She had read about the ceremony in her research for this trip. Apparently, they were being performed less and less, since the older generation was dying, and the younger people weren't interested in learning or carrying on the traditions. She saw the group of dancers just up the road. There were six of them, plus the leader, a very old woman Joan hadn't seen before. It was the same type of chant and response that she had heard during the *alim* ceremony. The old woman leading the chant had a very high, beautiful voice. It reminded Joan of the singer's voice in "Snow White and the Seven Dwarves"—high and crystalline. The chant and the colorful costumes, mostly woven of cotton in brilliant red with variations of stripes in yellow, white and black, were mesmerizing. She stood and watched for a long time. Presently, she heard Nigel's voice speaking softly behind her. She turned to see him with his camera, shooting photos.

"The mayor gave me permission to write an article and to shoot this," he said. "This is so rare, I had to do something about recording it for posterity. Maybe some day I can sell it to National Geographic, after the immediacy of the tragedy and the situation is over."

Then all at once, Joan realized the implications of this exotic performance. The chant took on a whole new sound in her ears, and she started to cry for the lives it honored. It was so easy to be in denial. She had practically forgotten Michael's dead body on the floor of the cave, killed coldly and deliberately, like the others.

"Here now, old girl," Nigel handed her a handkerchief, and she dried her eyes and blew her nose. She turned and threw her arms around him, squeezing the handkerchief in her fist. He gently put his hands on her back and held her while she shook with sobs against him.

"I think a drink would do us both a world of good," he said, pulling away but putting an arm around her shoulders and leading her away from the *hudhud*.

"I'm sorry, Nigel. It's just…"

"It is that, it's bloody hard sometimes, just to hang onto all the pieces."

A while later, they were back at the hotel bar drinking bloody Marys. Rosie walked slowly in, looking like a hollow shell of herself. Even her curly hair seemed pale and limp.

"Good morning, Rosie," said Nigel, smiling.

"Oh, not so loud," she whispered. "I feel so rotten. I can't believe how bad I feel." She slumped down into a chair across from them and lowered her head gently into her hands.

Nigel grinned at Joan and quietly got up and left. In a minute, he was back with a small tin, motioning to Manny, who was walking past the entrance to the bar.

"Bring us a tea service for the lady, but without tea. Just hot water," he requested.

When Doming appeared with the tea tray, Nigel scooped a large spoonful from the tin and stirred it into the hot water in the teapot.

"The best hangover remedy in the world," he said softly. "Cinchona from China, ginkgo from Japan, tamarind just to sweeten up the bitterness. It really works." He poured a cup of it and set it in front of Rosie.

"Drink up, you poor dear," he said.

She took a sip and scowled. But then she drank some more.

"It's not really too bad," she said.

In just a few minutes, she smiled at Nigel, "Thank you, dear sir. I'm actually starting to feel better."

At exactly twelve o'clock, Val joined them and pulled up a chair. He took a teacup from the tray, asked "May I," poured a cup and took a large swallow. He sucked his cheeks together and looked at everyone with a sheepish grin.

"Someone must have a hangover."

The four of them laughed as none of them had in a long time, letting out the intense feelings of stress and sadness. Guests at a couple of other tables looked up at the commotion and started laughing along, even though they didn't know what they were laughing at. Rosie slapped her hand over and over on the table with mirth, tears of joy pouring down her cheeks.

"It really is good for more than just hangovers!"

When he finally was able to stop laughing regain control of himself, Val dried his eyes with his napkin and said, "I'm sorry, but there is a serious reason why I'm here."

"We realize that, Val, but that certainly was therapeutic, I'm sure, for all of us," said Joan.

"Yes," Val continued, "but these murders and the theft are deadly serious. Senator Vital just called. He had met with the President and informed her of what happened. She was terribly upset. They both agreed that, for now, this must not reach the press."

He looked at Nigel. "We're counting on your help to keep this quiet. You can be sure that there will be ample reward for your assistance in this matter."

"Of course. I'm happy to do whatever I can," said Nigel.

"The Senator is sending a special group of security investigators to Banaue, both to search for evidence and to guard the treasure from additional attacks until it can be moved. He said these men are well trained, very capable, and dangerous to whomever they find to be guilty of this crime. They will be arriving this evening.

"He asked that all of you, and especially you, Joan, give them your utmost assistance in their investigation."

"That goes without saying," answered Joan. "I'm pleased at this decisive response. President Aquino and the Senator are to be praised for reacting like this."

* * *

Joan lay curled in bed with Paul lying behind her, his arms around her. The curls of his beard tickled her neck. There was a knock at the door. Who could that possibly be at this hour? She woke from her dream and glanced at the clock. Five a.m. Someone knocked again. She got up and put on her robe as she walked to the door. Manny looked very embarrassed when she opened the door.

"You must pardon me, madam," he said, "but some gentlemen have arrived, and one of them needs to speak with you. It seems to be a matter of some urgency."

"Yes, of course, Manny. I'll just put on some clothes. Where is the gentleman?"

"In Room 115. His name is Teodoro Monsod. He felt the meeting would be more discreet in his private room. But I can assure you, madam, that he means no embarrassment to you."

"Thank you, Manny. Tell Mr. Monsod that I will be right there. And would you please send us some tea?"

"I already took the liberty to do that, madam."

Joan dressed and walked down the hall to Room 115, which was only two doors from hers. The door was slightly ajar, and she knocked it open a bit farther.

"Come in, please," said a deep, masculine voice.

She opened the door and walked in. The voice belonged to a man who could be a movie star. He was taller than six feet, with a muscular physique just shy of looking overpumped. He had dark, curly hair and a small mustache. Who was that actor? Yes, he looked a little like Andy Garcia. He crossed the room and extended his hand.

"Thank you for coming at such an ungodly hour, Miss Webster," he said as he shook her hand. His hand felt powerful, but he kept it in check. "But the sooner we know what we are up against, the sooner we can apprehend these murderers. I am Captain Teodoro Monsod, a chief investigator with the Philippine Special Forces," he smiled a movie star smile, "but please call me Doring. Won't you sit down? May I offer you some tea?"

After he had poured tea for each of them, he continued, "You must understand that we are here, as you Americans say, incognito. None of us are in uniform, as that would attract too much attention. There are eight of us: six who will make sure that no one disturbs what remains of the treasure. They will not look like guards and will not necessarily stand at the entrance to the cave brandishing guns, but they will be here and there, and you may continue your work in complete safety."

He paused, "Are you comfortable? Can I order you anything else?"

"No, this is fine," answered Joan. "And I assume that you and another member of your group are the investigators?"

"Correct. Lt. Felicisimo Pedrosa will assist me in that endeavor."

He spent the next hour asking questions and taking notes. It was evident right away that Joan couldn't help much with details of the crime itself, but he wanted as much information as she could give concerning the treasure and the items that she knew were missing. She finished by giving him the names of the other members of her research group, as well as that of Nigel, and he let her go, asking her to get her group back into their routine, except that he would like to see each of the others at seven, eight, nine, ten, and eleven o'clock, in no particular order.

It was after six in the morning, too late to go back to bed, although she felt she could definitely use some rest. She talked to each of the others and filled them in, then she went for a run by herself. She didn't feel like company right now. She needed some time alone. The fabulous treasure that she had discovered, that had given her so much excitement and celebrity, had turned into a hateful thing. Someone's greed and indifference to human life had taken so much away from her, even though she hadn't been touched physically. And repercussions of the treasure had taken Paul away from her, although she now realized that something else could have probably triggered the same thing. She had to get through this on her own. She knew she could, but God! She was anxious to get beyond this little dead end of a town and back to Manila and civilization.

14. BONTOC

Paul had been exercising his back and his leg and each day putting a little more weight on the foot, until he could walk around the room with crutches. But today was different; today he was being released! Millie came into the room and brought him some clothes Rudy had gotten from the hotel room—jeans and a red polo shirt, a little more worn and rough around the edges than the ones Loring wore, and tennis shoes. She smiled and left the room and closed the door. His heart was pounding with excitement as he sat up and pushed each leg into the jeans. They felt very strange on his bare legs, yet wonderfully familiar. He reached up over his head and pulled on the shirt. He walked across the room to the little chair he had seen for so many weeks and sat down. He bent over and pulled on his sneakers and tied them. Not a twinge in his back. He was healed!

Loring had strongly suggested he use a cane for a day or two, until he regained his sea legs. You will feel a little wobbly at first, he had said. Paul picked up the cane, opened the door and walked out into the hall. It was an actual hall that opened to the right on a small lobby with a desk. Next to the lobby was the nurse's room, where Millie sat filling out a form. She looked up and smiled that angelic smile.

"Praise be to God! With his care, you are well again!" She got up from her desk, put her arms gently around him and kissed him on the cheek. "I've prayed for this day, Paul, and it has come at last." Her eyes glittered with tears.

He embraced her awkwardly, hitting her on the back with his cane. "Oh, I'm sorry, Millie, I…"

She stepped back from him and looked him up and down. "You look good standing up, Mr. Webster. It suits you," she laughed. "Now go, and move your legs and breathe the air. I'll see that the things in your room are moved back to the hotel. Do you trust me with your computer?"

"Of course, I…"

"Go ahead, now." She turned and walked down the hall.

There was a screen door at the entrance to the clinic. He opened it and stepped out onto the covered porch and stood looking up and down the street, breathing in the smell of pine trees. He made an ungainly descent down the two wooden stairs, and then he was on solid ground.

Paul had arranged to travel up to Bontoc the next day, but until then, what to do with his newfound freedom? He had asked Rudy not to tell Joan that he was being released today—he didn't want her making a big deal about this. He was nervous about seeing her in any case, but this whole treasure thing loomed so large, he decided that he'd have to see it for himself. Joan would probably be at work in the cave, but that would be a better way to see her than having her helping him out of the clinic. He headed up the road towards the turnoff to the cave—Joan had given him so much information that he felt he had already been in the cave. They had erected a railing to help the museum staff get up and down the slope to the cave, so he figured he could handle it well enough, too. As he turned down the trail that led to the cave in one direction, and the rice terrace where he had fallen in the other, a powerful looking young man in a sport shirt and slacks approached him.

"Can I help you, sir?" asked the man. He was chewing gum and seemed relaxed, but the question was more of a challenge than an offer of assistance.

"No, that's all right," Paul answered. "I know the way."

"The way to what, sir?" There was a little more menace in the man's voice this time.

"I'm going down to the cave to meet my wife," said Paul.

"And who would your wife be, sir?"

"Joan Webster."

"Oh. Mr. Webster. I'm sorry. We haven't met before. I see you have a cane. Here, I'll accompany you to make sure no harm comes to you."

They walked together down the trail, and the young man explained that he was part of the security force sent up after the murders and robbery. He asked Paul all about his accident with great interest. Everyone in Banaue knew about Paul's accident. Paul realized that this was the first of many, many episodes of reliving the accident through others. He was out of the clinic, but he would carry the accident with him forever.

They reached the pit, and the guard took Paul's cane and then started climbing down the ladder.

"Turn around and come on down, Mr. Webster. Just go slow. I'm here to help you."

With great hesitation, Paul started to climb down, and then he realized that this was not a problem. There was no pain. He was merely climbing a ladder as he had done dozens of times before. He smiled to himself as he reached the bottom of the pit. The guard handed him his cane.

"I'm fine now. I can go on from here. You can go back up, and thanks for your help."

He turned and started into the cave. It had a sloping rock floor, and he could tell that the wooden railing had been recently installed. As he worked his way down the shaft, it turned left and grew darker. But then he noticed a string of electric lights running along the ceiling on the left. Fifty feet past the turn, Paul's heel skidded on the stone floor, and his feet started to fly out from under him. He grabbed onto the railing with both hands, and his cane clattered loudly to the floor, the sound reverberating around the tunnel. Oh, God, he thought, Joan said the cave is full of bats! I hope that noise didn't startle them. It was then that he realized the railing had held, and he wasn't on his back on the stone. He cautiously pulled himself upright, mentally searching for feelings in the bones in his back and leg. Everything seemed all right. I guess Loring is right, he thought. I'm as good as new, but I'd better be careful. I'm not as surefooted as a goat; not that I ever was, he added to himself. He picked up his cane, took hold of the railing and started back down the tunnel. He went down carefully, noticing a small trench on the right with running rainwater. When he reached a tall, natural arch, he gratefully stood up straight and stretched. The slope became steeper, slowing his progress. And then he saw it: Joan's descriptions, while accurate, somehow hadn't communicated the magical effect of the spreading pool crossed by a lovely Japanese bridge with the huge red torii gate on the other side. He stared in wonder; the whole scene was illuminated by lights coming from inside a net-covered structure behind a tall bamboo fence. Yamashita's treasure!

All was quiet. The clamor of his dropped cane had been too far up the tunnel to disturb the bats. He could hear the faint sounds of modulated conversation coming from what must be the museum offices beyond the fence. He regained his breath, hiked down the remainder of the slope and up across the bridge. As he entered the office quarters, he saw a figure ahead of him. With that hair, it had to be Rosie. She turned, and seeing him, rushed towards him.

"Paul?" she shrieked in as quiet a whisper as she could master. "You're out of the clinic!" She squeezed his arms and then gave him a hug.

"Rosie, I'm well again," Paul whispered back with joy. "Where is she?"

"In the back with the Ifugao photographer. Oh, she'll be overjoyed to see you!" She took his hand and led him back through the maze of packing crates, Asian art and office furniture.

When they reached Joan, she was turned away from them speaking to the new photographer. Paul dropped Rosie's hand and went on ahead. "Joan," he said softly.

She turned, and her eyes grew bright with excitement.

"Paul!!" she cried softly, and ran to him. She threw her arms around him and kissed him all over his face, then kissed him gently on the mouth. Finally, she stopped and looked at him.

"Are you all right? Do you need to sit down? Is it still painful? Why didn't you tell me you were getting out today?"

"Because I knew I'd be peppered with questions like that and way too much attention. Yes, I'm feeling fine. No pain. In fact, I'm spending too much time being delighted that I'm well again."

Joan looked at Rosie. "Thanks, Rosie, for bringing him to me. I'll talk to you later."

As Rosie left, Joan introduced Paul to the photographer, then led him through more maze to a sort of private office space. She put her arms around his neck and kissed him long and hard, pressing her body against his. Paul put his hands on her back, but didn't really return the embrace.

"I'm not really ready for that yet," he said.

She pulled back, still holding him, and looked at him.

"I've got something I need to do first. I'm leaving tomorrow," he bit his lip. "Then, maybe, well, we'll see."

"Whatever you need, darling," she sighed. "Where are you going? For how long?"

"I'm going north, not far from here, up in the Mountain Province. It isn't very many miles, but it's worlds away. I don't know how long I'll be there. Maybe a month, maybe two, but I have a story that needs to be told; the opportunity for my book has finally found me."

"Is it dangerous?"

"It might be. But I'll be careful."

"I hope so. I want you coming back to me of your own accord, not leaving forever because something outside of us happens to you."

"When I got out of the clinic, I didn't know where to go at first. And then I realized I had to see you. I wanted you to see that I'm back on my feet. I wanted to see your lovely face. I also wanted to see this treasure that's changed your life so," he looked around. "How about a little tour?" He smiled, "I've been told that you give a treasure tour like nobody else."

She hugged him again, "It's great to see you smile, Paul," she said, blinking back a tear. "I'd love to show you some Asian antiquities worth a few billion dollars."

After an hour's glimpse at a veritable museum in crates, Joan brought him back to the entrance of the office area.

"You're leaving in the morning?"

He nodded.

"Then let me buy you dinner tonight. You don't have any other plans, do you?"

"No, my date pool is especially empty right now," he smiled. "Sure, I'd love to have dinner. Oh, I just realized. Do I still have a bed in our hotel room?"

"Of course you do. And if you want to keep your distance right now, you know I'll honor that. I'll meet you at seven in the bar."

"Seven o'clock, then."

* * *

Returning to town, Paul looked in at Val's office to say hello and tell Val about his plans to venture up into the Mountain Province. Val was noncommittal about the NPA, but said that he felt that Paul would do good works wherever he was. Paul asked Val to watch over Joan to the best of his ability, and Val said he was happy to completely accept this responsibility. They made their goodbyes, and Paul walked to the hotel, where Manny was so delighted to see him that he knocked over a large floral bouquet in the lobby. Paul had lunch on the deck, looking out at the rice terraces that were so indelibly printed, in so many ways, in his memory. He spent the afternoon reading and taking notes, then, around four o'clock, his reading brought back Millie's story to him, and he knew he had to see her.

When he arrived at the clinic, the little room that served as lobby and reception was alive with noisy, excited men. Blood dripped across the floor and down the hall as far as Paul could see. Millie and Cece were running back and forth up the hall and into the reception, trying to quiet the six or seven workers who had evidently brought in the patient, a co-worker who had nearly cut off his leg clearing brush with a machete. Finally, Loring came out, his neat white coat covered with blood.

"Quiet!" he shouted. "Out! Out! Out, all of you! Your friend will be fine, if you will let me sew him up!"

Sheepishly, the men filed out.

Millie paused, and looked at Paul. "Do you need anything, Paul?"

"It'll keep until you're free. Go help Loring. I'll wait here."

Half an hour later, Millie returned, blood spattered on her dress.

"I'm sorry to keep you waiting so long," she apologized. "I'm such a mess, but I didn't want you to wait longer. What is it you need? Are you in pain?"

"You're beautiful, as always," said Paul. "I'm fine. I just need to talk to you for a few moments. Can you come outside?"

"Of course, but what is it?"

Paul opened the screen door for her and led her to the shade of a large pine tree near the road. "I just want you to know that I love you."

Millie started to say something, but he cut her off. "Don't worry. I got over my infatuation. I don't want to marry you anymore. I finally realized that was a dream. A very nice dream, but a dream, nonetheless."

He took her hand. "I love who you are. I love the way you cared for me. I love your courage in telling me your story. You know I'm going up into the Mountain Province tomorrow, and I couldn't leave you without saying all this."

She smiled and put her arms around his neck and kissed him. Paul's face felt hot, and Millie's body pressing against his made him dizzy. He was about to pull her to him for more when she backed away.

"You're a wonderful, intelligent man, Paul. I'm glad that you got past the dream. Your dream must be Joan. And you should know that I have a new dream. His name is Rudy. We're engaged to be married."

She stepped back and took him by the hands, "I will never forget you. And I will see you when you return to Banaue. Until then, may God be with you."

She glanced down at herself and grimaced. "I must go clean up now."

"If you ever need anything…"

"Thank you," she turned and went back into the building.

* * *

At five to seven, Paul walked into the hotel's restaurant. He carried the cane, but didn't use it. In spite of the season, several tables were filled with guests, and, in the far corner of the room, Joan was already seated, drinking a glass of white wine.

"I thought I'd beat you here."

"Do I seem over eager, Paul?"

"On you, it's very attractive." He sat down and ordered a bourbon on the rocks from the waiter. When his drink arrived, he raised his glass to Joan.

"To all things mending," he said. He took a swallow of whiskey and looked back at Joan. She didn't make a sound, but he could see her lips moving, I love you. She sipped her wine, and her eyes sparkled in the candlelight. She put down her glass and dabbed at her eyes with her napkin.

"Dammit, I told myself I wouldn't let you make me cry."

"I didn't mean to. I didn't think it would move me so much to see you. But it has. You look wonderful."

She smiled and lifted her glass again. "And here's to a safe and successful trip to…. Where are you going?"

"I'd rather not say, but thanks for the wishes. I'll be back before you know it."

The waiter came for their order and they stopped to look at menus. When he left, Joan said, "At least I'll be busy while you're gone. It looks like I'll be going to Manila in a week or so to arrange for moving the treasure. The roads should finally be passable by then. The government is providing a wing of the National Museum for a temporary exhibit and continued cataloguing of all the pieces. We'll be able to complete the work much faster down there."

"What'll they do with the cave when the treasure's gone?"

"There's talk of turning it into a historical monument to the War and the Arts in Asia. They'll probably build a small museum here in Banaue. It would definitely be popular with tourists."

"What about the theft and the murders?"

"The security group that's here in Banaue right now is investigating them, but doesn't seem to be making much headway."

"Oh, one of them must be the fellow I encountered. He wasn't in uniform, but was definitely guarding the entrance to the cave. He helped me down the slope and the ladder once he knew who I was."

"Their commander feels that they will attract less attention if they aren't in uniform. But they are soldiers in the Philippine armed forces. They arrived in a Humvee, which they keep somewhat out of sight."

"Yeah," said Paul. "I suppose a low profile makes the most sense."

Their salads arrived, and Paul ordered another round of drinks. Joan had suggested the Filipino Style Caesar Salad, and it was delicious.

"It's the *bagoong balayan*," she said. "It's anchovy sauce, which is very popular. So it's natural that a Caesar salad would be popular here, as well. By the way, have you met Nigel, Nigel Barclay, yet? He's quite an excellent chef and knows all about lots of Asian food, since he's lived here for years."

"As a matter of fact, I did meet Nigel. He dropped by the clinic a couple of weeks ago to pay his respects. Once I got past the shock of imagining I was seeing Emory alive again, we had quite an interesting chat. Of course, he wanted to know all about the accident and how I was feeling and so forth. When he came in, I was at the point that I was putting weight on my leg, so he never saw me on my back in traction. We were chatting amiably, when he interrupted me, and, looking somewhat embarrassed, said 'Pardon me, old chap, but I have something I need to put to you.' I stopped and waited, and he finally continued with, 'It's my understanding that you and Joan are somewhat on the outs.

If that is the case, I wonder if it would trouble you too much if I, er, as you say, courted her?'"

"Paul, I can't believe this!"

"It's true. Before I could answer, he said, 'I know I'm considerably older than Joan, but I must tell you, Paul, that she's quite an amazing woman, so I would appreciate it if you might tell me how you feel about this.' Well, I was as shocked as you are now, but on thinking it over, it goes with the territory. This is just the kind of thing Emory would have done in a similar situation, and we both know that Nigel has a lot of Emory's genes."

"So what did you tell him?"

"I told him that, yes, I was sorry to say that we were on the outs, as he put it. I also said that whether we were together or not was of no consequence, because in no way could I or would I say that you might be courted by anyone. You are your own person, and you are the one to make such a decision. He seemed satisfied with this, and, since he had accomplished the main thing he had come for, we exchanged pleasantries, and he left."

"Wow! That's incredible! But, you know, it does kind of explain why he's been so attentive lately. The poor man thinks he actually has a chance at replacing you," she reached across and squeezed Paul's hand. "No one will ever replace you, darling."

Paul smiled, but said nothing. But he could feel his heart pounding harder than it had for a long time.

After dinner, they strolled out onto the wide deck. The sky was clear, and a growing moon shone down on the terraces, cutting the dark with vivid patches of light. The air here was unpolluted, and the moon and stars felt unreal, they were so bright. The night seemed filled with magic. Paul put his arm around Joan's shoulders, and she leaned against him. He felt like he was a honeymooner. He turned and kissed her lips, and they stood together a long time in an embrace that filled the longing of months. Her breath was warm against his ear, and she whispered,

"I love you so, Paul. There'll never be anyone else. Only you."

"You know I could never leave you, don't you," he whispered back and held her against him for a dizzyingly long time.

Finally, Joan pulled back to look at him.

"Well, soldier, we have just one night together before you go off to war."

* * *

That wonderful night had been exactly one week ago. Today Paul lay on his belly in the pine needles on the floor of the forest, parting the branches in front of him to see better. His leg was throbbing slightly after the four-mile hike to get here, and he reached in his pocket for a small bottle of pills. He put one in his mouth, sucked up some saliva and swallowed it.

The others were about ten yards in front of him, also lying in the low growth beneath the pine trees, looking down the slope toward one of the main trails between Bontoc and Sagada. However, they had rifles, not a notepad and ballpoint pen.

He had convinced Loring to put him in touch with Roberto Dagatan, the leader of a small band of NPA operating in the vicinity of Bontoc in Mountain Province, a few miles and mountains north of

Banaue. The Mountain Province and Kalinga, the neighboring province to its north, had been NPA strongholds since the late Sixties. When Paul was finally discharged from the clinic, he had arranged for a ride to Bontoc. Insik, as Roberto was known, had sent a young cadre to meet him there and lead him back to their campsite. Insik was a native of Bontoc, and had been an active NPA leader there for more than twenty years. Because of the difficult mountainous terrain, the area that now included the Mountain Province, Kalinga-Apayao, Benguet and Ifugao resisted the advances of the Spanish for three centuries. In 1908, the Americans named the whole area the Mountain Province after the Spanish *la montañosa* and divided the province into four in 1966. In modern times, the mountainous region had proven to be a similar thorn in the Philippine government's side, with the successful growth of NPA forces working to bring justice to the indigenous people who had very little voice in the national scheme of things. Insik had joined the NPA when he was only fourteen, angered by the injustices he saw daily in his family's barangay. Insik, whose nickname meant "Chinese" in Tagalog, was called that because he had one great-grandfather who had migrated from China, and Insik inherited his genes. His skin was much fairer than others in his family, and his eyes had a definite northern look to them. His face was round, almost moon-like, and his short, stocky body seemed pudgy, but he was nothing but muscle and strong as a bull. The government had put a price on his head, but even though he was known throughout the region, no one turned him in—he was much loved, for the honor he gave his family and his people. Paul spent a week at the campsite, listening to Insik's history and the problems that still persisted for his people. Even though the Marcos regime had ended, Cory's policies were still based on much that came from the Senate, and the Senate was made up primarily of members of the wealthy families who owned most of the Philippines. Cory herself was from one of those families, and she didn't always understand the real needs of the poorest of the poor. In fact, in some ways, it seemed like martial law was still in effect, because the AFP continued to have more power than it knew what to do with, and certain individuals in the military took advantage of the situation. Just recently, an AFP squad had begun to extort money from several villages in the area, and, when not compensated according to their demands, had even murdered three civilians to make their point. That was why today, Insik and his cadres, with Paul following, were lying in the brush waiting. One of the elders in a village nearby had told Insik that the squad was coming today to collect its protection money. This was the only way for them to reach the village, and Insik's NPA group were here to make their point.

Something tickled Paul's hand and he looked down to see a small beetle struggle up the side of his hand, then hurry across and down the other side to disappear into the pine needles. That was when Paul heard the sound of voices coming from the south, down the trail. They grew louder, and then he saw nine soldiers walking up the trail toward Insik and his cadres. They were dressed in uniform, but they walked like a group of young men sauntering to a bar. They were laughing and joking with each other, looking for all the world like schoolboys, except for their uniforms and guns. They were speaking in Tagalog, and he didn't recognize any of the words except "money" and "good." He saw sergeant's stripes on one man at the front of the group. As the guns went off, every bird in the vicinity took off in noisy flight, adding to the chaos.

He saw the sergeant twist from a bullet in the shoulder, then jerk back and collapse when a second bullet hit him in the head. Two other men fell to the ground. The rest, terrified, turned and ran, two of them dropping their weapons. A late bullet caught the slowest in the thigh, and he screamed and fell on his face. Then there was silence, except for the moans of the wounded soldier. Paul smelled the gunpowder in the air. He would never feel the same about fireworks again. Insik got to his feet and skidded down the slope to the trail, followed by the others. He walked past the three dead bodies to the wounded man, and Paul thought he was going to execute him, but he merely gave him an envelope and spoke a few quiet words to him. Meanwhile, the other cadres collected the guns and ammunition that were still there. Insik motioned to Paul, and he got up and stretched his sore leg and worked his way down to the trail.

"Are you okay?" asked Insik.

Paul nodded.

"Do not be ashamed if you feel sick," Insik said. "We know you have never seen men die before. And, for me, it is not easier, eh. It happens when there is no other choice, only."

As they started their hike back to the campsite, Paul realized how strange and terrible it all was. One minute, several men were walking along, laughing, sure of their youth and their lives. Seconds later, three of them would never see the sun rise again. He hadn't pulled the trigger, but, by being there, he had approved of it. The law in the United States would hunt them down and execute them or send them to prison for a very long time. But perhaps, here in the Philippines, the law was made for a very few. In the last few weeks, he had heard things far beyond his

242

comprehension. He had learned of a legacy of atrocities that somehow changed his kneejerk tendency toward civility. He knew Insik was not a villain, not a bloodthirsty man. The night before, he had been sitting, writing by the light of the fire, when Insik interrupted him.

"How do you spell 'extortion,' eh?"

He looked up and saw Insik writing something himself. He had never seen Insik write before. Paul spelled extortion for him, and Insik said thanks and started writing again. A short time later, Insik got up and walked around the campfire and handed Paul a piece of paper.

"What do you think, Paul?" he asked. Does this one look okay to you, only?"

"What is it?" asked Paul.

"It's a message to say why we will do this thing tomorrow."

Paul looked down at the crudely printed message.

"This is the answer we make to those who would hurt us with extortion and murder. Let the mountain people live in peace."

15. ST. PHILIP NERI

As Joan ate her breakfast of fruit, toast and coffee, she read through her notes for the administrators at the National Museum. They would need to know in great detail what was expected of their staff, and tomorrow Rudy was driving her down to Manila to meet with them. Val had made the decision to use several small trucks to move the treasure. He definitely believed in erring on the side of caution. The first trucks would be arriving in Banaue in three or four days. Boy, as the senator insisted she call him, had finally convinced her to spend her time in Manila with Vicky and him, so she didn't need to bother checking into a hotel.

Joan glanced up from her notes and noticed Manny standing at the entrance to the dining room. The concierge seemed agitated. He looked at her, and then to each side, and then left. She took a bite of toast and went back to her notes. A minute later, he came back and approached her table.

"Madam?"

She put down her pen and looked up. "Yes, Manny. What is it?"

"Oh, I hate to trouble you, but... Oh, never mind. It's probably nothing." He turned to leave.

"No. What's troubling you?"

He leaned closer and whispered, "Well, you see, this seems so foolish, but, you know that strange vehicle the new guards have parked down below the hotel?"

"The Humvee. Yes, what about it?"

"Well, I don't know why I didn't think of this before, but I saw that same vehicle on the night of the murders."

"Are you sure? Maybe it was another Humvee."

"Oh, no, Madam. I remember that when I saw it parked out in the rain, I peered into it, because I hadn't seen a vehicle like it."

"And?"

"And it had a little statue of St. Philip Neri on the dashboard. I thought it was strange not to have a statue of St. Christopher or the Blessed Virgin, but it was St. Philip Neri. My priest told me he's the patron saint of certain military special forces. And this new Humvee, as you call it, has the same."

Just then, a girl from the front desk came in to tell Manny that he was needed by a guest.

"In a minute! I'm *talking* to a guest!" he answered, then looked at Joan, who nodded, and back at the girl, "I'm sorry, I'll be right there."

When the girl left, Joan asked quietly, "Have you told anyone else about this?"

"No, no one."

"What about your priest?"

"I didn't say why I wanted to know about the saint."

"Then I'll take care of it. Please don't say anything to anyone. Not even to Val."

"I have sealed lips, Madam," he smiled at their secret.

"Go help the other guest, then."

"Yes, Madam."

Joan picked up her coffee cup, but she was shaking so hard she had to put it down. So these soldiers killed Michael and the guards, she thought. It was a shock, but it made sense. The murderers had obviously known what they were doing, and these men were well trained, or else why would the senator have trusted them to investigate? The senator! He must have sent them up here! How would these soldiers have known the location of the treasure without him? And now he'd sent the same men back to supposedly investigate the crime and guard the treasure! How ironic! These soldiers were guarding the treasure from themselves! She should go to Val—he'd know what to do. But then, Val seemed to agree with what the senator had said about the NPA. Maybe Val was involved in this, too! No, he couldn't be. She wouldn't believe that he would allow his own villagers to be murdered. He must be as in the dark about this as she had been. But now, she had evidence! But what evidence did she have? The testimony of a hotel concierge and a good luck charm on a dashboard? The army had hundreds of Humvees—probably many with dashboard saints. If this was the patron saint of the military, it could be a popular item at the PX, given the Filipino predilection to fill their cars with decoration. No, it was too early to go to... Who could she go to? Val certainly wouldn't have the ability to arrest these men who were well-trained assassins. Someone in Manila. The Manila Police? But she knew one thing—corruption was everywhere within the military, the police, and politics. And the senator would have powerful allies in every corner of the administration. But she knew one person she could trust. Cory Aquino was above the corruption. From her meetings with Cory, Joan knew she was absolutely to be trusted. She couldn't go to Cory with the information she had, though. She'd have to find something else. Something that tied the senator to all this. She'd have to go ahead with the plan to drive to Manila tomorrow for her meetings. She'd have to stay in the dragon's lair and somehow find something incriminating that would give her an ironclad reason to talk to Cory. She knew this was her only choice, and with this knowledge, she became calm. She picked up her coffee cup, drank the cold coffee, signed her check and left for the cave.

After a fitful night of sleep, Joan woke at four and dressed for running. It was the darkest hour of the night, but the moon and stars illuminated the dirt road leading away from the village. She had run this way often since arriving in Banaue, and had no trouble negotiating its grades and curves. She ran until she developed a light sweat, then turned to retrace her steps. The previous evening, she had arranged to meet Rudy at the car at seven for the long drive to Manila. She had already thought long and hard about how she could find hard evidence that Boy was truly involved in this horrific crime. What kind of motive could he possibly have? He certainly didn't need the money—he was richer than God. Owning part of the treasure might give him something of a rush, but Joan didn't think that could be a strong enough motive for someone as powerful as a member of the Philippine senate. It was obviously not a crime of passion—it had been methodically planned and meticulously carried out. There was also the added risk of having several others involved—they would assuredly be paid well for their roles, but the chance of information leaking out was still there. Perhaps Captain Monsod worked closely enough with the senator that he had seen correspondence that gave him the location and situation of the treasure. Maybe this was just a case of some ambitious and ruthless soldiers being in the right place at the right time.

Joan arrived back at the hotel, no wiser nor more confident than when she left. It was after six by the time she showered and changed into a sleeveless blue silk dress comfortable enough for the eight-hour drive, and she'd still be presentable at the Senator's mansion. She took her bag and went down to the restaurant for coffee. As she sipped the hot coffee, Captain Monsod spotted her from the lobby and came in.

"May I join you for a moment, Mrs. Webster?" he asked, pulling out a chair and sitting as he spoke. He was dressed in a khaki work shirt, blue jeans and well worn cowboy boots. "I understand you're driving down to Manila today."

"Yes, we're getting preparations ready to take the treasure down to the National Museum."

"Hmm, yes. Well have a safe trip. Driving through the Cordillera, in any season, is always hazardous."

"And I've not seen you dress so casually before," observed Joan.

"We've gotten word that there have been activities north of here that may pertain to our investigation. It'll probably amount to nothing. Just a little jungle excursion, I'm afraid," he looked at Joan thoughtfully. "You have not heard of anything happening, have you?"

Joan frowned, "Why would I...?"

"No reason," he got up from the chair. "I must be off. I'm sure you'll be fine. Rudy is very trustworthy."

As the captain left, the waiter refilled Joan's cup.

"Thank you, Doming. And would you ask Manny to see me for a minute?"

Captain Monsod must be fishing for something, thought Joan. Manny arrived in scant minutes, asking what he could do for her.

248

"Manny, I just wanted to tell you that Captain Monsod and his men are heading north to investigate some activities they heard about. As I recall, Bontoc and the Mountain Province are to the north, right?"

"Yes, madam. Very much so."

"Well, perhaps you might know someone who could make sure the people in Bontoc know that they are coming."

Manny smiled, "I am sure that those in Bontoc will be gratified to receive this news. Thank you, madam, and drive carefully."

Just before seven, Rudy came into the restaurant, picked up Joan's bag and a box lunch he had ordered for the trip. Joan followed him out. The big, black Mercedes sat at the front entrance, shining in the morning sun, and Rudy opened the door for Joan. "It's going to be a beautiful day, mum."

"I hope you're right, Rudy." God, thought Joan, a beautiful day is the least of my worries.

* * *

They had been driving for nearly two hours and were approaching the broad, southeastern edge of the mountain chain where the jungle merges with the endless fields of corn, bananas and pineapples in the Cagayan Valley. Joan looked up to the front, and saw the back of Rudy's head, his hands on the wheel, on task as usual.

"Rudy, how long have you worked for the senator?"

"Well, Mum, it must be close to eight years now," he replied.

"Do you like working for him?"

"The Senator saved my life, Mum. I owe everything to him."

"Is that so?"

"Yes, Mum. You see, I'm not proud of it, but when I was young, I was kind of a wild kid. I grew up in Manila and used to kind of live on the streets. I didn't have to; my pop was a cook for Mrs. Vital's parents. I grew up in the shadow of their mansion, in the servants' quarters, which were plenty nice, compared to the way a lot of people live. My pop was a fine father, but I thought he was scum, because he was a servant. I swore I'd never be a servant, and, more and more, I hung out on the streets and palled around with a bunch of other kids, looking for kicks. We learned to pick pockets, mostly. And just hung out, smoking pot and looking for girls."

"Didn't your father know where you were?"

"Oh, yeah, Pop knew where I was. Even though it's huge, Manila is really a small town, if you know your way around. He'd track me down, and twice he took me home, but I just ran away again.

"So, anyway, I met these guys, and they told me that picking pockets was for small fry, and they showed me how to steal cars. So I stole cars for a couple of years, and the money was way better. I was a big deal guy. I had money, and I always had a girl on my arm, and I thought I was pretty cool stuff.

"When I got busted, I thought I was too cool to even go to jail, and I just laughed at everyone and wouldn't tell them anything. And I wound up in prison. Well, that was some shock! But I still thought that everyone else was wrong, and I was just being jammed on. One day, a couple of the other cons busted me up, real bad, and I ended up in the hospital. They thought I was going to die. So my Pop came to see me, and he cried all over me, and he said he'd find a way to help me if only I got well.

"Rudy, you don't have to tell me…"

"No, it's okay, Mum. I really like you. You and your husband. You're really good people, and you've been really fair to me. Actually, it feels kinda good to tell someone.

"So Pop goes to the Vitals, and they go to their daughter and the Senator. Two days later, I get moved to a private hospital, and I'm lying there, thinking how cool I am, and in walks the Senator, and he beats the hell out of me. Not with his fists, and he could, 'cause he's a strong guy, but with his tongue. He tells me what a nothing I am, and he tells me that I can be something if I do what he says. So I turn in all the guys in the gang, and they put me on probation, and I'm to work for the Senator, and if he so much as burps, I'm back in the bamboo hut, if you know what I mean."

"So I do what the Senator tells me. He's tough, but he's been fair to me. And now it's really paying off. Now I've met the person for me. Did you hear that Millie and I are getting married? And I owe it all to the Senator. And of course, to you."

One way or another, I have to find a way to prove that Senator Vital is innocent, thought Joan. Or I have to implicate him beyond a doubt in these awful crimes. He'll either be my best friend or my worst enemy.

* * *

Rudy turned into the drive, and Joan shielded her eyes from the late afternoon sun. The gatekeeper waved to them, the gate swung open, and

Joan was staggered all over again by the opulence of the landscaping of the Vitals' home as they passed under the canopy of palms up the long drive. The car stopped at the front entry, and Rudy hurried around to open Joan's door before the butler had time to do it.

Joan took Rudy's helping hand and got out of the car.

She barely had time to say, "I'll see you later, Rudy," before the butler whisked her across the terrazzo and into the house. The vestibule was a fabulous solarium filled with orchids, small palms and banana trees. She followed the butler across the polished floor until Vicky rushed into their path. She looked beautiful in a flowing silk gown of tangerine and turquoise.

"Joan!" she exclaimed, throwing her arms around Joan and kissing her on the cheek. "I was beginning to think you'd never get here. Are you tired? You *must* be tired. It's such a long trip. " Come sit down," she urged as she led Joan into a sitting room furnished in lacquer wood and rattan.

"I know it's such a bore to ride all the way down from the mountains. I don't know how you stand it. Personally, I hate the mountains. They're just too far from everything! Baguio is all right. It's only a short drive. But no farther for me. You must be thirsty after such a long drive. Would you like some tea?" asked Vicky, turning to a maid standing in the corner of the room. "Carmen, Mrs. Webster would like some tea. I'm so happy that you're going to be in Manila now, instead of those awful mountains. I'll take you to the best stores. You'll need a whole new wardrobe now that you're in Manila, and especially now with winter coming, you'll need new things for the season. There are so many parties being scheduled with the new season coming! And with your treasure, you're already the talk of the town. Everybody wants to meet you. We'll have such fun!"

With Vicky's harmless chatter, Joan had nearly forgotten what her real situation was, and what she needed to try to do in this very house. Suddenly, she felt very tired, and very tense.

The maid, Carmen, was laying out the tea service as Joan said, "Vicky, if you don't mind, I'd rather have something cold. Would it be possible to have a vodka tonic?"

"Of course, you poor dear. I'm sure you never wanted hot tea at all. What could I have been thinking of? Carmen, I'm sorry, but would you take the tea away? And bring Mrs. Webster a vodka and tonic. And I'll have a lemonade."

She turned back to Joan. "I just don't even think about liquor. I always leave that up to Boy. I really think that drinking liquor is more of a man's domain. And, of course, Boy is late today. He knows perfectly well that you're arriving today, but he had some meeting that just wouldn't wait, and so I'm having to look out for entirely everything. We've put you in the Twilight Room. I've named all of the bedrooms for different times of day—each room is named for the time of day when it's at its best, and your room is just stunning right after the sun goes down and the lavender sky of twilight comes seeping in through the shutters."

Carmen arrived with the drinks, and Vicky lifted her lemonade, and said, "Here's to your having the time of your life in Manila," just as Boy walked into the room.

"Oh, darling, you're finally home. Look who's here! Joan and I have been planning on shopping 'til we drop!"

Boy crossed to Joan and kissed her on the cheek, "Welcome! Welcome! So Vicky's finally getting her way with you. She's been dying for a new project, and I'm afraid you're it." He patted Vicky on the cheek and gave her an affectionate kiss, then sat across the table from them. "Carmen, my usual, please."

Joan looked at Boy. He seemed completely at ease, happy to be home. He and Vicky seemed to have a very natural, relaxed relationship. He couldn't have authorized all those horrible crimes, but then, being a major player in politics, he was probably a very good poker player and...

"Don't you think so, Joan?"

Joan started as she realized Vicky was talking to her. "I'm sorry , I'm rather tired."

"You poor darling. I was just telling Boy that he needs to start thinking about slowing down. He's not getting any younger, you know, and he has to learn to delegate more assignments to his staff. He continues to try to do everything himself. He needs to moderate. That's the word: Moderate. Don't you agree, Joan?"

"Yes, Vicky. Slow down and smell the roses, as they say."

"There, you see, Boy? Joan agrees with me," she turned back to Joan. "We'll just have an early dinner, and then you can get some rest."

They sat and talked, or rather listened to Vicky talk, for another half hour. Vicky was excited to be involved with Joan's treasure, "in a roundabout sort of way," since she was on the National Museum's Board of Directors. It would be so exciting to see all the fabulous things that Joan had found hidden in the mountain. Boy continued to stump Joan— he spoke little, but his comments showed he was listening to the conversation. His mind didn't seem to be wandering, she thought, as it would if he were distracted by guilt or the fear of discovery. When Carmen came with the news that dinner was served, they moved into the small dining room, and Boy held the chairs for both women to be seated.

"Would you like a little Chablis, Joan?" he asked. "It goes perfectly with these mussels."

She nodded, and he poured the wine. She was beginning to relax, herself. She looked around the perfect little room. It was all glass and candles, with a heavy glass table, étagère and metallic lemon wallpaper. A large folding Japanese screen many museums would love to have stretched across the main wall, coloring the room with pale chrysanthemums. The étagère was filled with exquisite Chinese ceramics, and.... On the second shelf, proudly standing on a black, lacquer wood base, was a small, cusped bowl, a piece of Yaozhou ware—her bowl! It had to be—there couldn't be another piece like that! Still, she had to know for sure, she had to find the drill mark on the base that she knew must be there! She hoped she hadn't reacted too obviously when she had seen it. She glanced up at Boy and Vicky, but they were chatting about an upcoming dinner with Cory.

"Boy, could I have a little more of that excellent wine?" she said, hoping that there was no quaking in her voice.

"Happy to oblige," he replied, and leaned toward her with the bottle ready. She picked up the nearly empty glass to reach out to him, but her hand shook so, she had to put it down closer to him. "You *have* had a trying day," he commented, filling her glass, "but Vicky will soon get you into the swing of things."

Steeling herself, Joan picked up the glass and took a large swallow. "Thanks, Boy, that really is excellent wine. You must give me the name so I can get some myself. And you're right, it goes perfectly with the mussels, which, if I may add, are really wonderful. How do you do it all, Vicky?"

Boy laughed and said, "She does it all with a huge staff, and I'll see that there's a case of the Chablis ready for you whenever you want it."

They finished their dinner, and Joan excused herself from the table.

"Meling, would you show Mrs. Webster to the Twilight Room? Actually, I'm a little tired, too. I think I'll read a little in bed," she paused as Boy started to leave the room. "Boy, where are you going?"

"I'll be in my office, dear. I have a few things I need to finish."

"Men!" Vicky threw up her hands and said good night to Joan.

The maid led Joan to the north wing of the house and opened the door to what was actually a suite of rooms, with a bedroom, sitting room, bathroom, shower and walk-in closet the size of many rooms. The predominate color scheme was not, as she had expected, based on lavender, but a rich golden mauve that warmed and soothed at the same time. Vicky, Joan thought, had an eye for dazzling and an interior designer budget to match. The maid busied herself with adjusting the curtains, then turned and asked if mum would like the bed turned down.

"Yes, thank you, Meling. That'll be fine." She sat down on the edge of a small bamboo loveseat cushioned with pillows upholstered with a palm frond fabric. She sat there numbly while the maid finished her preparations.

"Anything else, Mum?"

"No thank you, Meling. I've everything I need," she paused, then said, "Good night."

The maid left and Joan sat there, her mind spinning with possibilities. Obviously, she had to make sure that it was the same bowl, even though she couldn't imagine a twin existing. She had to know. But what then? Go to the police. The items stolen from the cave had been missing for some time, and Boy could simply say it turned up in a shop, and he bought it. No, she needed some way to make an airtight case. She knew in her heart she was right, but the evidence so far was strictly circumstantial. She sat there for an hour, more than enough time for the kitchen staff to finish cleaning the dining room and retire to other chambers and duties. She kicked off her high heels and walked barefoot across the room. Most of the house was floored with polished tile, and it was cool to her feet. She quietly opened the door, slipped out and padded silently down the hall. The house was quiet. Not a sound except for the relaxing flow of water pouring across river rock in a Japanese fountain. She made her way back to the front sitting room, then on and around the corner, past the large banquet hall to the small dining room. The room was empty, with lights turned down so that only small indirect bulbs illuminated the étagère on the far wall. She approached it, noticing how elegant the bowl looked in the low light. There was a slight click when she opened the glass door, and she froze, then realized that it only sounded like an alarm bell because of the silence. She picked up the bowl, turned it upside down and saw her drill mark. She started to put it back, then paused when a reflection distracted her.

"Don't drop it! It's priceless, as you well know!"

A strong hand grabbed her by the shoulder, and the other hand deftly scooped the bowl from her quivering fingers and carefully put it back on its pedestal. Boy pulled her away from the glass case and spun her around. He had replaced the barong Tagalog with a white T-shirt emblazoned with "Virginia is for lovers," and his feet were bare, like hers. She started to cry out, but in her shock, only a small whimper emerged from her lips. Before she had another chance to make a sound, he pinned her arms behind her and clamped his other hand over her mouth.

"I'm surprised, Joan. Did you really imagine that a house like this would not have security cameras?

He moved Joan to the other side of the room and managed to open a door on the wall, then pushed her through into a room that was much cooler than the rest of the house. He kicked the door shut and turned on the light with his elbow. They were in a room full of wine. From floor to ceiling, all four walls were covered with racks and coolers full of wine bottles. There was a door on each side of the room, and a table and chairs and a small overstuffed sofa in the center. Boy pushed her down face first into the sofa and straddled her. His weight nearly knocked the wind out of her. She tried to turn her head to scream, but he forced her sideways, burying her face in the juncture of back and seat cushions. He pulled off his belt and lashed her elbows behind her, then picked up a cloth napkin from the table and stuffed it in her mouth. Satisfied she was under control, he got up and pulled a cell phone out of his pants pocket. He punched a couple of numbers, listened and then said,

"Rudy, it's the Senator. I need you in the wine room, on the double. And bring some rope."

He clicked off the phone, then sat down on one of the chairs.

"I'm afraid we have an unfortunate situation here, Joan. I made one mistake, and you found me out."

Joan rolled to the edge of the sofa and tried to spit out the gag. Boy got up, pushed her back, and continued.

"I saw that Yaozhou bowl among the artifacts from the cave, and I knew that Vicky would adore it. I gave it to her as a special private present, I said. And I asked her to keep it only in our bedroom, but you know women—she just had to show it off. I hadn't noticed that she'd moved it until you saw it. Oh, yes, I saw your eyes—I'm afraid you don't have much of a pokerface.

"You should know that she has no idea where it came from—she thinks I found it in an antique shop. "

There was a knock at the door. Boy got up, opened the door a crack, and let Rudy in. Rudy stopped short when he saw Joan lying bound and gagged on the sofa.

"But Senator..."

"I'm sorry, Rudy, but this is necessary. I know you think highly of Joan, but she's become a risk to me, to everything. I want you to tie her well, and I want you to take her out to the garage. Put her in the Mercedes, and wait for me. Oh, and get her shoes and bag from her room. She wouldn't be down in that cave without shoes.

"Rudy, I don't want her escaping. We'll leave for Banaue at first light. There's going to be another theft before the treasure is moved, and a final casualty."

Rudy sat down in one of the chairs and scratched his head, "But Senator, can't we...?"

"Just do what I say, son, and you won't be hurt. And if you just follow my orders and keep quiet about everything, neither will Millie."

"Oh no! Senator, no! Don't hurt Millie!"

"Of course I won't. Just do as I say. Understand?"

"Yes, sir."

Boy waited while the chauffeur trussed Joan's ankles, then when Rudy started to tie her wrists, Boy pulled his belt loose from Joan's arms and slipped it back on.

"I'll be back in just a few minutes, Rudy. Remember what I said," and he left the room and quietly closed the door.

Joan squirmed around and kicked her hobbled legs at Rudy. She made as much sound as she could through the gag.

"Oh, no, Mum. Please don't," he gently moved her back. "You don't know him. He's a bad man. He'll kill Millie if I let you go. He's killed other people. Please don't. I'll think of something."

Tears filled his eyes as he finished tying her hands and sat her up in the corner of the sofa. Joan looked into his eyes, and for the first time this evening, she felt there was no hope. Terror filled her, and she moaned through the gag.

The door opened and Boy came back in carrying a large glass. To Joan's amazement, Vicky was with him. She was wearing a black peignoir, and she had an expression on her face Joan had never seen before.

"You naughty girl, why did you have to be so curious? I'm really sorry about all this, but you have it all wrong. You think the treasure is for the people. Haven't you ever heard of 'Finders keepers?' And I was so looking forward to having fun shopping with you."

Boy crossed to Joan and held up the glass. "Just to be safe, here's something that'll relax you," he said, pulling the gag down and tipping the glass to her lips. She spit the water back at him. He grabbed her by the hair and pulled her head back, "*I said*, this will relax you," and he poured the water down her throat. She choked and swallowed and choked again. He lowered her back onto the sofa, standing over her, waiting for the drug to take effect. She could see Vicky standing casually behind him. The last thing she remembered was making love to Paul on a beach somewhere in Virginia.

* * *

Joan woke with a muffled groan and realized she still had the gag in her mouth. She was twisted uncomfortably on her side, and she could hear road noise below the carpet she was lying on. She stretched her head back and saw that she was on the floor in the back seat of the Mercedes. The tops of sugar cane rushed past the side window from her viewpoint, and she remembered the sugar cane plantations at the foot of the Cordilleras. They must be nearing the climb up to Banaue.

"Rudy, it looks like the lady is awake."

Boy's voice seemed very far away, but Joan knew that he was just sitting in the front seat. She still felt groggy, and the distant voice took her back to fond memories of sleeping in the backseat of their Packard sedan when her parents had gone on weekend drives. Her parents' murmuring conversations had given her a powerful sense of security, but today, in this car, that voice brought nothing but a fearsome ache.

"I know the gag is uncomfortable, Joan, but I regret that you must continue to have it, even though you won't be screaming for help. I simply don't want to listen to your pleadings or your arguments."

He paused, and then began again. "As I said before, what's happening here is very regrettable. I really do like both you and your husband, and if the situation were different, I would be one of your best friends and strongest supporters. But there's just too much at stake here. You can't imagine how much money it takes to keep Vicky happy, with the house and servants and trappings of a Senator. The wealth of both families was a start, but, since Marcos was ousted, the true source of millions of dollars of our budget has dried up. I thought many long nights, I'll tell you, before I decided that Yamashita's gift had to be at least partially mine. And Vicky's—she's a lovely woman, but she's very needy. There are many in the government who are suffering just like I am, now that we've lost our access to American foreign aid, but I was the lucky one with the opportunity."

They drove along in silence for perhaps fifteen minutes, then Boy said, "You can rest assured that no one else will hear this conversation. I trust Rudy implicitly. He's a good man and knows what he must do to maintain his health and the health of his loved ones. He's helped me through many scrapes before, and I know he'll not let me down this time either.

"At any rate, you should know that your death won't be entirely for nothing. With the evidence we'll have prepared to show that you were murdered by cadres from the NPA, Cory will sign the papers herself, allowing me to send death squads into the Cordillera to wipe out the resistance there, once and for all. So, you see, politically, your death will bring about a fundamental change in the administration's attitude about so-called 'people power.'"

Joan waited, but there were no more words from Boy. He had made his confession, and, as far as he was concerned, he was exonerated. He had sufficient motive, it seemed, to end another human life. She lay still on the floor of the car, tuned into its motion as they climbed through the miles of curves taking them back to Ifugao country.

The Mercedes pulled off the road and drove for a few hundred feet on what felt like dirt. Even from the floor of the car, Joan could see that they had reached Banaue—they were driving down behind the hotel. Rudy stopped the car and turned off the ignition, then opened his door.

The senator stopped him before he could hurry around the car and open the passenger door, "I'll stay here for now, Rudy. Tell the concierge we've arrived and find Captain Monsod. Have him meet me here at the car."

After Rudy left, Joan heard the sound of a cigarette lighter and could smell the smoke from one of the cigarillos the senator liked. He drew a deep breathful of smoke and exhaled slowly, "I'm truly sorry that things had to end this way, Joan. You're a talented woman, but you're one very bothersome loose end I just can't afford to ignore."

Joan clamped her teeth tight on her gag as she saw Monsod's profile pass the window of her door. He opened the senator's door, "I'm glad you're here, Senator. Something's going on. Three of my men have gone missing."

"Never mind that now. This is urgent," Boy replied. "Our big problem is in the back seat. I want you to take her down to the cave. Don't bring her back."

"Yes, sir," said Monsod, opening the senator's door farther and assisting him out.

"Report back to me when you're finished. I'll be in the bar."

Joan could hear Boy's steps as he walked up around the car. Then the rear car door opened, and Monsod stood there, looking down at her. He was still wearing the denims and boots he'd had on the day before. He shook his head and pulled his knife out of its sheath and cut the rope binding her ankles. He put the knife away and bent back down to pull her up from the floor, but first slid a hand up her leg to the inside of her thigh. Joan kicked him in the ribs, and he grunted in pain, then smiled at her.

"Game to the last, I see," he said. He grabbed her ankles and pulled her across the floor of the car, then took her upper arm in an iron grip and hoisted her out of the car to her feet. She stood numbly, wobbling after the hours of bondage in the car.

"C'mon," he said. He slammed the car door and started down around the back of the hotel toward the trail to the cave, pulling her along after him.

Finally standing, Joan now saw that the Mercedes was parked next to the soldiers' Humvee, pulled partly out of sight under a couple of spreading pines. Monsod jerked her along, and she stumbled to keep up. His grip on her arm was so painful it nearly brought tears to her eyes, but she wouldn't give him that satisfaction. Halfway to the cave, she began to mumble, forcing her mouth against the gag.

He stopped and looked at her, "There's no one here to save you if you shout," and he pulled the gag down around her neck, took her by the shoulders and kissed her roughly on the mouth. Joan pushed back and bit him on the lip, until she could taste his blood.

"Bitch!" he slapped her hard across the face, then turned and pulled her along down the trail.

"You're really going to take me down there and just murder me in cold blood?" she asked, panting to keep up.

"I'm a soldier. I do what I'm told. The senator wants you dead. I'm just following orders."

They reached the ladder entry to the cave. Monsod bent down and threw Joan over his shoulder like a sack, then climbed down the ladder.

"But I may need to do something that will add to the myth of the NPA, who we all know are committing this crime. I think that the investigators will find that the NPA sometimes rape their victims before they kill them," he flipped her off his back and held her in his arms, smiling at her, then dropping her feet to the floor and grabbing her arm again.

Joan thought about spitting at him, but she held herself in check as he pulled her down the stone slope into the cave. He reached the power switch and turned on the lights in the tunnel and the cave. Just a few steps past the power switch, Joan's high heel slipped on the stone, and she nearly fell, but Monsod's grip on her arm held her up. She cried out from the pain, kicked both shoes off and continued in her bare feet.

"I do like a woman in high heels," he said, but he kicked the shoes to the side and pulled her along.

Joan was recovering her balance, and now with her high heel shoes gone, it was easier to keep up with Monsod's pace. They reached the narrow archway, and Monsod pushed her through first, then followed along with no trouble. They reached the cave itself, and Joan was amazed, as she was every time she entered it, at the stunning grandeur of the place. The broad pool glistened in the lights, and the bridge arched gracefully across. They reached the bridge, and at the top of its arch, Joan screamed for everything she was worth. Monsod jerked with surprise, and Joan yanked loose of his grip on her arm. He pulled out his pistol to shoot, but the thunder of the bat colony as it left its corner distracted him. Monsod fired as Joan raced down the bridge and across to the office space, but his aim was off, and the bullet slammed into the back of a file cabinet ahead of her. At the deafening sound of the gunshot, the bats veered again, confused by the noise. Monsod turned in time to see the dark tidal wave sweep down and carry him bodily off the bridge. He approximated a backward swan dive as he fell, hundreds of wings and claws caught on his hair, his face and his clothes and landed, head first, in about a foot of crystal clear water. The bats took one more turn about the cave, then, calming, they flew back up to the roof and settled. As quickly as the cacophony had come, the cave was silent again, with no sound but a tiny dripping as the water entered the pool. Joan crouched behind the netting, having watched the entire awesome sight. She took a deep breath, then stood up and quietly walked back up onto the bridge. She twisted to the side, bent down and picked up Monsod's gun, which was still lying on the bridge. She looked down into the water and saw Monsod lying on his back, arms and legs askew, with several drowned bats still attached to him. His neck was twisted in an extremely unusual way, and he was very much dead.

Joan walked back across the bridge to the office space, where she found a matte knife on a light table and cut the ropes off her wrists. She rubbed her sore wrists as she started back up the path to the entrance of the cave. She still had Monsod's gun in her hand, and when she came to her shoes in the tunnel, she decided to ignore them for now and went on in her bare feet. Climbing up the ladder at the cave's opening, she saw that the sun was nearly setting, and she could hear gunfire not far away.

The shots were coming from up on the road, so Joan left the trail and hiked along the top edge of the terraces until she reached the area down below the hotel. She turned at the corner of the hotel and edged slowly up along the flank of the main building. Up ahead she saw the Humvee and the Mercedes. She circled them and saw a body lying in the underbrush next to them. She held out the gun, inched ahead and looked down. She gasped as she realized it was Val! Lakay Pawid lay on his stomach in the brush, a bullet hole in his back. She knelt down to check for a pulse, but Val was dead.

"Oh, Val, I'm so sorry," she whispered.

She stood up and looked around the vehicles. Seven of the eight tires had been slashed. Evidently, someone had discovered Val sabotaging them and murdered him. Boy is going to pay for this, she thought to herself. There was a volley of gunfire above, and then she heard a man's voice cry out, "Don't shoot, I give up! There's my gun. Don't shoot!"

Joan climbed the rest of the way up the hill and walked out onto the dusty roadway.

16. IFUGAO

Today was a special day, because one of the families farming southeast of Bontoc had given Insik some coffee and a piece of loin from a pig they had slaughtered. This morning the cadres wouldn't be settling for weak tea and a small ration of rice. The coffee was brewing now, and it smelled wonderful to Paul. He had put away his bedroll a quarter of an hour before and was finishing the notes from last night that were interrupted by falling asleep. Insik and the others were putting the camp back together after leaving it for most of yesterday when the warning came that a Special Forces unit would be in the area. As it turned out, nothing had happened. They hadn't seen a sign of armed forces, but Insik knew when to be cautious. The deaths of the extortionists would certainly cause some kind of response, however small.

Suddenly, Insik signaled to the group, and they grabbed rifles and hit the ground or took cover where they could. Paul could hear running feet approaching. It was only a couple of people, and they were running without stealth, not in the secretive manner he would expect from militia. Then he saw them—it was a woman and a small boy. It was Rosie! He stood up, and said, "It's all right, Insik. She's a friend of mine."

Rosie nearly collapsed in Paul's arms, and one of the cadres helped him sit her down to rest. Others cared for the boy, who didn't seem as winded as Rosie.

"Paul, they've got Joan and..."

"Get your breath back, Rosie. Don't try to talk yet," he said, although he was frantic to know what about Joan.

One of the young women with Insik's group brought Rosie some water to drink, and she drank it down gratefully, then choked and coughed.

"Joan found evidence that the Senator planned the theft and the murders, and the same security force he sent to "investigate" were actually the men who killed Michael and the others."

"Oh, my God!"

"Well, she went to Manila but the Senator caught her, and he's bringing her back up to Banaue. They plan to stage another robbery and kill Joan! Oh, you've got to help!"

"How do you know this?"

"Rudy managed to sneak a call to Millie and told her. Millie went to Val, and he sent me here. The boy is Nano, and he's the fastest boy in Banaue. He's been my very able guide. We got a lift a few miles up the Bontoc road, rested awhile, then we've been running through the jungle for most of the night. The driver who drove us up is the father of one of the murdered guards. His name is Dandy, and he'll do anything we say— he wants to avenge his son. He's gone up to Bontoc to find a truck. He'll have it back down waiting when you and your men get there."

Paul turned to Insik, "What do you think, Insik?"

Insik crossed his arms and said, "It sounds like an opportunity for an answer to another atrocity." To Rosie, he asked, "How many men are in this security force?"

"Eight, plus the Senator. But these are highly trained special forces soldiers."

"Well, in our way, we are highly trained, also. What do you all think? It will be dangerous, but does this sound like a fair fight to you, eh?"

The vote was unanimous.

"Miss Rose, would you and Nano like a little rice to eat? And then I think you should rest for an hour or so, before we take you back through the jungle. Okay?" Insik turned to go, then added, "Also, I want you to know how much respect we have for you who can run through our jungle in the night. That is not an easy thing to do for anyone, only."

When he had finished his rice, Nano shyly approached the NPA leader, "Lakay Insik, I am honored to meet you, sir. I know well of what you do for the people. Did I do well, too?"

Insik put his arm around the boy's narrow shoulders, "Nano, you make us all proud. Some day, when you get bigger, you will be a brave cadre, too, and you will learn how to fight for your people, eh?"

An hour later, they broke camp. They couldn't move at the rate of Nano and Rosie, but they moved at a very quick pace through the jungle, and Paul was amazed how she had run this route in the dark. The trail was often steep, and crossed ravine after ravine, going down one slope, encountering a stream bed and muddy footing at the base, then climbing up to the next ridge, where ahead of them lay yet another series of the same. He slapped at a mosquito and took a pain pill for good luck as he struggled up the next hillside.

They reached the road by mid-afternoon, and Paul gratefully squatted down to rest for a minute. He was learning that the typical way Filipinos squatted made sense. It gave you a rest, but kept you off the ground below, that might be muddy or full of insects. Insik and Rosie were discussing the whereabouts of the truck—he thought it might be waiting farther up, but both Rosie and Nano insisted that this was where they had been dropped off. The argument ended, when, five minutes later, a large flat-bed truck with wooden sidewalls came clattering down the road. The driver, Dandy, waved as he pulled to a stop. He had done well. Not only had he found a truck, but two men from Bontoc were in the cab, as well. One of them had a rifle, so now they had a total of six guns.

After a short discussion of strategy, everyone climbed into the back of the truck, and they headed south. It would be very slow going, but certainly faster than the trail. Last night, they had encountered three washouts, but Dandy knew he had room to avoid them, and the truck would do better than his car had. They insisted that Paul and Rosie ride in the cab, so that Insik could meet the Bontoc men and fill them in on what he knew.

Rosie sat in the middle and put her head on Paul's shoulder as the truck pulled away, "Don't let them hurt Joan," she said, just before she fell asleep in spite of the bouncing of the truck on the rough surface.

Don't worry, Rosie, he thought. No one's going to hurt Joan unless I'm dead first. He sat and stared through the mud-spattered windshield as the truck worked its way up and down switchbacks and through the edges of streams swollen from the rainy season, but all he could see was a slender blonde girl with very straight hair.

* * *

As they approached Banaue, the late afternoon sun was slanting sharply across the road, and they could hear gunfire in the distance. There was a knock on the back window, and Paul turned to see Insik motioning to Dandy. He leaned around the side of the truck and asked him to pull over.

"We'd best go on foot from here, and not down the middle of everything. I don't want to be caught in a crossfire."

They got down from the truck and followed Dandy and Nano to a path off to the left. As they grew near the gunfire, it became clear that it was coming from somewhere near the hotel. To the right, the sound of automatic weapons, and on the left, an occasional measured shot or two. Paul moved up next to Insik.

"It sounds like the soldiers are in front of the hotel, and their opponents are over here up ahead."

"You're right, Paul," answered Insik. "They seem to have some major firepower, too."

"But they don't know we're here yet."

"Exactly. We should be able to take out one, maybe two, before they know, eh? Keep Miss Rose and Nano here, and give us that chance only."

Paul dropped back and gathered up Rosie and Nano, then waited. The others moved quietly forward, aided by all the growth from the rainy season that shielded them. There was an excruciatingly long pause, and then a volley of gunfire came from the NPA, followed by shouting and cursing and more automatic gunfire. Paul ran forward, keeping low, until he reached Insik.

"Get down," whispered Insik. "Two are dead, but there are still two more. I don't see the Senator. And I thought you said there were eight."

Paul could see Kiwil crouched behind a large boulder ahead. Kiwil spotted him, and grinned. He dropped down low and scuttled across to Paul and Insik.

"Thank you, thank you, brave ones," Kiwil said. "With those two, plus the one that we shot, there are only two left, and the Senator, I am afraid, also. But we have wounded, too. I am sorry to say that we have lost Bingo Bulahao. And Mr. Nigel Barclay has a bullet to the leg. Now that you are here, we must take him to the clinic."

"I thought there were eight," said Insik.

"Hee, hee, hee. Lakay Pawid is a very smart man. He got medicine from Doctor Sanchez, and Manny fed it to three of them in their breakfast. They are sleeping in the hotel, tied up of course only."

"Where's Joan, Kiwil?"

"I do not know that one only. I think maybe the captain took her to the cave. We were too late to stop him."

"Where's Nigel? Maybe Rosie and one of your men, Kiwil, can get him to the clinic," said Paul.

Suddenly there was a voice behind him. "Ahoy, mate," answered Nigel. He was lying back in the bushes, invisible.

"I'm afraid I've had my share of skirmishes during my years in this bloody continent," he said. "I'm usually pretty good at lying low, but with all that automatic fire, a stray bullet got me in the thigh."

Paul dropped back up the trail a bit and rounded up Rosie and Nano, suggesting that Nano head north from the trail, circle around and get to his home to keep out of harm's way.

"We don't need you getting a bullet as a thank you for guiding Rosie, Nano."

Rosie put her arms around Nano and hugged him, then kissed him on the forehead, which drew a scowl from Nano.

"You've been a great guide and friend, Nano," she said. "I'll see you soon, as soon as the gunfire's over." She squeezed him again, then sent him running up into the bush.

"Can you help Nigel, Rosie? He's been shot in the leg, and he needs help to reach the clinic."

"Of course, Paul. But you need to go find Joan."

Just then the NPA and the Banaue men fired a volley in unison. Bullets flew all around the lone gunman in front of the hotel.

An automatic rifle flew through the air from behind the car the soldier was using as cover.

"Don't shoot, I give up! There's my gun. Don't shoot!"

"I'm going to find Joan. I'll see you later," said Paul, and he stood up to circle back to the trail to the cave.

"You're too late, shouted Nigel. "There she is on the road! By God, there's the real treasure—a woman who can take care of herself."

Paul looked up, and there was Joan climbing up from down behind the hotel. She was bruised and dirty, and her dress was torn in several places. She had lost her shoes and was barefoot, but she had a service pistol in her hand, her jaw set with determination and her eyes flashed with anger.

"You're a lucky man, Webster. You have an astonishingly good woman there."

Paul ran out to the road, but hesitated as he reached Joan.

"Paul!" she cried as they threw their arms around each other.

"You're all right! Thank God!" he said, and kissed her. They held each other a long time, and then Joan said, "Where is that asshole?"

"What?"

"The fucking Senator," she answered. "They killed Val! I found him down below the hotel, shot in the back." And then the memory of it came back to her and she collapsed into Paul's arms and sobbed on his shoulder.

As the last edge of the sun dropped into the jungle, and the early full moon brightened in the east, Paul asked, "What about the captain?"

"Yamashita's cave killed him."

"That accounts for the whole squad. We'd better check out the hotel. Maybe Manny knows where the Senator is. We'd better find him before he's able to escape in the dark."

They crossed to the hotel entrance and skirted around the furniture and bullet-scored autos that had served as cover for the special forces squadron. The lobby was a jumble of piled furniture, broken vases and cut flowers dying in puddles of water on the floor. Manny had the entire hotel crew, including the maids and some of the waiters, picking up, sweeping up and straightening up. When he saw Joan and Paul, he stopped what he was doing and crossed eagerly to them, taking Joan's hand in his and kissing her on the back of the hand.

"Oh, thank God, you're all right, Madam. We were all so afraid for you," he said, "and I'm to tell you that if you need him, Rudy has gone to the clinic to protect Millie and the others there. But if I can do anything at all...."

"Thank you, Manny. What you can do is tell us where to find the Senator."

"Well, now, I wish I could. He was sitting in the bar, drinking, for the longest time. Finally, he called me to his table and asked me if I'd seen Captain Monsod. I told him not since the Captain had joined the Senator outside. Well, he actually swore to himself! I heard him say, 'even Monsod's abandoned me.' Just then Lt. Pedrosa came up and informed the Senator that some villagers with guns were gathering outside. The Senator told him to get his men together and disperse the villagers. When the soldiers started out the front entrance, Kiwil and his men started firing. The soldiers stripped the lobby to cover themselves, and, what with all the gunfire and whatnot, the Senator just disappeared. I haven't seen him since.

"Perhaps I should've put sleeping powder in the Senator's drink as well, but, after all, he is a Senator. I'm sorry, Madam, if I let you down."

"Not at all, Manny," answered Joan. "What you did was dangerous, and we're all proud of you for your bravery."

Just then Kiwil came in, leading the last special forces soldier. "Manny, do you have another room for this evil one, eh? And have him tied well to the bed frame like the others are, only?"

Manny called two kitchen workers over and passed the prisoner on to them.

"Kiwil," asked Paul, "do you have any news of the Senator? Manny said he left when the shooting started."

"No, but time is short, eh? It is nearly dark, and we do not want him to escape, only. We will scout up and down the road with the help of

Insik and his people. And may I give my thanks for bringing them to help us, eh?"

"I'm happy I was able to help. After all, my wife was in real danger, too."

"That is so. I must go to start the search, only."

Joan turned to Paul as Kiwil left, "Where would you go if you had just been implicated in a huge crime that would end your life of high living, and you had just lost the only people willing to fight for you?"

"Well, if I had been drinking all afternoon on top of that, I don't think I would be dealing with too much reason."

"Exactly. Maybe he's just lurking about, hiding, without a plan left in his head."

"Interesting. Why don't we check out your theory before it's dark? I can't think of anything else to do."

They went out the front door of the hotel and started to circle back down towards the area where Val's body and the vehicles were. As Paul turned the corner, a shot rang out, and a bullet sank into the edge of the wooden wall. He ducked back, then dropped to his knees and reached out low, looking back around the corner. The Senator was sitting in the front seat of the Mercedes with a handgun aimed in their direction. Paul was low enough that he couldn't be seen. He raised up slightly, and another shot whizzed over his head. Then Boy got up and started running, shooting back behind him without aiming at anything. He continued to shoot until the gun clicked empty, then threw down the gun and ran off down below. Paul was up and after him, running through the thick grass and weeds like he hadn't run in years. Where in the hell is he going? thought Paul, as he realized that Boy was running toward the terraces. That's a dead end, pure and simple. He must be completely out of his head. He was closing on Boy, having less trouble fighting through the undergrowth than the big man. He dove and tackled Boy by the ankles, and both men skidded through the grass. Boy rolled over and kicked him in the arm, trying for his face. Paul pulled back, and Boy jumped up and moved farther down the slope. Paul caught him again, this time swinging him around by the shoulder and punching him in the face. Boy's nose spouted blood, and he slugged Paul in the stomach, doubling Paul up. Boy turned toward the end of the terrace still damaged by the quake. Paul caught him, and both men rolled down the steep slope, until they fell ten feet into the top terrace, sinking into the thick, green carpet of ifugo that lay in the pool. Paul choked on the muddy water and pulled himself up, punching the bigger man.

"What? You smug bastard!" shouted Boy. "You want to fall off the mountain again? Okay, I'll help you!" He caught Paul with a roundhouse right, and Paul went down in the muck and the rice. He inhaled more water and mud as Boy pushed him under, then picked him up by his clothes and dragged him to the walkway at the edge of the terrace.

"You think you can die twice, and get away with it?" he yanked Paul onto the walkway and started to push him off.

"You can't ruin Bonifacio Vital, a man that millions of people revere!" he shoved again, and Paul's legs slid off into space.

Boy climbed up onto the walkway and started to stomp on Paul's hands and arms. "Let's see how you do with a few hundred feet, not a measly seventy."

Paul started to black out, and his hands slipped across the top of the stone ledge, but he found a thicker stone and grabbed on hard, digging his fingers in. It was nearly dark by now, and he could just see Boy's outline towering above him. He heard a slight thump as a small, dark form landed in the Senator's shadow. Boy turned at the sound, and Paul saw something flash in the moonlight. The Senator spun back toward Paul, a look of surprise and amusement in his eyes. He tilted toward Paul, and, as he did, the precarious balance act ended, and the Senator's head and body separated and fell past Paul, curling silently through the air, side by side down the mountain in a graceful arc.

Paul waited a long time until he heard something hit the treetops below, then looked up to find Kiwil with his left hand outstretched, waiting to help him up. In his right hand, he held an Ifugao head axe.

He grabbed Kiwil's hand, and the powerful little man pulled him up onto the ledge. Kiwil's eyes glittered with tears that caught the moonlight. "He killed Val."

Paul reached out for Kiwil and put his arms around him. Kiwil's body shook as he wept for his friend. Paul was swept with the sadness he'd known when his own father died. He looked down across the terraces, remembering what Val had told them about headhunting there on the terrace wall, so long ago. He had said, "Today, we have learned to live in peace..., but there are still occasions when outrage demands retribution."

17. TANIG

Father Algarme squinted into the morning sun as he stood on the platform erected on the grassy field. The grass that was not hidden under the platform was still wet with dew, and the sun was low and directly in his eyes. Behind the priest the panorama of the Banaue rice terraces stretched, still mostly in early morning shade. In front of him Rudy Castillo and his best man, Dr. Florio Sanchez, stood looking into the sun as well, up the flower-strewn aisle between the ranks of folding chairs. The guitarist at the back started to play a lovely, gentle song. Paul sat on the aisle in the third row back, watching as a beautiful woman slowly walked down the aisle, holding a small bouquet of orchids. He smiled with gratitude as Joan passed, then took her place to the priest's right as Millie's matron of honor. Her pale blue dress shone in the morning light, and he couldn't remember seeing her look more lovely.

It was their first trip back to Banaue after Joan left for Manila with the treasure, accompanied by a military convoy ordered by President Aquino, and Paul finished his work in Bontoc. The Battle of Banaue, as Nigel had named it for the press, had cost the lives of three of Banaue's best citizens, four AFP soldiers and Senator Bonifacio Vital. Cory had sent a personal, unofficial letter of thanks to Insik and his cadres, promising to renew her efforts to address their concerns. Vicky had been sequestered in her family's compound in Quezon City and would never more be in the center of Manila's social whirl.

The guitarist began a new refrain, and Millie Estacion, accompanied by Luis Gahidan, the new police chief, started down the aisle. Millie was radiant with happiness, and Paul felt his throat swell with emotion. Her partner was shorter than Millie, but he was wearing his best barong Tagalog, and he proudly held her hand on his arm. As they walked by, Kiwil whispered to Paul, "Magic, eh?"

* * *

Joan looked across the rows of chairs filled with Banaue's leading citizens. On either side and behind the platform, more friends and neighbors stood watching the proceedings. Her eyes moved to Paul, who was intently watching the priest and the couple in front. His curly brown beard stood out distinctly in the sea of glistening black hair. She realized he had always stood out from everyone for her. And she was especially proud of him right now. He had finished his book and found an agent. A university publishing house had picked it up, and it had been well received by historians and politicians alike. She had sent an autographed copy to Cory herself, and Cory had written her, calling it a revelation and vowing to do what she could to encourage communication between the administration and all organizations in support of true "people power."

The ceremony ended, and Rudy bent down and kissed his bride, and the crowd applauded them as they headed up the aisle. The occupants of the chairs flooded up behind them on the way to the reception, which would feature the mayor's mother singing a traditional Ifugao song. The wedding was to be a combination of Roman Catholic and traditional Ifugao, the *Tanig* in their culture. Joan saw Paul moving against the flow on his way to her. She joined him, and together they chatted with Loring and the priest for a few moments. The two men were in a hurry to get to the reception as well, and they were left alone on the platform, gazing out across the still water and green shoots of rice stretching far below them.

"You look breathtaking today," said Paul, holding her hand in his.

"I feel like I just married you again," replied Joan. "I really like the feeling."

"So do I," he took her in his arms, and they stood there for a long time, just holding each other. "I never get tired of telling you I love you."

They kissed a kiss of years together, and Joan said, "Well, shall we head over to the reception and congratulate the newlyweds?"

"Seems like an appropriate thing to do."

As they walked up the road to Banaue, Joan put her hand in Paul's. His hand felt warm and strong. "Oh, by the way, said Joan. "In all the fuss, I forgot to tell you that Joe called last night. He told me that the museum commission is all hot on doing an exhibition on Burma, or Myanmar, as it's now called—it just changed its name. They want to make sure that its art isn't destroyed by the growing unrest, and they think we're just the couple to handle it. Feel like a little more travel?"

END

ACKNOWLEDGMENTS

This novel places fictional characters in actual places and against some historical events. While the bulk of the action takes place in and around Banaue, Ifugao Province, the Philippines, many liberties have been taken with the specific geography and reality of Banaue. The author takes great pride in the many Filipino friends he has had throughout the years, and it is his intent to honor the country and the people of the Philippines.

I'd like to thank the following people for their kind assistance in my research for Stairway of the Gods:

Mark Fenn, San Francisco Asian Art Museum, and Stephen Stokes and Richard Bailey from Oxford Luminescence Research Group, University of Oxford, for sharing some of their knowledge on identifying ancient artifacts.

Karen Zoller, MD, and Michael Strauss, MD, for assistance in keeping Paul's injuries and recovery more realistic.

The following three books were exceptionally helpful to my knowledge of Philippine history and politics:

The Philippines: Land of Broken Promises by James B. Goodno, Zed Books Ltd., 1991.

Red Revolution: Inside the Philippine Guerilla Movement by Gregg R. Jones, Westview Press, 1989.

Rebolusyon! A Generation of Struggle in the Philippines by Benjamin Pimentel, Monthly Review Press, 1991.

Quote, page 199: from July 26, 1986 issue of "New York World"

Quote, Page 213: Teodoro Agoncillo, History of the Filipino People (Quezon City, Philippines, Garotech Publishing, 1990). pp. 230.

My utmost gratitude to Helen Borgers, Jim Kline, Jim Scott, Emily Warren and Vincent Patti for their enthusiastic support and insightful editing assistance.

To Monica Matulich, whose editing and public relations talents provided me with a wealth of knowledge to help me polish the final manuscript. And thanks for finding the perfect title.

And finally, to my wife, Laurel Scott, for her loving energy, phenomenal proofreading and editing skills and unflagging belief in the book that kept me going through many long hours and days.

GLOSSARY

Alim (all eem') Epic poem of the Ifugao performed when persons of high rank are ill.

Alyog (all' yog) A god of the Ifugao Underworld who causes the earth to quake.

Amaterasu (ahm a' tur os oo) A sun goddess and one of the chief Shinto deities.

Ampual (am' puu all) The chief god of the Fourth Ifugao Skyworld.

Armed Forces of the Philippines (AFP) Consisting of the Army, Navy and Air Force of the Philippines.

Atis (ah tees') A fruit; in some regions of the world, known as the sugar-apple or custard-apple; looks slightly like a pine cone.

Baguio (bog' ee o) City in northern Luzon, Philippines.

Banaue (bon now' ā) Capital town in the province of Ifugao, Philippines.

Barong Tagalog (ba rong' ta ga' log) Formal garment of the Philippines, mainly worn by men; very lightweight and worn untucked.

Bontoc (bon tok') 242 Town in the province of Mountain Province, Philippines.

Bulul (bu lul') Hardwood figures of human shape; sometimes used for healing, but more often connected with rice harvest.

Carabao (care' a bow) A large buffalo of Asia having large, spreading horns; a water buffalo.

Communist Party of the Philippines (CPP) The leading Communist party in the Philippines. An underground political organization founded in 1968.

Daya (dy' ah) The Upstream Region in Ifugao mythology.

Dongla (dong' la) A tea plant of Asia.

Himong (hi mong')Ifugao war dance ceremony.

Hudhud (hud' hud) A long Ifugao tale sung during special occasions, often as a tribute to the dead.

Ifugao (ee' pu gow or ee' fu gow) Province in the Cordillera Administrative Region in northern Luzon, Philippines.

Ileus (ill ee' us) Gastrointestinal condition that often follows trauma or surgery, generally only lasting a few days.

Ipugo (ee' pu go') In Ifugao language, means "people of the earth," also name for the Ifugao rice.

Lakay (lok aye') Grandfather; term of respect for elders.

Lingling-o (ling' ling oh) Ifugao jewelry in the form of a broken circle; brings luck and improves fertility.

Luzon (lu'zon) Largest and most economically and politically important island in the Philippines.

Mamah-o (ma ma' o) Ifugao priestesses allowed to recite myths for curing sickness.

Mombagol (mohm bag oll') The chief Mombaki who chants the Ifugao Alim.

Mombaki (mohm ba' kee) Ifugao religious specialist, literally "sayer of prayers."

Narra Timber tree, also known as padauk.

New People's Army (NPA) The armed wing of the Communist Party of the Philippines. Formed on March 29, 1969.

Nueva Vizcaya (nwā' vah viz ky' ah) Province of the Philippines situated southeast of Banaue, between Manila and Banaue.

Payon di a-ammod (pie ohn' dee ah' ah mod') Ifugao for the "fields of our ancestors."

Philippine Constabulary (PC) Para-military police force of the Armed Forces of the Philippines.

Sagada (sah god' ah) Town in the Mountain Province in the Philippines.

Seto (sea' toe) Japanese ceramic style that started around the beginning of the Kamakura period (1185-1333) in the region of Seto; distinctive because they were the only ceramics of the period that were glazed.

Shinto (shin' toe) An ancient Japanese religion based on nature worship.

Susano'o (soo sah' noh oh) Shinto storm of summer.

Tanig (tah neeg') Ifugao term for wedding ceremony.

Tapis (top ees') Wraparound skirt or sarong worn by Ifugao women.

Tapuy (tah pwee') Filipino rice wine originated in Ifugao province.

Torii (tor' ee) Traditional Japanese gate usually found at the entrance to or inside a Shinto shrine; literally, bird perch.

Tsukuyomi (soo koo yoh' mee) The moon god in Shinto and Japanese mythology.

Wigan (vi' gan) One of the Ifugao gods of the Upstream Region, also known as the god of good harvest.

Yaozhou ware (yow jhu') China, Northern Song period (960–1126); one of the most elegant of Chinese green wares.

ABOUT THE AUTHOR

VIC WARREN is a Clio award-winning advertising executive with 30-plus years in the travel industry, best known for creating the Alaska Airlines Eskimo logo. In the 90s, Warren collaborated with several illustrators and turned his talent into writing and designing more than 100 children's books. His fascination with the Philippines began in his college years in Seattle and culminated with collecting tribal art from the Cordillera Mountains that he found in the marketplaces of Manila and Baguio. Vic's same interest in ethnic art led him to uncover the legendary story of WWII General Yamashita's treasure said to be buried in the Philippines.

He is currently at work on two more novels: *Saffron*, a sci-fi adventure that reads like mainstream fiction deals with the discovery of a race of underwater humans off today's California coast; and *Hong Kong Blues*, which takes a newly-married couple through the streets of Hong Kong in a Hitchcock-style thriller.

Warren lives in Kailua-Kona, Hawaii with his wife, Laurel, and their three-legged cat, Oscar. To learn more about his novels, *Stairway of the Gods, Saffron* and *Hong Kong Blues*, please visit www.vicwarren.com.